CW00515285

Whittington Manor

Claire Voet

PNEUMA SPRINGS PUBLISHING UK

First Published in 2010 by:
Pneuma Springs Publishing

Whittington Manor
Copyright © 2010   Claire Louise Voet
ISBN: 978-1-907728-06-8

This is a work of fiction. Names, characters, places and incidents are either products of the author's imagination or are used fictitiously. Any resemblance to actual events or locales or persons, living or dead, save those clearly in the public domain, is purely coincidental.

Pneuma Springs Publishing
A Subsidiary of Pneuma Springs Ltd.
7 Groveherst Road, Dartford Kent, DA1 5JD.
E: admin@pneumasprings.co.uk
W: www.pneumasprings.co.uk

A catalogue record for this book is available from the British Library.

Published in the United Kingdom. All rights reserved under International Copyright Law. Contents and/or cover may not be reproduced in whole or in part without the express written consent of the publisher.

Whittington Manor

In Memory of all those courageous men and women who fought to protect England during World War II and, in particular, the civilians who lost their lives rescuing our war heroes from Dunkirk.

ACKNOWLEDGEMENT

I should like to thank Pete, Linda, Brian, Alison and my family who supported and encouraged me to write this story.

With much love to you all. C.V

One

Sarah Whittington-Lambert waved goodbye to the last of her party guests as they drove down the long winding gravel driveway. She looked out onto the grounds from the main drawing-room window. They were wonderfully designed, perfectly manicured, with symmetrically patterned lawns and hedges, and the riots of colourful plants were in full bloom now that it was early spring.

Whittington Manor was located in the rural outskirts of Portsmouth, between Portchester and Fareham, and boasted eighteen opulently decorated rooms. The house was over four hundred years old and had been inhabited by the Whittington family for the last two centuries.

A small smile crept across Sarah's face. It always gave her a sense of peace as she stood looking out at the grounds she and Joe had worked so hard on. It was easy to recall the desperation of the war. It still sent chills down her spine as she remembered the terrible tragedy her mother and Annie had endured and her brief and dreadfully unhappy marriage to Edward Hamilton.

There were also those endless days without Joe... It had all been so difficult then. The world was such a frightening place, full of desolation, continuous heartache and worry.

She looked down at her hands, and at her wedding band embedded with dainty diamonds. She had worn it every day since Joe had placed it on her finger. They were still beautiful hands; graceful and useful, thank goodness, but nevertheless they were the hands of an eighty year old woman. She had lived long and survived hard times as well as many long and happy years.

Henry, the old black and white sheep dog, walked up the entrance steps, panting and looking sad that all the guests had gone and deserted him. He gave a half-hearted deep bark forcing Sarah to snap out of her dreamy state of mind. She called out to him and he continued his waddle into the drawing-room. She patted him on the head and he then made a bee-line to his basket close to the fireplace and flopped down in a weary heap.

It had been a long day but Sarah never tired of seeing her closest friends and family. It warmed her heart how they spoiled her and always gave her

6

such a fantastic birthday party. It was as if her family was expanding almost every year, with ten grandchildren and three great grandchildren only recently born.

She turned from the window and looked at Joe's portrait hanging above the open fireplace. He looked important and proud. He had been thirty when that portrait was painted. His golden curly hair slightly ruffled and his mischievous sparkling green eyes seemed to follow her from wherever she watched in the room. It was as if he was constantly looking at her, watching out for her as he had always done when he was alive. She smiled warmly at him. If only he had been there today to celebrate her birthday, it would have been a perfect day. It was hard to believe that he had been gone ten years. There wasn't a day that passed when she didn't think about him or long to hear his voice and feel his warm caressing hands, yet despite the feeling of emptiness in her heart, she continued her life with a smile on her face, just grateful that she had shared those many happy years with him and they had raised four beautiful children together.

Sarah walked across the spacious room. The high ceilings and tall windows gave the room elegance, while the warm creams and subtle peach tones of the walls and curtains were a perfect back drop for the two very large light brown chesterfield leather sofas placed in an L shape facing the fireplace. The plump deep red velvet cushions on the sofas and the soft dim lamps placed around the room gave a warm and homely appeal. A huge thick red and cream Persian carpet lay under an antique, oval, wooden coffee table. An old rocking chair stood closest to the fireplace with a red velvet cushion matching the ones on the sofa and was shaped with an indent as if Joe had just recently got up from it. He used to love to sit there, smoking his pipe and gazing into the fire. Not far from the fireplace stood a grand ornate wall unit with a drinks cabinet, displaying the finest Edinburgh crystal glasses and decanters, containing liquor such as brandy, whisky, sherry and of course port, which was Sarah's favourite tipple.

Sarah opened the drawer below and carefully took out an old photo album. Its cover was faded and worn and she gently dusted it off. Sitting down on Joe's rocking chair, she slowly and delicately opened it. She ran her fingers softly over the first photo, which was of Joe standing on top of Portsdown Hill. Her lips curled into a soft fond smile. Portsdown Hill had been their special place, the place where they had first met, shared their first kiss. She had barely been more than a child then. So much had happened after that photo was taken, and it was on that very same day that England had declared war on Germany. It was odd... it seemed so long ago, yet she remembered it as if it was yesterday.

7

*****

`I just don't think it's fair, Mama... What is so wrong with me wanting to become a nurse?' Sarah pouted, folding her arms tightly in front of her and perching herself down on the cold, chesterfield leather sofa. The fire was not lit and there was a slight chill in the air now that the sun had gone down.

Lady Laura Whittington took a sip of her tea, placed the cup and saucer down on a small oval wooden coffee table in front of her and gave a heavy sigh. `Sarah, if I've told you once, I must have told you a thousand times, there is nothing wrong with wanting to be a nurse .... It's just, it's not what your father and I had in mind for you.' The tone of exasperation in her voice matched her facial expression.

It was clear to see where Sarah had inherited her stubbornness and determination. They were two of a kind. They also shared the same fiery auburn hair, deep hazel brown eyes and soft creamy-coloured skin with a smattering of freckles.

`So what exactly did you and Father have in mind for me?' Her arms were now unfolded but the deep frown was still creasing the middle of her forehead.

`With the threat of war coming, we really don't want you putting yourself in danger. Who knows? With medical skills you could be sent off to work in very dangerous locations. Darling, you really must listen to me.' Laura walked over to where Sarah was sitting and sat down next to her, the leather sofa gave a familiar creak. She picked up Sarah's hand and placed it gently in her own. She was doing her best to reason with her but it was so tedious. Sarah pulled her hand abruptly away and folded her arms again. `So why did I have to study so hard? Why did you go to so much trouble for me to have private tutoring, if I'm to do nothing with my education?'

Laura turned to face her, their eyes met challengingly. `Because one day you will find yourself a well-educated and loving husband, just like I did when I met your father, and being well-educated is a good thing. It means you will be able to talk knowledgeably with your husband and also join in conversations at dinner parties and other social functions. A good education never goes to waste, my dear.' Laura glanced at her watch, they had been having the same discussion for almost an hour and she was still not making any progress.

`I don't want to get married, neither do I intend on chatting to pompous people at dinner parties. I just want to be a nurse and you have no right to stop me, Mother!' Sarah jumped up from the sofa, she was just as tired of the conversation and there was only one thing for it, she would have to take the

8

matter into her own hands, when the time was right of course. She stormed out of the room, brushing shoulders with her father in the doorway. Their eyes locked for a second, as he searched her face for an apology. Eventually, it came. `Sorry Papa,' she grimaced before continuing through the door.

`And what was all that about?' Lord Whittington asked his wife, with a trace of amusement. He was a tall and handsome man for his age, with dark blue eyes and a thick head of grey hair which gave him a distinguished look.

Laura threw her hands up in the air with despair. `She's still insisting that she wants to be a nurse.'

`Well that's absurd! She's only sixteen years old. She can still carry on studying for now. That will keep her out of mischief and in a few years she will be married anyway.' He lit his pipe and gave a series of short puffs.

Laura walked back to her favourite arm chair, nearest the window and sat down. She looked weary as she rubbed her tired forehead. `I'm not so sure.... She's very head strong, William.'

`Head strong maybe... but I am the head of this family and it's time she learnt that. Anyway, I have far more important things on my mind. I've just been reading today's newspaper.' He sat down in the matching leather arm chair next to Laura. `You do realise what will happen if Hitler goes back on his promise not to invade Poland?'

Laura sighed. 'I do, William. It really doesn't bear thinking about. I feel sick inside with worry and especially for Charles and Thomas... and there is still no news from Thomas.' Her voiced trailed off wistfully.

Thomas at the age of twenty had been in the navy for two years now. The last the Whittingtons had heard was that he was heading for the South Pacific. Charles was working as an accountant in Fareham, but for sure if war broke out, he too would be called up for service. Everyone was still saying that war wasn't imminent but reading the newspapers and listening to the wireless, it certainly felt like it.

Sarah marched into the large well- kept kitchen with its sparkling brass pots and pans hanging neatly above the stove. An oak wooden cabinet stood tall and full of crockery on the far side of the room. Everywhere you looked jars were labelled and neatly displayed, every item in the kitchen had its place. She slumped down on a wooden chair, and putting her elbows on the oak wooden kitchen table, she cupped her hands over her face and groaned.

Annie was watching her closely from where she was standing next to the stove. `My, my, Miss Sarah, whatever is the matter?' Annie, the housekeeper, was a plump comfortable looking woman with rosy cheeks and a warm smile who was born and brought up in Portsmouth. Annie

Philpot had joined the Whittington family fifteen years ago and loved caring for the Whittingtons. She was the kindest person Sarah had ever met. Nanny, she called her. She had called her that since she was able to talk, although she wasn't her Nanny, but she was as good as. Her own nanny who had cared for her up until she was thirteen had retired three years ago, Sarah had called her Nanny number two, always putting Annie first. She loved Annie dearly.

`Life isn't fair, Nanny' she helped herself to one of Annie's homemade, freshly baked biscuits laid out on a baking tray cooling on the kitchen table.

`Oh you are right there little'un.' She wiped her hands on her starched white apron and then stroking Sarah's arm affectionately, she smiled at her with her brown soft doe like eyes.

`I want to do something with my life, Nanny. Is that so bad?' I just want to be a nurse but it seems that I am to be married in a few years instead. Nothing more is expected of me. If I had been born a boy then I could do whatever I want, maybe even become a doctor. It's so unfair.'

Annie gave a wry smile. `Your Mum and Dad just want to keep you safe, that's all. If that 'itler carries on marchin' through Europe, taking over countries, gawd only knows what will 'appen 'ere,' She suddenly looked very worried at the idea as she went back to her baking.

Sarah got up from the table and followed her. `I know, Nanny and that's exactly why I want to be a nurse. They will need as many nurses as they can get if there is a war. I want to help other people not stay hidden away in the unrealistic protective world that I live in.' Why didn't anyone understand? Not even Emma understood and she was her best friend. All Emma wanted was to marry and have children.

`Ere 'ave a cup of milk.' Annie handed a glass of milk to her. Her hands were still covered in flour.

Sarah sipped her milk and smiled thankfully at Annie.

`D'you feel better, now?' She was growing up fast but she was still a little girl in Annie's eyes and the idea of her putting herself in danger frightened Annie too. She understood fully why Lord and Lady Whittington had been so opposed to the idea of Sarah becoming a nurse, although she would never have told her that.

`Not really, but talking to you always helps.' She shrugged her shoulders. If only she could speak to her parents the way she speaks to Annie, life would be so much simpler.

The Lambert brothers, Joe and Tommy, came marching up Portsdown Road in Portchester, on their way home. They were chanting triumphantly, `We won, we won, Pompey won!'

`I can't believe we beatem four one!' Tommy was still laughing as they opened the front door and went inside `The Laurels.'

There were no house numbers on any of the houses in Portsdown Road. They were recognised simply by the house name. The Lamberts had been lucky to have secured a rental agreement in that street when they had moved from their small terraced house with an outside toilet in Summer Street, in Portsmouth, six months ago. The houses in Portsdown Road were semi-detached and modern. There were three bedrooms, although one was a tiny box room but at least they had the convenience of having a proper bathroom located upstairs as well as a good sized back garden, although it needed some attention as the weeds were taking over the patchy lawn.

At nineteen years old Joe was turning into a handsome young man with his blond curly hair and attractive green eyes. There were many girls in Portchester that had their eye on Joe Lambert but he was far too shy for all that malarkey and although he quite liked Jessica Bishop who lived down Medina Road, he still hadn't plucked up the courage to ask her out yet, unlike Tommy who had no problem with asking girls out. Tommy had more girlfriends then he had had hot dinners. He was slightly chubby and smaller than Joe even though he was almost two years older but he was cheeky and charming and the girls loved him.

`What time dyou call this?... And take off those muddy boots' Audrey Lambert scolded them as they walked through the front door.

`Sorry Mum we've been celebrating. It's not every day Pompey wins the cup,' Joe was beaming at her while doing as he was told and takingg off his boots. Audrey looked tired. She had been up half the night looking after Maureen's baby who had a touch of colic.

Maureen glared at her brothers as they walked in the front room. 'Can you lot shut-up! You're gunno wake the baby in a minute. It's taken me hours to get her off to sleep... I've got no life of me own, not like you two who's been out partying at some stupid football match all afternoon.' At the age of sixteen she had shocked everyone when she came home pregnant and rumour had it the baby's father was a sailor from Portsmouth. Audrey had told everyone in the neighbourhood her daughter had married young and her husband was away at sea, not that anyone believed the story of course.

'Shouldn't have got yourself knocked up then' Tommy laughed, challenging his sister. It gave him great pleasure in winding her up whenever possible.

'Comen' sit down and eat your tea, all of you…now' Audrey demanded, raising her voice as she brushed a lock of chestnut coloured hair from her green eyes.

Maureen looked perplexed as they sat down at the dining table. It was as if she was struggling to try and work something out and finally, she looked at Joe and frowned. 'I dunno who Pompey were even playin' against. Come to think of it…. who really cares anyway? I mean why is football so bloody important to you two?' She felt annoyed that she had even spent a few moments thinking about it. If there was one thing she hated, it was football. A bunch of grown men running around kicking a ball and when it went in the net they all hugged and kissed each other. Yuck! She shuddered at the thought.

'Oh for gawd sake Maureen, it were Wolverhampton everyone knows that' Joe glared back at her in frustration.

'And it's important to us because we love it' Tommy added, with sarcasm in his voice and a fake smile siding with his brother.

'What did I tell you about swearing, Maureen? Nice girls don't swear, do you 'ere me?' Audrey chided and she placed a plate of bread and jam on the table.

'What you talking about, Mum? she ain't a nice girl,' Tommy smirked.

With fury in her eyes, Maureen stood up, her fist clenched leaning over the table and just as she swung her arm in Tommy's direction, Audrey caught her flying fist in mid air.

'Now sit down and stop this at once… the pair of you.' Audrey shouted. She was exhausted and couldn't be doing with their carryings on. She had dark lines around her tired green eyes. The sleepless nights of caring for baby Nancy and the worry of a possible war breaking out was taking its toll.

At that moment they all looked up to see Frank walk through the lounge door. His big muscular frame filled the doorway. He too had been to the match.

'What a result lads – hey.' He walked past the boys and gave Audrey a peck on the cheek before he sat himself down at the table ready for his tea. His hair was a mixture of grey and blond streaks and his face looked rugged and weather beaten from working outdoors. He had large, smiling, deep brown eyes, surrounded by laughter lines, as Audrey affectionately called them. He had an easy-going nature, everyone loved Frank Lambert.

As usual the family had eaten their dinner at lunch time which was normally a good substantial meal. Supper was served later in the evening which was usually a cooked snack such as eggs on toast or something similar and tea was invariably bread with home made cake that Audrey had baked that day. The boys nodded in agreement with their father as they devoured their mother's freshly made tea cake.

`I saw our Ed at the match. We went for a drink in Pompey after the match. It was bedlam getting out of the place...It was packed, Audrey.' Frank helped himself to the bread and jam in the centre of the table.

`Was it? Packed with football mad men I suspect' Audrey rolled her eyes and Maureen nodded in agreement.

`Well, ain't nothing wrong with that. It's good to see so many people enjoying themselves, it makes a change. Everyone you speak to these days is talking about bleedin' 'itler and war.'

`Do you think there will be a war?' Joe asked his father with a look of concern. Tommy joined in the conversation. `The way that 'itlers is carrying on, I'm sure there will be a war,' he said, taking a large bite from the slice of tea cake he was holding, forcing the rest of the cake to crumble away onto his plate.

Frank glanced up at him. `You're most probably right son – most probably right.' He took a gulp of his tea to wash down the last slice of bread and jam.

Maureen moved closer to her father, sitting down on the spare old wooden chair next to him. `Will we be safe 'ere Dad?' she asked with an obvious tone of fear to her voice.

They all looked at Frank, even Audrey, searching his face for the answer. There was a moment of endless silence before he spoke. Like everyone, he was just as much in the dark and this time he didn't have the answer. Who could predict what Hitler would do next? It seemed likely he wasn't going to keep his promise and would invade Poland anyway. They were all in this together, the nation and the whole world it seemed.

`Well, we are safer than those poor sods in Portsmouth,' he finally replied, after giving it a great deal of consideration.

`Some of those poor sods, as you call 'em, are our family.' Audrey piped up pouring him a cup of tea from the teapot with a colourful tea cosy.

`Don't you think I know that, Audrey? We'll just 'ave to help 'em best we can... But I'm thankful we don't live there no more.' He took a large bite of tea cake and pushed it to one side of his mouth so that he could continue talking. `You know moving from Summer Street to here was the best decision we ever made... Look around you... we got a nice 'ome, don't we?' His words were muffled by his munching. He looked around the room with pride. All he had ever wanted to do was provide for his family. He worked long and hard hours on the land to put a roof over their head and food on the table and he was proud of it, and even more so now he had moved them away from down town Portsmouth, and drunken sailors who had made his daughter pregnant. He was more than happy to be living in Portchester and especially now with the threat of war hanging over them.

`Still the same old tatty furniture but it's a darn site bigger than the house in Summer Street, I'll give you that.' Audrey agreed.

Baby Nancy let out a cry from upstairs and Maureen rolled her big brown eyes and pushed a blond curl from her face. `I've just sat down for me tea' she moaned.

`Go and get her and bring her down 'ere. I'll watch her after I've brought the washing in so you can eat your tea in peace,' Audrey said, taking a sip of her tea. Maureen got up reluctantly and made her way upstairs to get the baby.

Audrey placed her cup carefully down on the table and eyed Frank closely. `There's talk about evacuating all the kids and mothers with babies,' she whispered softly in hopes that Maureen wouldn't hear her. Her eyes were still fixed on Frank and Joe and Tommy listened with interest, their eyes suddenly lighting up. `Do you think we should send our Maureen and baby Nancy?' Audrey asked.

Frank shook his head. `No — there will be no need for that. Like I said it's safer 'ere than Portsmouth and they are building those Anderson shelters everywhere now.'

`I think they would be safer if they go, Dad.' Tommy nudged Joe in the ribs for help.

`I agree Dad, it might be for the best.' Joe added in a desperate attempt to convince him. It would be heaven on earth if they could get rid of her and that screaming baby of hers too.

`They will be fine here... enough said on the matter' Frank looked annoyed at them all and got up from the table and wondered over to his favourite thread bear arm chair. He picked up the day's newspaper. It was rolled and scrunched up resting precariously on the arm of the chair. Maureen had used it to swat a fly earlier that afternoon and the remains of it were still splattered over the back page.

Audrey went out to the back yard and looked up at the sky. There were some ugly black clouds forming in the distance. Looks like rain she decided as she went about taking in the washing. She felt something smooth and fury around her right ankle and glanced down to see Tabby the cat weaving himself lovingly around her. She reached down and smoothed him. `I s'pose you're hungry.' He began purring loudly as if in answer to her statement.

She reached up for Maureen's yellow dress and the baby's little white socks and tears began to well up in her eyes. What was going to happen to them all? She couldn't bear the thought of Joe and Tommy being sent off to war. What would happen to Maureen and the baby? Would they really be safe in Portchester? It wasn't that far away from Portsmouth. It was only a short bus ride away. And what about the rest of the family who were still in Portsmouth? There was Shirley her sister and her two girls, Mum and Dad who were too old to travel anywhere now, Ed and Betty....

`It's just not right,' she mumbled under her breath. Everywhere you went there was only one word on everyone's lips ... War. How can one man be responsible for so much misery? How dare he turn peoples' lives upside down. How dare he storm into those countries and try to take them over. The whole of Europe was getting dragged into all this terrible misery and not just Europe but as far away as Russia too. He's a lunatic that flaming maniac, Adolf Hitler, she thought angrily as she strutted into the house with the washing basket under her arm and Tabby following hungrily behind her.

Two

Emma Howlett had just finished piano practice and gently closed the lid of the old grand piano, being careful not to trap her fingers. At the age of sixteen she was already quite a talented pianist. She rushed to collect her light weight coat shouting out down the long hallway, `I'll be home before dark, Mama.' Not waiting for a reply she dashed outside and was surprised to find how warm the summer air was on her skin. Rain had been forecasted but the sky was bright blue with only the odd white wispy cloud hanging around. It was actually colder inside Bowood House than it was outside. She contemplated turning back and leaving her coat at home but decided against it. It might be chilly later, if the weather forecast was right.

She walked down the street leading from her house and cut through a little path lined with neatly pruned hedges. There was an aroma of roses around or was it honeysuckle? She couldn't quite decide but whatever it was it was lovely. The pathway led out onto the grounds of Whittington Manor. Ignoring the front door, as she always did, she ran around the back of the property to the tradesmen's entrance. Going to the front door would mean being greeted by the butler and then she'd have to wait an age while he fetched Sarah. Very often she would be left making polite conversation with Lord and Lady Whittington. Entering through the tradesmen's door was a far better option and more than likely Annie would be out the back and would be happy to show her directly to Sarah.

Annie was bending over the hot stove and didn't see Emma arrive. She was deep in concentration waiting for her vegetable soup to reach simmering point while stirring it continuously.

`Hello, Annie.' Emma wiped her feet on the little black carpet just inside the back door, it was left there for the staff or delivery people to clean their feet. Her rosy cheeks glowed from running and her long dark hair was neatly braided, she looked clean and fresh in a pale pink dress with a white lace collar.

Annie looked startled for a second. `Oh 'ello my love, 'ow are you?'

`I'm very well, thank you, Annie. Is Sarah home?' Emma liked Annie, she wished she had a housekeeper or even a nanny like her but her own nanny had now retired and their housekeeper was far too formal, she only spoke when spoken to and only did what was expected of her, unlike Annie who was always happy to stop and chat and help whenever she could.

`Well, I haven't seen her for a little while mind, but I think she's in her room. Wait there while I take me pot off the fire and I'll find out.'

Emma smiled at Annie. She still remembered her from when she was a little girl. She had been five years old when her father had made friends with the Whittingtons. Lord Whittington and the Admiral had met at a social function and had hit it off from day one, just as her mother and Sarah's mother had. Emma was an only child. Her father a retired Navy admiral had met her mother late in life and although Florence Howlett was much younger than her husband, she had experienced complications during child birth with Emma and was unable to conceive another child.

Emma walked into Sarah's bedroom to find her lying on her bed with her head in a medical journal. `What are you doing inside on a beautiful day like this?' Emma enquired with a frown, reaching over to look at what she was reading.

`I'm just reading. I got these magazines from the newsagent. They order them for me now. It teaches you how to do first aid in this one... look!' She smiled, handing Emma the magazine.

`Disgusting! That's truly ghastly, Sarah.' Emma screwed up her nose as she looked at a graphic photo of a woman with a severely burned arm.

`Oh you are so squeamish, Emma, really.'

`So where do you want to go?' Emma asked, changing the subject and closing the magazine, trying to forget about the horrific picture.

`Portsdown Hill, maybe? We've not been there for months.' It had been one of their favourite places to visit for a while but like most places it became a little boring and they changed their walks, sometimes to the park or to Portchester Castle.

The girls quickly made their way down to the kitchen to find Annie still busy cooking.

`Annie, we're going out for a walk. I don't know where Mama is, can you please tell her for me?' Sarah asked, as she tidied up her hair, looking at her reflection in the kitchen window.

`Your mum is 'avin' a lay down, she's not sleeping too good at the moment but I'll be sure to tell her when she gets up... And be home before dark, mind,' she shouted after the girls as they ran across the lawn to the front of the house and started to walk down the gravel driveway chatting animatedly.

By the time they had reached Portsdown hill their mood had turned somewhat sombre as they spoke about the prospect of war looming ahead. `Do you think there will be a war Emma, your father must know more than most being a retired Admiral?'

`He says he has it on very good authority that it doesn't look good, but that's all he says. If war is declared Father wants us to move to Devon.'

`Devon? How on earth, am I going to see you when you are in Devon?' Sarah looked horrified at the idea.

`I don't know, Sarah', Emma sighed. She really didn't want to leave Portchester or Sarah for that matter.

`But why can't you stay here? It's not that dangerous. It's not as if we live in Portsmouth.'

They placed their coats on the grass and sat themselves down. `With my father's heart condition it would be better for him to be away from it all.'

`I suppose.' The thought of Emma going away was simply too depressing to even contemplate.

They had been so engrossed in their conversation they hardly noticed the view in front of them. From the top of Portsdown Hill the view spread as far as Portsmouth, The Solent, Gosport, Isle of Wight and even beyond on a clear day. The hill was covered with grass and heathland, while below when looking up the hill the huge chalk pits embedded into the hill were in full view. The forts of Portdown Hill stood covered in moss looking weather beaten. They were built as a result of the 1859 Royal Commission, to defend Portsmouth of a possible attack from France.

Both lost in their own thoughts neither of them had noticed a boy sitting not too far away from them. He was perched on a large stone and was quietly sketching something on a note pad. He looked almost as if he was in a trance as his pencil danced back and forth over the paper. He too hadn't noticed the girls sitting a short distance from him.

Finally Emma spotted him and nudged Sarah gently. `Look at him, what do you think he's drawing?' They both stared at the boy with curiosity and as if he could sense them watching, he turned momentarily and glanced at them. The girls quickly turned away giggling nervously.
`Ask him what he's drawing?' Emma challenged Sarah.
`No, I don't even know him. You ask him?' Sarah was still giggling.

`Alright.... I will' Emma stood up and smoothed the creases from her pink dress.

`No Emma, please don't. I was teasing!'

Emma cleared her throat with a little polite cough. `Excuse me! Sorry to interrupt you.' The boy turned and looked at her, a little surprised and bemused. `Yes' he was wondering what she was about to say next.

`My friend and I were just curious as to what you were drawing?'

`I'm drawing the view,' he returned Emma's smile and then tried to look at Sarah who was hiding behind her. She wished the ground would swallow her up, Emma was enormously embarrassing. His blond curls were blowing in the wind and she could see from where she was sitting that he was extremely handsome, which made the situation even more mortifying.

`May we look?' Sarah's cheeks turned scarlet listening to Emma. The boy signalled them both over and a moment later the two girls were admiring a brilliant drawing of the view in front of them.

`It's wonderful' Emma exclaimed with enthusiasm. `Yes, it is' Sarah agreed nodding her head.

`What's your name?' Emma asked. The boy looked a little awkward and overwhelmed by all the attention they were giving him.

`Joe Lambert.' His cheeks coloured almost the same shade as Sarah's.

`So are you an artist?' Sarah enquired after plucking up the courage to speak and cocking her head to one side to get a better view of his drawing. Joe laughed.

`No, it's a hobby I s'pose. I work on the land with me dad, whenever he needs me that is.' He continued drawing as the girls stood and watched over his shoulder.

`Do you live round 'ere?' he asked. He found it easier to talk to them while he was drawing. Looking them in the eyes was far too unnerving.

`Not far' they both replied in chorus.

`And you?' Emma couldn't resist being nosy. He was very intriguing and he had a strange accent which made him even more mysterious.

`I live down Portsdown Road.' He shuffled on the uncomfortable rock and then continued to draw again.

`Do you draw people?' Sarah asked out of curiosity. Her father once knew an artist and she could remember looking at his portfolio, many of his portraits were of people, some of them famous some not, but it had impressed her how he had managed to capture their features so well.

Joe turned and looked at her. Her voice was as soft as silk. He gazed up into her pretty hazel eyes. She was the most beautiful girl he had ever seen, even prettier than Jessica Bishop, he decided.

`I could draw a picture of you.... if you like?' he offered shyly.

19

`Now?' Sarah blushed profusely at the idea.

`Well it's a little late now, gotta go home for me tea soon. I could tomorrow if you like, though?'

She hesitated for a moment and smiled at him. It would be exciting to have him draw her portrait. `Alright that would be very kind of you.' He chuckled at the way she spoke. She didn't sound like she was from around here, far too posh, he thought.

`What time?' she asked nervously. Their eyes met again and there was an unfamiliar chemistry between them that neither of them recognised. It was almost as if they already knew each other, yet they had never met. It was odd but wonderful at the same time.

`Anytime tomorrow afternoon... Say after dinner?' Sarah was puzzled for a moment and then realised that he had confused dinner time with lunch time. She agreed, smiled at him and turned around to walk down the hill with Emma.

`Oh my goodness Sarah, you have just made an engagement with a complete stranger' Emma stared at her in utter amazement as soon as they were out of earshot

`Well I need some fun in my life.' Her eyes were dancing with excitement.

Joe stood up and started to make his way back home, thinking of the girl with the auburn hair and the pretty hazel brown eyes. Who was she? Where did she come from? He had never seen her before and he often went up Portsdown Hill. He decided he wouldn't say a word to anyone about her. If he did, no doubt he would have Maureen in tow tomorrow, having a look just to be nosey or annoying, one of the two, or worse than that Tommy. Oh my God Tommy, he would chat her up from right under his nose if he wasn't careful. No, this was his secret. He just hoped she would turn up the next day.

As he took off his muddy boots inside the house, he suddenly realised he didn't even know her name. How could he have forgotten to ask her name? She knew his. `Why hadn't he asked her?' He was no good when it came to girls, Tommy was so much better at all that, and then he smiled. This time he had done it. He had a date tomorrow, well not really a date as such but it was a step in the right direction he decided and his smile broadened.

`What you grinning about? Your tea's nearly ready' Audrey had spotted him standing in the hallway.

`Nothing, Mum' he sat himself down at the table next to Tommy who was ploughing his way through a cream cake.

Just then Frank came in carrying a large piece of paper rolled up in one hand and a pencil in the other. `What the 'ell is that?' Audrey asked watching him pin it up on the wall.

`This is a map of all the countries and I'm gunno put a circle round each country that 'itler has taken over... so we can keep a close eye on the bugger, if you know what I mean.'

`We don't need no stupid map to find out what's 'appening, you only 'ave to go outside and hear everyone talking on the street, to know what's going on.' Audrey sat down at the table and poured herself a cup of tea. `I saw Rose Gladstone from up the top of the road this morning,' she said, `and she were in bits, crying her eyes out the poor mare. Her Colin has just gone and joined up and he's leaving home in a few days.' She took a sip of her tea, tutting to herself.

Tommy looked a little sheepish and placed his tea cup down with caution. `Mum, I've got something to tell you. I went to Pompey today.'

`Oh yeah' Audrey looked non-plus as she took a sip of her tea not aware of the bombshell he was about to drop.

`I've signed up with the Navy. I think it's for the best.' Audrey stared at him in disbelief, her mouth open, trying to place her cup down with out looking at it. Frank turned around, with his pencil in his hand. `Well, that's a good choice son, better than the army.' He turned around again and drew a circle around Czechoslovakia.

`Good choice son. Is that all you can say?...A good choice son?' Audrey shrieked, after Tommy's words had finally sunk in. She knocked her cup as she stood up from the table, spilling her tea all over the table cloth and then stormed off to the kitchen.

Frank put down the map and rushed after to her. He found her bent over the kitchen sink, crying. She reached for her handkerchief in the front pocket of her pale blue pinafore and blew her nose, then turned to look at him with sheer desperation in her eyes.

`It's 'appening already, Frank. Our family is being torn apart.' He held out his arms to her and she walked over to him. He held her tightly as she cried in his arms. There was nothing he could say to comfort her, no words like *it will all be alright* or *don't worry*, there was nothing anyone could say, the future was far too uncertain.

Three

Charles Whittington was in the drawing-room talking to his father when Sarah almost stumbled in on them. They had large plans spread out all over the table. `I think we should have three beds on this side and here is an area for a table and some chairs, and over here we could put a small kitchen area,' Charles explained in detail to his father. He looked like him in many ways. He was as tall as his father and of the same build and his light brown hair also carried a hint of auburn which he had inherited from his mother. They were discussing the plans for their private air-raid shelter that was to be erected to the back of the property. Lord Whittington was voicing his ideas too.

Sarah was spying on them through the crack of the door. She had left her hairclip in the room on the table right next to where they were standing but there was no way she was going to go in there to get it and risk them asking her where she was off to. She would just have to use another one she thought. She had told Annie she was meeting up with Emma and another friend to have a picnic and she already felt guilty for lying. The less people that saw her the better it would be. For sure they would not be happy to learn she was meeting a boy she didn't even know on Portsdown Hill. She was relieved her mother was still out visiting a sick friend, at least she wouldn't have to make excuses to her.

Looking in the mirror she straightened her cornflower blue dress and fiddled with her hair. It was tied back in a bun with a few stray wispy curls here and there, framing her pretty round face. Quickly dashing up stairs, she grabbed another hairclip from her dressing table, fixed it in her hair, and ran back down again. `I'll be home before dark' she called out to Annie, as she dashed out of the kitchen not giving her time to ask any questions.

Sarah felt a light fluttering of nerves and excitement in her stomach as she made her way to Portsdown Hill. As soon as she reached the top of the hill, she saw him sitting there, waiting for her, perched on the same small rock as the day before with his pencil behind his ear and notepad at his side. She stopped to catch her breath and her heart fluttered just as her stomach did. He was only drawing her portrait she told herself calmly over and over again as she approached him, but there was no denying it, Joe Lambert was exceptionally handsome.

She sat down on the grass next to him, her cheeks rapidly turning pink. For a moment they didn't speak while they each caught their breath and tried to calm their nerves.

`Your friend ain't with you today?' he said, breaking the silence and trying to make polite conversation.

`No, she has gone on a picnic,' she replied shyly, looking at him out of the corner of her eye.

`So, you still want me to draw you then?' he asked, looking anywhere but at her.

`Yes, please' she shuffled around, positioning herself in front of him.

This time he had no choice but to look at her. If he was going to draw her, he would have to. She was even more beautiful than yesterday he thought as he reached for his pencil, blushing slightly.

`Just turn your head a little' he instructed. He started to make light sketching movements with his pencil on a clean sheet of paper that rested on his note pad. He made swift short strokes and Sarah watched in amazement as her features miraculously started to develop on paper.

`I never asked you your name?' He appeared more confident now. It was easier to talk to her without her friend around.

`Sarah Whittington.'

`Whittington? Rings a bell... Now where `ave I heard that name before?' He scratched his head with the end of his pencil as he tried to remember.

`I live in Whittington Manor....My father is Lord Whittington,' she announced proudly.

In shock he dropped his pencil. My God she was from that huge posh house that stood on the edge between Portchester and Fareham. He had walked past there on many occasions on his way to Fareham and he remembered the sign that read `Whittington Manor' in large black letters, placed at the bottom of the long sweeping driveway. Once, he and Tommy had climbed the oak tree next to the sign, to see if they could see inside the house, but they were spotted by someone walking past and were told to get down. So she was from there, that huge house.

He picked up his pencil that had rolled on to the grass next to him. He was lost for words, not really knowing what to say next. What do you say to the daughter of a Lord?

After a moment he managed to regain his composure. `Did you go to school nearby?' Suddenly he was curious about her. Where did daughters of Lords go to school?

`No, I didn't. I studied at home, although I would have much preferred to go to school. One can make more friends at school, so I've been told.'

`Well I dunno... I hated school and I don't have many friends neither.` The more he thought about it the more he realised that apart from Keith Tucker from Castle Street and George Smith who now lives in Gosport, who he hardly saw these days, he didn't really have any friends, not even in Portsmouth where he used to live. He was too busy for friends, working for his father and drawing was enough for him. He was different from Tommy, he was quiet and a bit of a loner and he was happy that way.

Sarah studied him as he worked on her portrait. His green eyes twinkled and he had big strong hands. `Forgive me for asking, but why are you not working today?' she was just as curious about him as he was about her. She hadn't much knowledge of working class people, her parents had seen to that.

`I only work a few days a week... When me father needs me and today is not one of those days.'

`Oh I see.'

Her politeness amused him. She was different from other girls he knew. `So what do you do with yourself all day then?' he asked, trying to imagine what her life must be like living in that big white mansion.

`I play the piano. I have my studies and I read medical books'

`Read medical books? What dyou do that for?' he asked. It seemed an odd thing for someone to do, unless they were a nurse or a doctor of course.

`I want to be a nurse.' There was a deep sadness in her eyes as she turned her head the other way. Joe waited for a moment until she was ready to look back at him again.

`So, why are you sad about that?'

`Am I?' she looked surprised that he had noticed.

`Your eyes look sad.'

`My parents have forbidden me to be a nurse. They say it's too dangerous with the possibility of us being at war soon.'

`But that's even more the reason to be a nurse. We're gunno need nurses if we go to war.'

At last she had found someone who understood her. `My point exactly, but unfortunately my parents don't see it that way.' No one saw it that way, not her parents, her brother, Annie or even Emma, the only person who had agreed with her so far was Joe.

`How old are you?' he asked. To him, she looked to be around his own age but perhaps she was younger, which would explain why her parents weren't happy with her being a nurse.

`I'm sixteen.' She straightened her back as if to make herself look older.

`Anyway, I have already decided... I will be a nurse no matter what they say. They will just have to get used to the idea.' She sounded determined.

It seemed unfair of her parents, stopping her doing what she wanted to do. Maybe it was hard for her living in that lonely mansion, never going to school, and what harm could come to her being a nurse anyhow? Joe thought as he watched her closely.

`So.... What about you? What would you like to do?' She asked with intrigue.

`Me?' He replied with a short laugh, as if it was funny that anyone should ask him what he wanted to do. No one ever really cared what Joe Lambert wanted, he was just Joe Lambert who worked on the land with his father and lived down Portsdown Hill.

`I used to dream of being an artist, when I was young that is, but round 'ere.... well... working with me dad, it's the best I can get right now.' He shrugged his shoulders as if accepting his lot in life. `I guess I won't be working on the land for much longer, mind. The way that itler is carrying on.... I'll soon have me marchin' orders.' Sarah suddenly felt a pang in her heart, they had only just met and it seemed silly that she was afraid for him, but she hated the idea of him having to go and fight in the war. Life was so unfair, why did people have to put their lives at risk?

Her thoughts drifted to Thomas at sea. `My bother is in the Navy, we haven't heard from him for quite a while now. His whereabouts are kept secret.' She looked sad again and for a moment she looked as if she were about to cry.

`It's most probably safety reasons why they ain't allowed to say nothing.' Joe gave her a reassuring smile. She smiled back at him and waited for him to finish drawing her, neither of them saying another word.

`There you go!' he handed her the portrait he had so carefully drawn.

`Joe that's truly magnificent, it almost looks like a photograph of me.' He sat down on the grass beside her. He liked her. She was easy to talk to and she wasn't silly like most of the girls her age. They continued to chat for a while longer and the longer they chatted the more he realised how special she really was. Every now and then her arm would brush against his or a waft of her fragrance drifted his way and he yearned to touch her, put his arm around her but he knew it wasn't wise to do so. It was strange to think they both live in Portchester, yet come from two entirely different worlds.

As the sun started to set and there was a slight chill in the air. `I should go, it's getting late,' Sarah sounded reluctant as she stood up and smoothed down the back of her dress where it had creased from sitting on it. She didn't want the afternoon to end. She could have talked to him all day and night. He was easy going, happy go lucky, even witty at times. There was nothing pompous about him. He didn't talk about politics, financial affairs and boring topics like most of the young men her parents had introduced her to at parties and social functions they often attended. No, Joe Lambert was different from anyone she had ever met and he made her feel special, unique, like she was only person that mattered and she liked that.

`I'll walk you back if you like.' Joe offered, picking up his pencil and notepad. Sarah rolled up her portrait, so as not to damage it, and slipped it into her dress pocket.

Joe frowned and staring at her hair, he moved closer to where she was standing. `Stay still... don't move... There's something in your hair.' Moving even closer, he cupped his right hand over a part of her auburn shiny hair.

`What is it?' Her eyes were wide and anxious.

Carefully, looking like he was picking something out of her hair, she stood very still in front of him, trusting him, too frightened to move a muscle.

`What is it?' she asked again, sounding panic-stricken.

`It's just a ladybird, that's all.' He unclenched his fist, as if to let it go, and she sighed with relief. As he turned to her, he touched her face, making soft stroking movements with the back of his fingers over her delicate creamy-skin. He couldn't resist the yearning he had had all afternoon to touch her. He had a sudden irresistible urge to kiss her. Gently pressing his lips on hers, much to his amazement, she responded to him. A few seconds later they looked at each other, both bewildered by what had just happened, and without saying a word, he took her hand and they began walking down Portsdown hill.

Stopping half way, Sarah suddenly turned and stared at him with a look of realisation on her face. `I didn't really have a ladybird in my hair, did I?'

She asked suspiciously, narrowing her eyes. He started to laugh and then shook his head from side to side.

`Oh......You!' she shouted, running down the hill chasing after him, as he ran as fast as he could from her. Just as he reached the bottom of the hill, he collided into an old lady, nearly knocking her off her feet. She grabbed onto her handbag with fear. `You want to watch where you're going, young man!' she scolded him, looking both angry and shocked at the ordeal.

`Sorry!' he shouted back as Sarah caught up with him, panting and laughing hysterically with him. They laughed uncontrollably with tears streaming down their faces, until finally they calmed down and continued to walk, holding hands once again.

Before entering onto the grounds of Whittington Manor they stopped and looked at each other. Joe had a solemn expression on his face. `Sarah, can I see you again?' He had to see her again. She was the most beautiful girl he had ever seen.

`Yes, I would like that very much.' Her voice was soft and caressing.

`Can I see you on Saturday? We could go to Portchester Castle if you like?' She nodded, in agreement.

Before she left him, he kissed her gently once more, and then leaning against the old oak tree, he watched her walk up the long gravel driveway to Whittington Manor.

Sarah dashed inside with a spring in her step. Her mother was just walking down the sweeping staircase as she walked through the front door into the large foyer. `You look a little flushed my dear. I hope you are not sickening for something?'

`I'm fine, mama... really... I am fine' she was beaming from ear to ear.

Laura frowned. `Dinner will be served soon so don't disappear' she instructed, sounding somewhat puzzled at her daughter's behaviour.

Sarah dashed up stairs and didn't stop running until she was safely in her room with the door firmly closed behind her. She flopped onto her bed in a daze, still smiling. Joe Lambert was the most handsome boy she had ever seen and he had just kissed her, not once but twice. She could hardly wait to tell Emma and she laughed at the thought of her friend's reaction.

Two weeks later, on a dreary Monday morning, the Lambert family were up very early to say goodbye to Tommy before he headed off to Portsmouth dockyard to join the Navy. Maureen sat at the table watching her brother polish off the big plate of eggs, bacon, tomato and fried bread that Audrey had got up extra early to prepare for him. Although she couldn't stand him, Tommy was still her brother after all, and the thought of him in danger worried her.

What if she never saw him again? What if this was her last memory of him – eating his eggs and bacon, and all those terrible things she had said to him would go with him if he died, she thought as tears clouded her eyes. As if knowing what she was thinking, he turned and looked at her. `Don't worry our Maureen, I'll be alright, and if war does break out, I could be a war hero, you never know,' he said, grinning cheekily at her.

Joe poured himself a cup of tea. He wasn't sure how he felt about his brother going away. He would miss him that was certain, and Tommy joining up, only made him realise that he too might be faced with leaving soon. Why now? At long last he had a girl, a girl of his own. The last thing he wanted to do was go away.

`Hold open your hand lad.' Frank said, as he pulled out an old looking farthing from his pocket.

`I won't be needin,' no pocket money where I'm off to' he said, laughing at his father.

`It's not pocket money, you daft sod, it's me lucky farthing. It kept me alive in the first war and it's gunno keep you alive if we have another.'

`Thanks Dad' Tommy said, sliding it into his trouser pocket.

`Well - I spose it's time' he said, as he stood up straight pushing his shoulders back. Audrey appeared in the room, she couldn't bear sitting at the table with him. It was like watching him eat his last supper, except this was breakfast. She stood staring at him through her tears, her little baby who she had rocked to sleep at night. She remembered taking him to school on his first day and putting sticky plasters on his knees from the scrapes and cuts of the playground, and there he was standing in front of her, all grown up and going off to serve his country.

`Bye, Mum.' Tommy flung his arms around her and she let out a sob, as the others stood watching, each with tears in their eyes. Even baby Nancy, in Maureen's arms started to cry.

`You take good care of yourself and don't skip meals... you'll need to keep your strength up. And I want a letter every week, do you ere me?' She pulled away from him, giving a chance for the others to hug him in turn. When it was Maureen's turn for a hug they both hesitated awkwardly. It was like calling a truce and hugging the enemy except she wasn't the enemy at all, the enemy was waiting for him elsewhere should the inevitable war break out.

28

As Tommy Lambert walked down Portsdown Hill, on his way to catch the bus to Portsmouth dockyard, he looked at the familiar houses he had walked past so many times over the past few months. Would he ever see them again? What would happen if war broke out? He wondered as he reached the end of the road and gave one last wave to the family who were standing at the garden gate, before he turned the corner and walked towards his unknown future.

Sarah and Joe had been almost inseparable during the last few weeks of the summer, even if it meant just snatching a short stroll after Joe had finished work or a few minutes to kiss on top of Portsdown Hill, after Sarah's studies, but somehow they always managed to find the time to be together. The best days were when Joe wasn't working or Sarah had no obligations to fill and they could spend all day in each other's company. They often went up Portsdown Hill or sat in the grounds of Portchester Castle, looking out to sea, chatting and kissing. Joe so far had managed to keep Sarah his secret for fear that the others might ruin everything and follow him out on his sacred dates with Sarah. She was his first love and he, hers. Their love was undeniably special and it was almost a miracle how their paths had crossed in the first place. Apart from telling Emma, who found it all rather thrilling, Sarah had not said a word to anyone. Amazingly enough she had managed to keep Joe her secret.

Annie had noticed Sarah's sudden happiness, but wasn't quite sure why, and was waiting for the right moment to ask her. Her parents had been far too busy with the new air-raid shelter and worrying about Thomas, to notice anything different about their daughter. The Lamberts had also been preoccupied with their worries too, what with Tommy going away and the threat of war, but for Sarah and Joe, war was the last thing on their minds. All they could think about was how much they loved each other, although they were both very much aware the road ahead of them would not be easy, and that was without a war.

*****

Two and a half months later

On September 3rd 1939, Sarah had never felt happier as she took a photograph of Joe standing on top of Portsdown Hill. He was pulling funny faces and teasing her. Finally, he managed to stand and pose normally, just long enough for her to take the photograph.

He held her close and kissed her tenderly. `Sarah, I think it's time we told people about us. I don't care what they think. I wouldn't care if your father was the King of England, it still wouldn't change 'ow I feel about you... 'ow about we start now, and I take you home to meet me mum and our Maureen?' Sarah stood looking at him worriedly contemplating the consequences. `Me dad might not be home yet, but still you could meet the others.' He said grinning at her. He had never felt surer about anything. His confidence rubbed off on her and her look of worry broke into a broad smile. `Alright let's do it' she said, sounding resolute.

They walked hand in hand, down Portsdown road towards The Laurels. `It's not a big posh house like yours mind and it may not be too tidy neither' he said, starting to get nervous as they approached the house. Sarah stopped and faced him, placing her finger on his lips.

`Shush, it's your home and it's your family.' As long as she was with Joe, she couldn't care less where she was, or who she met, they couldn't be that bad, and certainly couldn't be as stringent as her own parents, she thought.

`Is that you Joe?' Audrey called out from the front-room.

`Yeah it's me. I've brought home a visitor, Mum,' he said, as Sarah stood next to him blushing, her new found confidence suddenly rapidly draining away.

They walked into the front-room together. `Mum, this is Sarah.' Sarah's lips twitched with a nervous smile.

`Ello.' Audrey extended her hand with a broad warm smile and Sarah returned the smile and shook her hand.

`Pleased to meet you, Mrs Lambert.'

Maureen turned instantly, with a look of surprise to hear her high-class accent.

`Where do you live my love?' asked Audrey.

`I live on the outskirts of Portchester,' she replied, feeling that it was a little inappropriate at this moment, to say she lived at Whittington Manor. Audrey eyed her closely. Pretty girl, but a bit la-di-da, she thought.

`You want a cuppa?' she asked, being friendly.

`Thank you, that's most kind' Sarah answered, standing awkwardly in the doorway of the front-room.

`Come `n' sit down' Joe said clearing away a pile of socks waiting to be darned that were strewn over the best part of the old chocolate brown sofa. The two matching arm chairs in front looked just as worn as the sofa did, with its thread bear arms, snags and stains.

She sat down next to Maureen and looked around the room. There seemed to be a lot of junk on top of the old fireplace that looked like it had accumulated over time, - empty cigarette packets, an old hair brush, a pair of small black gloves. Opened post was wedged in the oval brass frame of a mirror that hung above the fireplace. On one wall there was an old dresser, displaying an expensive looking dinner-set, but there wasn't much else of value. The furniture looked worn and tired, as if it had seen better days. The Lamberts worked hard to pay the rent at The Laurels and there was very little over after pay-day, especially for buying luxuries such as furniture.

Joe made a mad dash out to the kitchen to find his mother. `What dyou think of her, Mum?' he whispered as she filled up the kettle to go on the stove.

`Very nice, our Joe... She's ain't from round ere though, is she?'

`No, Mum. I need to tell you something.' Joe said hesitantly.

`Oh - and what's that?' She turned and looked at him curiously with a frown on her face. Perhaps she had some deep dark secret. Perhaps she had a baby like Maureen did or worse than that perhaps she was married and having an affair with Joe.

`She's from Whittington Manor, her father is Lord Whittington.' Joe blurted out.

`Oh my gawd! Why didn't you tell me you were bringing her 'ome? This was worse than all the things she had previously thought. Quick fetch the best china out the cabinet.' She pointed anxiously to the dining room door, next to where Joe was standing. `Mum relax! She's ain't like that. I mean yeah - she's got a posh accent, but she's a nice girl, really. She ain't stuck-up, if you know what I mean.'

`No, I don't know what you mean. Fetch the best china come on! - Oh my goodness and the 'ouse is such a mess. I was just starting me darning when you turned up. What is she gunno think of us? You should of told me she was comin' And a daughter of a Lord!'

`So ow long you known my brother then?' Maureen asked Sarah, having the time to interrogate her now everyone was out of the room.

`A few weeks... We met on Portsdown Hill when he was drawing. He drew a picture of me, too.' she added proudly.

`Hope you kept your clothes on' Maureen hooted. Sarah blushed.

`Our Joe's quiet and it's the quiet ones you gotta watch out for. Our Tommy on the other hand, well he's the one for the ladies. If you stick around long enough and play your cards right you might see him when he gets leave. He'll show you a good time, but you better be careful with the both of them or you'll end up in the same situation I was in.'

Sarah looked confused and was still blushing. Same situation?

`Yeah - Up the duff... Bun in the oven.' Sarah was still none the wiser, she was a strange girl. These were not the sort of conversations she was used to having, not even with Emma, who could be a little conspicuous at times.

`Pregnant'. Maureen rolled her eyes. It was obvious she didn't speak the same language and she wondered how her brother could communicate with her. She was pretty and he was probably getting what he wanted, although come to think of it, perhaps not, she was a bit stuck up to be doing it. Perhaps he was just hoping she would one day. She sat staring at her and Sarah felt very uncomfortable. She was relieved when Joe and Audrey walked back in the room.

`Now 'ow dyou like your tea? Joe likes his weak, like dishwater' she chuckled.

`Whatever is more convenient, Mrs Lambert' Sarah replied, still feeling nervous.

`So, Joe tells me your father is a Lord.' Audrey said, trying to make polite conversation. `What's a Lord?' Maureen asked, frowning at her mother.

`Someone important... Now shut-up' Audrey said, glaring at her.

`So your house is the big white one, just as you leave Portchester, in the direction of Fareham?' Audrey asked just to make sure she was thinking of the right one. Maureen's eyes grew wide.

`Yes, that's right,' Sarah replied shyly.

`Oh my gawd... she's loaded n'all!' Maureen whispered in her brother's ear, and he nudged her in the ribs to be quiet.

Just then voices could be heard coming from the street and Audrey stood up. `What's all that noise going on outside?' she said, placing her tea cup on the table and walking over to the front door. She could hear Frank's voice outside the front door. He seemed to be calling out to someone and talking very loudly. Frank pushed open the door just as she tried to open it and they banged in to each other.

`Oh it's you, making that racket. Come and meet our guest' she said, grinning at her husband. `Guest, what guest? Frank walked into the front-room to find Sarah sitting on the couch. She stood up as soon as she saw him.

`Ello, love. Frank Lambert' he announced, stretching out his hand for her to shake it.

`Pleased to meet you Sir. I'm Sarah Whittington' she replied timidly, blushing, while shaking his hand.

`Sarah's our Joe's friend and she lives at Whittington Manor. You know, that big white house on the way to Fareham,' Audrey informed him with a knowing wink.

`That's a very nice house,' Frank said, raising his eyebrows and looking impressed by what his wife had just told him. He wondered how she had become friends with Joe, he seemed the most unlikely type of friend for her. His thoughts were interrupted by his wife.

`Anyow, Frank, what was all that noise about just then, when you were coming in?'

`Oh that... I was talking to Alfred Jeffery three doors up.' He reckons there's some important news coming on the wireless soon. So if you don't mind,' he said looking at Sarah,

`I think it's best we tune in, just in case.' With that he brought the wireless in the front-room and started to twiddle the knobs to get a clearer reception.

`It's Neville Chamberlain, he's gunno make a speech.' Frank said anxiously.

`Who?' Maureen whispered into Joe's ear.

`The prime Minister... gawd sake... don't you know anything, Maureen?'

They all huddled around the wireless, listening intently to the words of Neville Chamberlain. Little did they know that what they were about to hear would not only go down in history, but change each of their lives forever.

"This morning the British Ambassador in Berlin handed the German Government a final note stating that, unless we hear from them by 11 o'clock and that they were prepared at once to withdraw their troops from Poland, a state of war would exist between us. I have to tell you now that no such undertaking has been received, and that consequently this country is at war with Germany".

Audrey gasped, clutching Frank's hand tightly. Joe put his arm around Sarah and held her close, and Maureen sat looking baffled, trying to make sense of it all.

With much emotion and almost in tears himself, the Prime Minister then concluded his speech with the following words...

"May God bless you all. May He defend the right. For it is evil things that we shall be fighting against - brute force, bad faith, injustice, oppression and persecution - and against them I am certain that right will prevail."

Frank stood up looking deathly pale and walked out of the room not saying a single word. The rest of them sat looking at each other in despair.

`That's awful,' Audrey said at last, her voice barely a whisper. `What's gunno 'appen now?'

Tears filled Sarah's eyes as she looked up at Joe in fear. What does that mean for you? Will you be called for service soon?

`I expect so.' He nodded mournfully, devastated at the thought of leaving her, but he clearly would have no choice. Their lives were about to be turned upside down.

Four

The Whittingtons apart from Charles, who was working at the time, stood on the platform of Portsmouth station as they bid farewell to the Howlett family. The station was packed with children who were being evacuated to the countryside, and there were more arriving in droves, each one carrying a suitcase and a small brown box containing a gas mask. To some it was like a holiday or a school outing as they chatted excitedly amongst themselves. Others looked subdued as they stood quietly in a queue to get on the train. A few appeared dazed with tear stained faces after having said goodbye to their parents. Some children were only three or four years old, clinging desperately to their older sibling, not knowing what would happen once they arrived at wherever they were going.

The teachers were busy ushering them onto the train and the parents who had come to say goodbye, were being pushed to the back of the platform by the crowds as they anxiously called out to their children with heart felt messages, *"look after your brother, don't forget to brush your teeth morning and night, mummy loves you very much, don't you forget that I love you son, remember to write"* The messages fell on deaf ears for the hubbub of the station was deafening as the children boarded the train.

Lord Whittington shook hands firmly with the Admiral, Laura embraced Florence and Sarah hugged Emma tightly. `I'm going to miss you so much.' Sarah brushed away her tears `I'm going to miss you too.

`Please be sure to write to me, won't you?' Emma smiled ruefully through her tears.

`Of course I will, every week, I promise.' Emma hugged her again and whispered in her ear. `I want you to keep me informed about Joe, all the gory details do you hear me?' Sarah nodded. The girls chuckled at their little secret, and with that the Howletts boarded the first class section of the train.

As the whistle blew and the heavy black steam train chugged slowly out of the station, children could be seen hanging out of the window in a last attempt to say goodbye or catch a final glimpse of their parents.

Lord Whittington placed his arm gently around his daughter's shoulders as they made their way out of the station. `We *will* visit them my dear.'

`I hope so Papa,' she said, with a sad smile trying to put on a brave face.

`It might all be over by Christmas,' her mother said, sounding hopeful, if not for her daughter's sake but for her own. The endless silence from Thomas and the waiting for Charles' call up papers were taking their toll on her. She was looking withdrawn and tired and the dark coloured fox fur that sat loosely around her shoulders made her skin appear even paler than usual. Lord Whittington appeared just as tired as his wife. He was looking much older these days, Sarah thought as she looked up into his weary blue eyes.

When the Whittingtons returned to the manor they went their separate ways, each carrying on where they had left off earlier that day. Lord Whittington had some business letters to finish writing in the library and Laura went to the drawing-room to finish her tapestry, she loved to sew and it helped her to relax. Sarah headed straight for the kitchen. There was only one person she wanted to speak to right now, other than Joe of course but he was working, and that was Annie.

She walked into the kitchen to find Annie busy preparing the evening meal. She had a colourful array of fresh vegetables in front of her on the kitchen table, ranging from bright orange carrots to dark green broccoli. Annie picked out the most attractive looking carrots, putting them to one side and then selected each potato carefully, checking there were no roots or eyes in any of them, before organising them neatly in a row ready for peeling. Everything Annie did was to perfection. You only had to look around the kitchen to see how extremely clean and organised she was.

`Come'n sit yourself down my love,' Annie said, with a sympathetic smile. She knew saying goodbye to Emma wouldn't have been easy for Sarah and her heart ached for the poor girl. She herself had grown fond of the friendly bubbly young girl who had come to call for Sarah almost daily, for so many years now. She could remember when the two of them would play contentedly for hours in the garden as small children. Annie would watch them playing in the distance from the kitchen window whilst she cooked. They loved to play hide and seek, hiding amongst the trees and shrubs on the grounds of Whittington Manor. They also used to dance around the rose bushes singing `ring around the roses.'

`It was terrible, Nanny - I'm missing her already'. She watched Annie peel the carrots.

`I know my love, let's just hope this terrible war will be over soon and she'll soon be back.'

`Nanny, there's something I want to tell you but I need you to promise me that you won't tell anyone, especially my parents.' Sarah's big hazel eyes were wide and apprehensive. Annie frowned. If it was anything untoward she would have to tell the girl's parents, there was no question about it. She owed it to Lord and Lady Whittington to tell them anything that could harm their daughter.

`Nanny, please! Do you promise me?' Sarah pleaded, breaking Annie's train of thought.

`Alright, what is it Miss Sarah?'

`I'm in love,' she said with a huge beaming smile that faded as quickly at it appeared.

`I see, and who might you be in love with? 'Annie asked, eyeing her closely.

`His name is Joe Lambert and he lives in Portsdown Road.' Sarah got up and closed the door, and then returned to her chair again.

`Oh and d'your parents know about this Joe Lambert?' It was unlikely, the way she had just closed the door and with her speaking so softly, Annie thought.

`No of course not, Nanny,' she replied in a harsh whisper, looking at her as if she were insane. `They want to marry me off to some haughty, self-important man who wants me on his arm to show off at dinner parties…love doesn't even come into the equation,'

`Oh Miss Sarah, I'm sure it's not as bad as all that, and I'm sure your mum and dad want you to marry a man you love,' she said looking sorrowful at her. `Anyow, tell me about this Joe Lambert then.' If she wasn't to tell the Whittingtons, she should at least find out if he was a decent boy, and if he wasn't, then perhaps she might have to break her promise.

`He's so handsome, Nanny and he comes from a nice family too. Joe works with his father, Frank and his mother Audrey is so kind, they make me very welcome,' she said enthusiastically. `They come from Portsmouth you know,' she added, wanting to impress Annie further, knowing full well that that was where Annie was from.

`Wait a minute... Did you say the boy's mum's name is Audrey?.. Audrey Lambert?' she said, as her eyes widened with surprise.

`Yes, that's right, Audrey Lambert.'

`I know Audrey Lambert, she lived down Autumn Grove when she was a girl, we went to the same school, although she was two years below me mind. She married a chap called Frank and they moved to Summer Street then.'

`That's right, Joe's father is called Frank. They are not bad people are they, Nanny?' Annie shook her head.

`No my love. The Lamberts are good people,' just not upper class, Annie thought but didn't dare state the obvious, she was just happy that she knew who the lad was and decided it best to keep Sarah's secret safe for now. The lad most probably would be called up for service soon anyway, and God only knows how long he would be away for. As if she could read Annie's mind, Sarah looked at her with big sad eyes. `He will probably receive his service papers soon and the time we have together is precious. I don't want my parents making things difficult for us. I am not going to tell them about Joe until he comes back from the war.' She had clearly given the subject much consideration.

`Just be careful. I'm sure he's a nice lad n'all, but don't go getting yourself into trouble before he goes away. You don't wanna be getting in the family way,' she warned sternly.

`Annie, of course not and Joe isn't like that,' blushing at the very idea, she was starting to sound like Maureen.

`Well, just be careful mind, that's all I say, and your secret is safe with me,' she waved her finger at her as she picked up a potato to peel.

Audrey Lambert was hanging out her washing, talking reluctantly to Phyllis Grimshaw over the garden fence. As usual Phyllis was in her curlers, Audrey wondered if they were glued to her head. She tried to remember a time when she had seen her without them, and apart from at Phyllis's son's wedding four years ago, when Audrey remembered seeing her big yellow curls, there was no other time she could recall.

`They're starting to call it the phoney war, so I've heard,' she said, as she stood propping up the garden fence with her left arm, the top of her pink floral pinafore showing. She always wore the same pinafore. Either that or she had one for each day of the week. `I think we will die of boredom not 'itler's bombs,' she scoffed.

It was as if she wanted bombs to drop on them, Audrey thought. Audrey was just thankful nothing was happening in Portchester and hoped it never would.

`I mean, it's been what, nearly four months now since Chamberlin declared war and it's as quiet as a mouse round ere, nothing's 'appening. Dunno even why all these men are joining up. Probably be all over soon,' she continued to complain, watching Audrey hang out her clean white sheets on the line. She had always been envious of Audrey's clean sheets, how did she ever get them that white?

`Well, it maybe quiet round 'ere in Portchester but at sea there's plenty going on. The *Courageous* was torpedoed and sunk off the Hebredies not long ago. That ship has been harboured in Portsmouth on many occasions, I remember from when I lived there. Some of those sailors were from Portsmouth you know.' One of them could have been baby Nancy's father, she mused but not wanting to say it out loud. `And to think how those poor families must be suffering.' She continued pegging out the rest of her washing. `And another thing,' she said, continuing to put Phyllis Grimshaw in her place after her comment that nothing was happening. `There was a report of a plane scrap recently, just over Southsea, so the Germans are coming this way,' She pegged the last item of washing on the line and turned to face her.

`And what 'append?' Phyllis asked curiously. This was all fascinating gossip. She hadn't heard any of this and reading newspapers wasn't her thing.

`Our boys scared 'em off, that's what 'appened.'

`I hear they will be giving out ration books soon, 'ave you heard about that Audrey?' She asked, hoping this time she knew something that Audrey Lambert didn't.

`Yeah, me sister mentioned something to me about it. Sounds a bit complicated to me,' She picked up her empty basket, ready to walk inside, just as soon as she could get away from Phyllis.

`Yeah, sounds a bit complicated to me n'all. Apparently, you got different coupons for different foods, like your dairy, your meat and so on, and you 'ave to give it in to the shop keeper. There's only so many vouchers you can use at one time.'

`That'll be so you are rationed to fair portions daily or weekly, I spose.'

`*Fair*?' Phyllis retorted raising her eye brows. `This bloody 'itler as a lot to answer for.' At last Phyllis Grimshaw had said something Audrey agreed with.

`Yeah, he does that.' Audrey replied nodding her head.

Phyllis stood up straight. `Anyow, best get on. Got me windows to clean today. I always clean me windows on a Tuesday, can't 'ang around chatting, much as I'd love to, mind. Cheerio.' Phyllis said, as if it was Audrey who was holding her up with idle chit-chat.

Even 'itler wouldn't stop Phyllis Grimshaw from cleaning her windows on a Tuesday, or stop her chatting for that matter, Audrey mumbled under her breath as she went indoors.

The house was spotlessly clean. Audrey had given it a good going over from top to bottom, whilst Maureen and the baby had gone to visit a friend, and Frank and Joe were at work. There was a feeling of peace and calm over the house as she looked around and heard the clock ticking softly on the wall.

Tabby was laying stretched out almost the full length of the sofa and had buried his face under his paw as he snoozed contentedly. Audrey reached above the fireplace and took down Tommy's letter wedged in the mirror. She had received it three days ago and had read it countless times. It was the only comfort she could find, reading the words *I'm fine Mum*, it was all she wanted to hear, it was all she had to cling on to, and it was only a matter of time before Joe would be off too, she thought as she sighed and started to read the letter again.

Although most people were well aware of the terrible atrocities that were happening overseas, as Phyllis had pointed out, there appeared to be very little happening in Portchester that showed there was actually a war going on. Apart from the looming barrage balloons in the far distance, rationing just starting in the shops, and the obvious lack of young men on the streets and in public places, everything was pretty much the same. Anderson shelters stood empty, and when the occasional siren sounded, people barely looked up, for they knew it was only a practice run. People were also getting careless with their gas masks, often using the little brown carrier box for other things, like their lunch instead of their gas masks. Nevertheless, there were those who said it was only a matter of time before the dreaded air-raids would start, and with Portchester being so close to Portsmouth, they would get rained on too.

`Have you read page two?' Charles asked his Father, appalled at what he had just been reading in the newspaper.

`Page two? No, not sure that I have.' Charles and Lord Whittington often spent time in the library. It was the one place they could relax without the women intruding on them, often referring to it as the *gentlemen's quarters*.

He was reading about how the Nazis had smashed windows of every Jewish shop, looted homes, destroyed synagogues and terrorised people.

And it said that some thirty thousand Jews had been taken off to labour camps.

'It's despicable' Charles said, then sighed as he paused from reading. 'How can they behave in such a way? I just don't understand how they can get away with it. Something has to be done.'

'Well, it's no secret that the Nazis don't like Jews... but yes I agree, something has got to be done about it,' Lord Whittington said at last, looking up from a letter he was reading.

'And I intend to help', Charles added with determination. 'Father, my papers arrived this morning. It seems that I am to report to Hilsea Barracks for duty on Monday morning.' There was a moment of silence before Lord Whittington spoke.

'I suppose it was inevitable. When are you planning on telling your mother?'

'I thought this evening, after dinner, as Sarah will be there too.' Lord Whittington walked over to Charles and rested a hand heavily on his shoulder. 'Your mother is not going to take this lightly old chap. You know what she has been like over Thomas. Thank goodness we received a letter to say he was alright, I was beginning to fear for her health,'

'I know Father, but we are at war, nothing can be done about me going away.'

Lord Whittington sat back down in the chair opposite him, suddenly looking as if he had aged ten years. He loved all three of his children but he and Charles were the closest, they were two peas in a pod, similar in character in many ways.

'I could speak to the authorities. I know people in high places... I'm sure there will be a loop hole somewhere... If I... Charles interrupted him.

'Father, I must go, it's my duty. I can not stand back and let those animals for want of a better word, they don't even deserve to have the title animal, take over the world. I want to serve my country.' He sat with his hands stretched out in front of him on the table with a look of determination in his eyes.

With tears brimming Lord Whittington's eyes he looked away for a moment. 'I'm very proud of you, son,' he said quietly trying to hide his emotions. He turned back to Charles and looked choked. He took a swallow as he fought back his tears.

'I need to get my affairs in order before I go away, I want my half of the accountancy business protected plus my stocks and shares, and I have to make a will too,' Charles said, lighting up a cigarette and trying not to get caught up with his father's emotions. At least he wasn't married that was one less problem to contend with, leaving a wife behind would have been simply another worry on top of leaving his parents.

Lord Whittington wrote down the contact details of a solicitor and handed it to him.

`Edward Hamilton is the chap for the job. He's a young fellow but knows his stuff, just like his father did. He recently replaced William Hamilton, who sadly passed away a year ago.'

`Edward Hamilton. I will contact him in the morning, thank you Father.

`I'm popping out to the shop. Maureen's upstairs... be back soon,' Audrey shouted out to Joe and Sarah who were in the front- room, as she grabbed her coat and shut the door tightly behind her.

`Looks like we're alone,' Joe grinned at Sarah. They began kissing passionately, as Joe's hands strayed to places they both knew he shouldn't be touching. Just lately their passion was getting difficult to control and they were snatching any moment of privacy they could get. It was too cold up Portsdown Hill or Portchester Castle and everywhere else they went there were too many people, people that might recognise her and tell her parents.

After drawing for breath he nuzzled his head on her neck and fondled her breasts as she stroked his hair. He moved his body almost on top of her and she could feel him becoming aroused, their passion was spiralling out of control. Just in time they were interrupted by Maureen's heavy footsteps coming down the stairs, and as she reached the bottom, they quickly jumped apart. Sarah looked flushed as she tried frantically to straighten her skirt and Joe sat up with his hair ruffled and his shirt half unbuttoned.

`Oh I beg your pardon did I interrupt something?' Maureen smirked, putting on a posh voice and giving an evil chuckle as she passed them on her way to the kitchen to make a cup of tea.

`I hate her! I really do.'

`She's not that bad. Charles annoys me quite often, and I suppose I will miss him when he goes away, just as Maureen will miss you. Realising what she had just said her eyes misted over.

`What's with the sad face, I don't have me call up papers yet, do I?' He pulled her into his arms. `Yes, but you will. I can't imagine being without you Joe,'

`I can't imagine being without you either. Who would want to leave a beautiful girl like you behind?' He kissed her again and then started to kiss her neck whispering sweet nothings into her ear.

`I love you' she whispered back, breathlessly.

`Oh for goodness sake, put her down,' Maureen sneered as she walked passed them again with a cup of tea in her hand.

Just as Joe was about to shout at her, Audrey walked through the front door. Once again their moment of passion had been interrupted, but as long as they were together that was all that really mattered. Every night before she went to sleep she would lay in bed for hours thinking of him, savouring each kiss and every touch as if it was the last.

Five

It was the winter of 1940 and the media were calling it the big freeze. There were icy blizzards in Portchester and Fareham causing the roads to be treacherous. It was bad in Portsmouth too. The snow was causing havoc and Langstone harbour had completely frozen. Train services had been cancelled. It was the worst winter since 1881.

Charles had been in the army for five weeks now and the Whittingtons had no idea where he had been sent to, but the worst news for Sarah came when Joe announced that he finally had a letter that morning, asking him to report to the barracks in Hilsea for duty in five days time.

`Apparently, I'm gunno be in the *gunners* and I've got me training in Whale Island' he reiterated the letter glumly.

`Whale Island, that's only down the road, it's near the Isle of Wight. Does that mean I can still see you sometimes?' Sarah asked with hope.

`I don't think so, Sarie.'

She loved the way he often called her Sarie. `It might be only down the road but I've heard they work you hard and then as soon as you are trained, you're off to gawd knows where.' He folded the letter up and put it back in his pocket.'

`I just don't know what I'm going to do without you, I will be going out of my mind with worry,' she looked up at him with tears in her eyes and her bottom lip quivered.

`I don't fancy it meself, if I'm honest... I hate to leave you, Sarie' he pulled her close and kissed her tenderly on the lips.

The next few days passed too quickly, and although they tried to make the best of their time together, it wasn't easy, with stolen moments of passion, and the weather so bitterly cold outside meant they couldn't even go out.

Joe and Sarah spent their last day together at The Laurel's. Audrey and Frank had been considerate and stayed in the kitchen for quite a while, keeping out of their way for the young couple to spend as much time as possible together.

`I can't bear to see him go off' Audrey said, as she pottered around the kitchen trying to keep busy for fear she would fall apart at the seams if she didn't. Having both her sons at war was breaking her heart and she looked anxious and tired.

`There's nothing we can do love. We just gotta pray he'll stay safe and sound just like we do for our Tommy,' Frank replied in a low voice from behind his newspaper. It gave him goose bumps, whenever he read the stories in the papers about how England and their allies were losing against Hitler's army. He felt as if his sons were being sent to the slaughter house but he played it down and tried not to tell Audrey too much information.

`Sarie, it's getting late, I'll walk you back,' Joe said, regretfully. He wanted the day to last forever, but he didn't want her to have trouble with her parents if she arrived back after dark. From what Sarah had told him, it wasn't a good idea to cross them, especially Lord Whittington.

Sarah grabbed her coat and then knocked quietly on the kitchen door to say goodbye to Audrey and Frank. `I just wanted to say goodbye to you' a lump caught in the back of her throat. Audrey rushed over to Sarah, wiping her hands clean on her apron.

`You take care of yourself Sarah, and whenever you want to come and visit us you are very welcome, d'you 'ere me?' Audrey hugged her tightly and for a moment she could hardly breathe.

`Yeah, you're more than welcome' Frank added, as he stood up from the kitchen table and held out his hand for her to shake it.

With tears in her eyes, Sarah took Joe's hand as they walked out of `The Laurel's' for the last time, not knowing how long it would be before they would return together again.

When they reached the old oak tree at the bottom of the long sweeping driveway to Whittington Manor, they stopped and faced each other, neither one of them wanting to say goodbye or to be faced with this painful moment. Big white snow flakes began to fall on them.

`Sarah, I need to ask you something... please be honest with me?' he took her hands in his own and looked deep into her wide eyes. `Are you ashamed of me?'

Sarah looked horrified at such a suggestion. `Joe, why would you think such a dreadful thing?'

`It's just you've never taken me to meet your parents and I know we kept it... I mean... us a secret in the beginning... but you know my family now' he turned away from her, looking in the direction of Whittington Manor. She gently turned his head to face her.

`Like I said to you before, my parents are not easy people and I didn't want them ruining our time together. These past few months have been precious to me and well if they had known...' She paused trying to find the right words.

`You mean they wouldn't approve of me.'

`No... well yes... I mean. Look... that's their problem, I know better and it's what I think that matters. I love you Joe and nobody will get in the way of my love for you, not my father or my mother... no one. You must always remember that,' tears were gently rolling down her face.

`Then if you are so sure and you really love me,...will you marry me when this stupid war is over?' Sarah looked away from him so that he couldn't see the uneasy look in her eyes. She gave a heavy sigh and then looked back into his wide, hopeful, green eyes. `I want to marry you Joe, more than anything in the world, but my parent's won't allow it and I'm too young to get married without their consent.'

`Then we'll marry on your twenty-first birthday' he said, determinedly. The corners of her mouth rose into a radiant smile. `Are you asking me to marry you?' she asked coyly as she swayed her coat from side to side flirtatiously.

The snow began to fall harder and Joe got down on one knee, taking her hand in his own. `Sarah Whittington, will you marry me on your twenty-first Birthday?' His eyes were twinkling and his hands were shaking, she wasn't sure if it was from the cold or from nerves. Fresh tears of joy began to cascade down her cheeks.

`Yes! Joe Lambert... Yes! She shrieked with happiness. `I will marry you on my twenty- first Birthday!' she was laughing and crying both at the same time. He picked her up and swung her around in his arms, as she continued to squeal with delight. He too had tears of joy in his eyes.

`You know what this means don't you?' he said, excitedly, placing her safely back on her feet.

`What?' She giggled.

`It means we're engaged. I don't have a ring to give you now, but I will when I get back, you'll see. You'll have the best ring... the very best for my girl,' he said, beaming at her and kissing her again passionately and breathlessly on her lips.

The wind started to pick up and whistle around them and Sarah shivered. The sky had grown dark and more wintery. They both knew it was time for them to say goodbye and it was even harder now, now they had made a firm commitment to each other. It was serious now, they were engaged, all bar a ring of course but in their hearts they were engaged to be married.

`Promise me you will write, Joe.' Tears were still streaming down Sarah's face but the tears of joy and happiness had faded into tears of despair and sadness.

`I promise!' They kissed each other in desperation.

`Stay safe Joe, come back to me... Promise me you will come back to me.' A sob caught her throat.

`I'll be back, I promise. No Jerry's gunno get me. He gave a wry smile. As they started to walk away from each other, Sarah ran back to him and threw herself in his arms, one last time. `I love you Joe' she grabbed hold of his coat in desperation.

`I love you too. Now go! It's cold, you're shivering,' he ordered, as he turned and pretended to walk away. He had to be strong now, it was the only way. A lump caught in his throat and he brushed the tears away from his eyes with the cuff of his coat. He couldn't look at her any more, it was too painful, but as Sarah walked up the drive to Whittington Manor, he couldn't resist seeing her one last time and so he turned and walked back to stand under the old oak tree. He stood watching her with his eyes squinting through the snow and his own tears. His heart was heavy. He wished he didn't have to leave her. Once this war is over, we will be married, he told himself over and over again, as he walked slowly home.

`And where have you been? My goodness you are frozen to the bone' Laura exclaimed, looking at her daughter in horror. `I will ask Annie to make you a cup of cocoa, and your father and I want to speak to you in the drawing-room.'

`Oh please not now, Mama' she sniffled, still wiping away her tears and blowing her nose in her hanky.

`The fire is lit and you need to warm up. Was she crying? or were her tears from the bitter cold? Laura wandered as she observed her closely.

Sarah sat down on the edge of the leather sofa next to the roaring fire, warming her hands, they were stiff and numb from the cold. Tears rolled softly down her face as she stared into the big angry orange flames. The pain of saying goodbye to Joe was cutting at her heart like a knife, and whatever her parents wanted to speak to her about, it really didn't matter any more, nothing mattered any more, only Joe staying safe and returning to her was important.

Her parents entered the room together, as if united in force and Laura handed Sarah a cup of steaming hot cocoa.

`Now... Young lady. I think you have some explaining to do.' Lord Whittington sat down on his favourite brown leather arm chair and lit his pipe. It was closest to the coffee table and he used the table in front of him for his tobacco packet and to place his drink, which invariably was a scotch in these harsh weather conditions.

Sarah glanced at him with big sad eyes and then stared back at the blazing fire.

`You've been seen fraternising with a young man on more than one occasion. You disappear for hours on end, without a mention of where you are going to, and today you walk in after dark, shivering from the cold may I add. Sarah what on earth is going on? And who is this boy you've been seen with?' His tone was a mix of anger and concern.

Sarah continued to stare at the fire. She felt numb and her heart was aching for Joe already.

`Your father asked you a question' Laura said, addressing her daughter sternly. `Who is this boy, Sarah?'

Finally, Sarah turned and faced her parents. `His name is Joe Lambert – and I love him' she added after pausing and taking a deep breath. There, she had said it. She had wanted to say it for months and it felt good to get it out in the open.

`And who is this Joe Lambert? What's his or his Father's profession?' Lord Whittington asked as he puffed on his pipe and frowned at his daughter. She rolled her eyes in exasperation. This was typical of him, all he cared about was profession, status and money.

`His profession is a land worker and so is his father's. Yes, they are land workers' she retorted.

`So you have been creeping around and tarnishing the Whittington name because of some land worker. Do you think I have spent good money in educating you, for you to mix with the likes of this Joe Lambert' He snarled angrily.

`So if he was a banker, an accountant, a solicitor, doctor or any of those types, then that would all be alright, would it Father?' she raised her voice to him and glared with wild angry eyes. Her fear of him had completely disappeared. He was not going to stop her seeing Joe. The war could stop her but nothing else could.

`Sarah, have some respect. How dare you speak to your father in such a way,' Laura scolded.

`Sarah, what kind of a future can he give you? You are used to a different way of life to him, and you deserve the finer things in life. You are a Whittington my dear,' he was trying to reason with her and use a softer approach. The girl had obviously fallen off the rails and maybe it was his and Laura's fault. They hadn't been giving her enough attention lately, what with all the worries over Thomas and Charles, and of course her best friend moving to Devon hadn't help, he thought as he rubbed his chin.

`Unlike you father, I don't care about money. I love Joe for who he is,' she was still glaring at him through her tears.

`Maybe so, but I am certain that Joe Lambert cares about money. For goodness sake Sarah, wake-up! Can't you see why he is interested in you?' he said, raising his voice to her in frustration.

`Oh, wonderful! So he's a gold digger now is he, Father? He can't possibly love me for who I am. It's just my money he loves.'

`What your father is trying to say,' Laura started to explain.

`What my father is trying to say is that Joe wants me for my money, well let me tell you both something, he is the kindest, sweetest person you could ever meet, who comes from a wonderfully sincere and good family. That family know what love is. They don't marry for money or status, they marry for love!' She stood up and paced the room like an angry tiger ready to attack. `And another thing' she continued, still fired up. `We are engaged, so I don't care what you think... you can put that in your pipe and smoke it!' she yelled directly at her father.

`So why are you not wearing a ring?' Lord Whittington bellowed back, challenging her. He had been tolerant enough, but she was getting out of hand now. The soft approach was clearly not working and it was time to play her at her own game.

`Because... Because,' she began to reply, so furious that she couldn't find her words. How dare he mock her?

`Because he has no money!' he shouted at her, slamming his fist down on the coffee table in front of him and spilling his whisky all over the table.

`I won't have you speaking to me like this, child. You will never see him again.' He raged, his face was as red as a tomato.

`And I won't have you speaking about him like that,' Sarah sobbed, storming out of the room.

Lord Whittington sat forward clutching his chest and gasping for breath. `William, are you alright? Laura rushed anxiously towards him. `Shall I call the doctor, William?' He didn't reply. He just kept clutching on to his chest.

`William! Speak to me, William!'

`No, stop fussing woman, I'm fine. The pain is going now it just comes when I get angry, it's just an anxiety attack.' He caught his breath and sat up straight.

The Lamberts were up bright and early the following morning to say goodbye to Joe, just as they had done when they said goodbye to Tommy. "This feels like déjà vu" Frank said as he watched Joe tuck into his eggs, bacon, tomato and fried bread that Audrey had cooked especially for him. He said very little while he ate, he was lost in thought about Sarah, and what lay in store for him in the months to come.

Audrey sat in the kitchen crying again, she couldn't face Joe until the moment she had to say goodbye. It was all too painful, and now there would be two of them to worry about, she thought as she wiped her eyes. Maureen stared at her brother, watching his every mouthful wondering if she would ever see him again, regretting being horrible to him, just as she had regretted her arguments with Tommy.

`Now, I gave your brother me lucky farthing, and you're the lucky one, cause I'm gunno give you me lucky shilling, but I want it back mind, when you return after the war.' He passed the silver shiny coin over to him.

`I'll give it back' Joe flashed an anxious smile.

Frank went to find Audrey, it was time to say goodbye. She appeared in the front room, her eyes red and puffy from crying. `You keep safe, d'you ere me?' She hugged him tightly.

`Mum, if Sarah comes to visit you, look after her for me and if anything should 'appen to me, be sure to tell her.'

`Now don't you go talking like that Joe Lambert'

`Mum, it's important, look after her for me.'

`Alright.....you have my word, I will.' She hugged him one last time, her little boy all grown up and going to war and fretting about leaving his girlfriend. Why did this have to happen? Why did he have to leave home? It wasn't fair.

`Nothings gunno 'appen to you son, you got me lucky shilling remember! Oh and don't forget it's only on loan. If I run out of money you might 'ave to nip back with it.' He ruffled Joe's hair and then grabbed him tightly for one last hug. He hated to let him go. His last son to leave the nest and the one he spent the most time with. He was a good lad and didn't deserve to be sent out there; he swallowed and fought back his tears.

`Bye Sis... and give a kiss to Nancy from me when she wakes up' he was doing his best to hold back his tears. Somehow Maureen wasn't that bad any more and neither was the baby. He would sooner stay home and put up with them than go to war.

He walked out of the garden gate and stopped to smooth Tabby, who was in a pouncing position ready to leap out on an unsuspecting innocent robin hopping on the other side of the hedge in the neighbour's garden. He was not pleased to be interrupted by a friendly hand wanting to give him a stroke.

Everything seemed so normal. Joe glanced back over his shoulder at the street behind him. Except it wasn't normal, it was far from normal. He was off to fight for his country and he wished with all his heart he didn't have to go. He didn't feel patriotic and a need to fight for England like some men he knew, including Tommy his own brother who wanted to join up just in case a war broke out and now he was in the thick of it all. He didn't believe in killing or any of it but he had no choice, it was his duty. He wished he could have seen Sarah one more time. Just one more hug, one more kiss, one more time to smell her perfumed hair, but they had agreed that it would be too painful to go through another goodbye. He reached the bottom of the road, took one last look over his shoulder, giving a wave to his parents and sister and then made his way to the bus stop.

Six

By early April, Sarah had more than enough of being at home, attending endless piano lessons and reading countless medical books. She had received several letters from both Emma and Joe. Emma's letters were full of talk about Devon, the parties she had attended, and interesting people she had met. It was difficult to believe there was even a war going on when reading her news.

Joe's letters were brief and he appeared to be in surprisingly high spirits, joking about other soldiers in his unit, things they had said and done. He had left Wale Island almost a month ago but he didn't speak about his location, nor did he speak about the terrible scenes he was witnessing day and night. Instead his news was kept fairly light hearted for Sarah's sake and he never failed to say just how much he was missing her or how much he loved her, signing off with the words *all my love forever, Joe xx*. These were the very words Sarah clung to day and night. She kept his letters in a shoe box hidden away under her bed, and his photo, the one that she took on Portsdown Hill, was kept safely tucked under her pillow, so that she could kiss him each night before she went to sleep, not that she slept much. The endless images of Joe stuck in muddy trenches, the rattling fire of machine guns and the droning of heavy planes dropping their bombs, haunted her every night, sometimes causing her to wake in panic and scream out into the darkness.

It was the 10th of April when Sarah decided to do something about her life. Waking up one morning after another sleepless night to the sunlight pouring in through the crack in the curtains, she decided it was time to stop moping around and see if she would be accepted as a volunteer nurse at Queen Alexandra Hospital. For sure they would be needing help and she wanted to offer a helping hand. There was no point hanging around Whittington Manor with her parents any longer, she would go insane if she had to.

`You are looking very smart my dear' Laura commented, glancing over at Sarah's smart navy blue dress and matching shoes as she sat down at the breakfast table. Sarah had almost finished her breakfast. `Thank you mama' she replied, wondering if she should say where she was going but then deciding she really couldn't face an argument first thing in the morning.

`Any particular reason why?' Laura persisted, studying her from across the table.

`My God, what are they playing at out there?' Lord Whittington was furious as he read the morning newspaper. `Hitler has now invaded Denmark.'

`So now Norway and Denmark have fallen?' Laura enquired worriedly.

As her parents continued to discuss the morning's news, it was the perfect opportunity to say goodbye and disappear quietly from the breakfast table without any further questions asked.

Walking through the entrance of Queen Alexandra Hospital, situated on the slopes of Portsdown Hill, Sarah felt a pang in her heart as she remembered strolling past it on so many occasions with Joe.

She followed the signs to various parts of the hospital until she saw an arrow pointing to a sign that read *"Administration"*. As she approached the desk, feeling nervous, and her heart pounding, she saw a group of women ranged behind the desk, handling paper work and talking between themselves.

`Excuse me! I was wondering if I could speak to someone about volunteer work,' she said rather timidly. A chubby looking lady with a freckly complexion and brown curly hair, looked to be in her mid forties, wearing a nurse's uniform smiled at her. `I'm Sister Morgan. You can speak to me, would you like to come this way?' Sarah followed her into a tiny office, no bigger than a cupboard. It was packed with shelves containing files and paper work. There were papers scattered over a small old desk and two hard wooden chairs were placed next to it. `Take a seat... Miss?'

'Whittington, Sarah Whittington,' she replied, still feeling nervous as she sat down.

`Well, Sarah, what medical experience do you have?' The sister asked, studying her closely.

`I've learnt basic first aid and I have read many medical books, particularly about infectious diseases, orthopaedic problems and open and gangrenous wounds' she announced enthusiastically.

`I see and do you have any proper medical training?' `Not really' Sarah admitted reluctantly not wanting to lie and pretend she knew things she didn't. `But I'm willing to learn and I'm also willing to work long and hard hours.' The Sister liked her. She was well-spoken and appeared to be well-educated and she certainly looked anxious to start work. It was always good to have hard working staff, and perhaps if she proved herself she could train to be a qualified nurse one day, she thought.

`Would you consider training as a nurse in the future?' she was curious as to why she wanted to volunteer.

`Yes, I have thought about it on many occasions.'

`So why do you want to volunteer and not start training now?' She sat back in her seat as she continued to study Sarah with interest.

`I would like to gain practical medical experience first and with England at war I thought this would be the best time to start as you may possibly need more help.' She added, hoping she was answering her questions satisfactorily.

`Alright, when can you start?' Sister said, smiling broadly at her. There was no point putting her through the mill for a volunteer position, she seemed nice enough.

`Tomorrow, if that's alright with you' Sarah said, bursting into a huge smile.

`Wonderful - report to this desk at 9am,' She stood up and shook Sarah's hand.

Sarah was grinning. `Do I need a uniform?'

`We'll find one for you tomorrow.' She showed Sarah to the door and smiled at her once more.

Sarah arrived back at Whittington manor floating on a cloud. She ran inside and found Annie in the laundry room busy ironing a pile of crisp, fresh white sheets. `Nanny, you will never believe this,' she was panting from running upstairs to the laundry room.

`What is it Miss Sarah?' Annie looked surprised at her sudden entrance.

`I've been accepted as a volunteer nurse at Queen Alexandra Hospital,' she was still beaming from ear to ear.

Annie looked at her cautiously. `d'your parents know?'

`No not yet, but I'm not going to let them stop me,' she said with determination.

`Well if you want my advice, I would tell your mum first and be sure to tell her you're gunno stay working here and not in Portsmouth or somewhere else. That is what you want isn't it?' Annie asked with concern.

`Yes, I only want to work here.' She hadn't even considered working anywhere else other than at the Q.A, she was just happy to be working as a volunteer nurse that on its own was a dream come true.

`Well then, I think it will all be alright... and well done, you'll make a fine nurse, Miss Sarah' Annie went back to her ironing hoping that the Whittingtons would approve. The poor girl, it wasn't easy on her losing her best friend and her boyfriend, although that was probably a blessing in disguise, knowing the Whittingtons Annie thought as she folded up a sheet and placed it in the basket next to her.

Sarah found her mother in the drawing-room, reading. `Oh there you are Sarah, you missed your piano lesson my dear. Mrs Hopkins has just left... After I apologised profusely for your bad manners of course.' Laura peered over her book with a stern expression upon her face.

`I'm sorry mother, I completely forgot. I have something to tell you.' She said eagerly, walking over to where Laura was sitting.

`I've been accepted as a volunteer nurse at Queen Alexandra Hospital.' There was a deathly long silence as Laura stared at her, trying to take in what her daughter had just said.

`I see' she replied, eventually.

`Mama, it's what I've always wanted to do. I'm seventeen now, I can't stay around here playing the piano and studying things I already know. This will keep me busy and my mind occupied.' Sarah explained, wanting to say keep her mind occupied whilst waiting for Joe, but soon thought better of it. `And it's not far from here, it's not like I will be in Portsmouth or somewhere dangerous.'

`Maybe you are right my dear. Your father and I have been a little hard on you lately, but we were simply just looking after your welfare.' Laura spoke in a soft voice. She looked emotional, placing her book down on the arm on her chair. `You are a bright young lady and you need to keep your mind stimulated. One day you will make someone a wonderful wife.' She smiled lovingly at her daughter.

Sarah tried not to get caught up with her mother's comment about making *someone* a wonderful wife. She would be Joe's wife, not *someone's* wife but this was not the time to get into an argument again. At least she was making progress about her working as a nurse. `I will only be working a few days a week to start with.' She was so relieved that this was going well and her mother actually didn't disapprove. `What about Papa? Do you think he will be angry?' She asked, suddenly remembering her father and looking worried. `Leave your father to me. He has many worries on his mind. Sarah we only want you to be happy and if this makes you happy then you must do it,' she said as she walked over to her and put her arm around her, then placing a kiss on her forehead. At least she wasn't moping around after the land worker any more; perhaps this was exactly what she needed.

Sarah's first day at the hospital went smoothly. She worked in casualty with Cynthia Worthing, a tall, slim pretty girl with blond hair and pale skin. She was born and brought up in Fareham and spoke with an upper class accent. There was an instant affinity between the two young women.

`So, I take it you're not squeamish if you are volunteering?' Cynthia said with a friendly smile. `No I'm not squeamish. I've been looking at some quite grim pictures in my medical books.'

`Well, actually it's not too bad here, it's far worse over at Hasler or The Royal for wounded soldiers. We don't have many soldiers, it's mainly civilian cases at the moment.' Cynthia said as they walked down a long corridor towards casualty. That may change, if the Germans carry on the way they are,' Sarah pointed out.

`Yes, and if air-raids start, we will have our work cut out too, we'll get the overspill from Hasler and The Royal, I'm sure of it.'

Sarah learnt a lot from Cynthia and the other nurses. Everyone was kind and she had a good feeling about working at Queen Alexandra Hospital. She had learnt to dress open wounds, deal with sprains, help set fractures and broken bones, take blood and of course there was the general care like changing sheets, and the dirty jobs like emptying bed pans, which she never once complained about. The staff were impressed with her. She was a fast learner and had a caring and polite bedside manor with the patients.

`She will go a long way that girl,' Dr. Gregory said to the Sister who was on duty and in charge of Sarah that day. She was the same lady that had interviewed her. Dr. Gregory was an older gentleman with grey hair and blue eyes that were full of wisdom. He had a kind face and was well respected by his staff `Yes doctor, she works hard I'll give her that,' Sister replied as they both stood watching her from a distance as she changed sheets on a bed and helped a patient into his clean bed. `Train her as much as you can, she will be a godsend if these promised air-raids arrive,' Dr. Gregory turned on his heel and walked away.

On her way home after finishing a morning shift, Sarah decided to visit Audrey. She had been working at the hospital for two weeks now, and everyday she had been contemplating visiting her, but without Joe somehow it seemed a little strange. She was missing Joe dreadfully and although most of her days were filled with working at the hospital, it was at night when she lay in bed thinking of him that the agony caught up with her. Perhaps going to see Audrey would help, she thought as she turned the corner of Portsdown Road. She hadn't walked down that road since the last day she spent with Joe in February.

As she approached The Laurel's and walked through the little iron garden gate, she felt a wash of sadness come over her as she knocked on the front door.

Looking down she saw Tabby sitting next to her feet, watching and hoping for the door to suddenly spring open. She knocked on the door twice but there was still no reply.

`Looks like no one is home, Tabby.' She knelt down and stroked him. He wrapped himself around her body and she smiled at him as a tear dropped down her cheek and on to his thick glossy fur.

`Sarah, is that you my love?' Audrey appeared at the garden gate with two shopping bags, there was a tone of uncertainty in her voice. She could only see the back of a young girl bending down and she squinted against the sunlight to see who it was.

`Hello, Audrey, I thought you were out,' Sarah sprung to her feet looking surprised and wiping away her tears as quickly as she could. She reached out to relieve Audrey of her shopping. `It's alright, they ain't heavy. Well, this is a lovely surprise. Come inside and have a cup of tea.' Audrey opened the front door and Tabby bolted in before her, almost tripping her up. `You sit down on the sofa and I'll put the kettle on, I'll be with you in a mo,' she dashed off into the kitchen to unpack her shopping and make them a cup of tea.

Sarah stood in the door way of the front room it was all the same. The old brown comfortable sofa that she and Joe had kissed on during their stolen moments of passion, the two old worn arm chairs opposite the sofa, with their thread bear arms. The scattered junk on top of the mantle piece appeared a little tidier and there were a few more letters hanging from the mirror which she presumed were from Joe and Tommy.

As she sat on the sofa her heart ached for Joe more than ever. She stretched out her hand and ran it softly over the sofa where he had once sat. Tabby pounced up, grabbing her hand and thinking she was playing with him. She smiled at him and then stood up and walked towards the wall where Frank's map was still hanging. There were far more circles on it than the last time she had seen it. Her eyes glanced over the many countries, noticing there was also a circle around Norway, Denmark and Holland too. She remembered her father talking about the terrifying *blitzkrieg* they were undertaking in Holland and her heart went out to those poor people over there. She shivered as she wondered if Joe or Charles were there too. Her father had also said there were tanks and paratroops all over Holland and Belgium, and France were expecting to be attacked next. He felt sure that Charles would be somewhere in the area.

The circles were growing like an ugly disease. How can one man cause so much devastation? She thought as she turned and walked back to the sofa. Audrey interrupted her thoughts as she appeared with a tray of tea and biscuits, placing them on the little coffee table in front of them. She was using her best china for her important guest.

`So - 'ow you been keeping? Has our Joe been writing to you regular?' she asked, smiling broadly at her. She felt slightly overwhelmed to see Sarah sitting there, she was missing both her boys and she so desperately wanted them home. `Yes, he has Mrs Lambert. I've had many letters.' It felt strange having tea alone with her mother-in-law to be. She wondered if Joe had told her they were engaged but she was too shy to say anything, it wasn't her place to do so, it would be up to Joe when he came home to tell her.

Audrey poured the tea. `Now why don't we stop all this Mrs Lambert lark and just call me Audrey, that's what everyone calls me round 'ere, I'm just plain old Audrey' she said with a chuckle as she handed her a cup of tea.

`Do you know where Joe is?' Sarah asked wondering if she had more information. It was driving her mad not knowing where he was, at least if she knew which country he was in she could listen out for news in that area.

`My Frank thinks he might be close to France but we can't be sure of it, he's not allowed to say much you see, for security reasons I s'pose,' she smiled to reassure her.

`Joe said you've got two brothers away, are they alright?' she asked sipping her tea.

`We rarely hear from Thomas. He's not much of a writer and Charles has written regularly since he left, he's fine.' she placed her cup carefully down on its saucer. The house was unusually quiet and for the first time she could hear the clock ticking on the wall.

`How's Maureen?' She asked, more out of making polite conversation than really caring.

`Oh, she's fine. She's gone to visit her friend in Castle Street, she'll be back soon. Actually she's thinking of joining the land army,' Audrey said, offering Sarah a plate of biscuits.

`Oh yes, I read a leaflet about that. What is it exactly that they have to do? The leaflet was a little vague' Sarah declined the offer of a biscuit.

`Well it ain't easy work, not a stroll in the park I can tell you. They got a lot of diggin' to do, like diggin' up potatoes, harvesting the crops, ploughing fields, looking after the animals and that sort of thing.' Audrey explained.

Somehow Sarah couldn't imagine Maureen doing that kind of work, she seemed the most unlikely person to be digging on the land. `Not that she will definitely do it mind, she's just thinking about it.' Audrey said as if reading Sarah's thoughts.

Sarah noticed how tired Audrey looked. She seemed to have more grey hair since the last time she saw her and the circles around her eyes had deepened.

`So if Maureen does join the land army who will look after the baby?'

`Well me of course, she doesn't have anyone else, not that I mind though. She's a sweet a little thing is our Nancy, and she's walking now you know.' Audrey announced proudly.

`Anyow, enough about us, what 'ave you been up to since our Joe went away?' She asked eyeing her closely. Pretty little thing, it was obvious why Joe had fallen head over heels for her, and the way she spoke was quite charming, she was getting used to it now but she couldn't help wonder if she had told her parents about Joe. `I'm working as a volunteer nurse at Queen Alexandra Hospital,' Sarah replied breaking Audrey's thoughts. It felt good to say she was working as a nurse. At long last she was doing what she had always dreamt of and the only one who had ever supported that dream was Joe. `Oh! – That's wonderful news. Will be 'andy 'avin' a nurse around,' Audrey chuckled.

`Well, I'm just volunteering right now but I'm learning a lot and maybe one day I will be a qualified nurse,' she smiled at that idea.

They continued chatting for a little while longer, until Sarah realised the time and said she had to go. `Are you sure you don't want to stay and 'ave some tea with us? Frank and Maureen will be back anytime now.' Audrey hated to let her go. It was comforting to see her again.

`Thank you, but I really must go.' She stood up and straightened her skirt.

`Come and visit again soon, won't you?' Audrey insisted with a trace of desperation in her voice.

`Of course I will,' Sarah assured her. She was a kind lady and she felt sorry for her, she looked so tired and sad.

`You never know, our Joe might get leave some day soon,' she said, sounding hopeful as she opened the front door for Sarah to leave.

`That would be wonderful,' Just like Audrey, that was all Sarah had hoped and prayed for since the day he had left.

Seven

On the day Winston Churchill became Prime Minister he requested that all types of motor vessels were to be officially registered. Frank sat at the kitchen table telling Audrey all about what he had heard. `Our Ed reckons that any type has got to be registered, even really small ones. I mean - can you honestly imagine a little dinghy crossing the channel?' Frank said, trying to make sense of it all.

`Are they gunno use the Gosport ferry n'all?' Audrey asked, looking astonished.

`I expect so. It sounds to me like the government is getting desperate. I'm mean what good is a soppy little dingy or even the Gosport ferry gunno be to our lads out there?' Frank sounded annoyed. He felt useless and only wished he could help. The thought of all those soldiers and even his own sons being led to what seemed the slaughter house to him, preyed on his mind day and night.

`So what exactly are they expecting these boats to do then?' Audrey asked.

`Rescue all the troops that are getting forced out of Belgium, Holland and France. 'itler's driving them out and the government has gotta get them out quick and fast.'

`Oh gawd Frank, what if our boys are out there? I mean Tommy's ship could be out there too.' Audrey said in dismay, airing Frank's thoughts entirely.

`I'll tell you something, if I 'ad a boat, I'd go and fetch 'em back meself. I s'pose Churchill's got no choice but to do this.' Despite not really understanding how those little boats were going to help, he did have faith in Churchill. He believed he probably was doing the right thing.

On May the 13th Frank tuned in the wireless to listen to Winston Churchill deliver his first broad cast as Prime Minister. Just three days earlier, Hitler had invaded France, Belgium and Holland. Winston Churchill's message was not cheerful by any means but he had a knack for turning bad news to sounding inspirational, although the grim reality of war was really only just beginning.

`He's gunno be a good leader, you mark my words,' Frank said to Audrey as they began to listen to his speech.

"I have nothing to offer but blood, toil, tears, and sweat......... We have before us many, many months of struggle and suffering. You ask, what is our policy? I say it is to wage war by land, sea, and air. War with all our might and with all the strength God has given us............... Our aim is victory. Victory at all costs - Victory in spite of all terrors - Victory, however long and hard the road may be, for without victory there is no survival.......... I take up my task in buoyancy and hope. I feel sure that our cause will not be suffered to fail among men. I feel entitled at this juncture, at this time, to claim the aid of all and to say, "Come then, let us go forward together with our united strength."

Frank turned off the wireless. `It doesn't sound good but like I said, he's good for the job and if anyone can lead us out of this mess it'll be him,'

`Oh Frank - I just keep thinking of Joe and Tommy. I mean they're bound to be there aren't they?' A tear trickled down her cheek.

`I'm not gunno lie to you, Audrey...Yes they most probably are.' Tears were welling up in his own eyes. `They most probably are,' he mumbled again under his breath.

When the promised boats from Portsmouth were nearing Dover and the sun was just coming up across the water, it was an extraordinary sight as the men on those little boats gazed in amazement at the scene around them. There were ships and boats of all sizes, from dinghies, sailing boats, ferries and steamers. Every inch of the water was covered as the boats made their way to Dunkirk. Their purpose - to rescue men from Dunkirk, by ferrying them to the Navel ships that couldn't get close enough to the beach. Civilians, together with military, were about to put their lives at risk to save half a million men who were facing the brutal attack of gun fire and bombs, being driven out like rats with nowhere to run to, and neither the Lamberts or the Whittingtons knew if their sons were there in Dunkirk. All they could do was sit and wait and hope for the best.

At Queen Alexandra Hospital, Sister called a meeting. `We are to be prepared for large numbers of soldiers arriving any time. These soldiers will be critically ill and we will, with out doubt, need as much help as possible around the clock.'

Sarah sat listening with intensity as she continued to speak about the type of injuries they could anticipate.

'Now your squeamishness will be put to the test,' Cynthia whispered in her ear. Sarah had turned noticeably pale, but the change in her colour was more out of fear for Joe and her brothers.

The ships which survived the fierce air-raids returned laden with injured soldiers. The Whippingham carried 2,700 men on board, and The Portsdown was so heavy that is stood only a foot above the water as it docked into Portsmouth. Men were ferried quickly to hospitals, and as Hasler and the surrounding hospitals rapidly ran out of beds, more and more men were sent to Queen Alexandra.

Sarah was called to help in the surgical ward and as she entered the room she stood and gasped in horror. There were more than a hundred men filling the room. They were covered with blankets, as some of them shook uncontrollably and others had a blanket covering their faces, where they had just died. Some were delirious from fevers and others reached out to her. As she walked past them, a few whimpered and cried from agony. Others lay in various states of distress, some with missing limbs that had been blown off as they fled from the battle.

It was a horrific scene, and although Sarah had been prepared for the worst by Sister Morgan, on duty that day, she could never have imagined it to be as dreadful as this.

Even Sister looked flustered as she held out a dirty basin and showed her where to get rid of it. Sarah didn't flinch but merely followed her instructions, and continued to do so for the next eleven hours. On many occasions she was left alone to dress wounds and mop fevered brows as there simply weren't enough qualified nurses around.

It was way after midnight by the time Sarah had been dismissed through sheer exhaustion. Sister asked her to stay over in the nurse's quarters, as she would be needed again early the following morning. She had managed to slip out before the onslaught to get a message to her mother to say what had happened and that she could be away from home for a couple of days yet.

After drinking a watered down soup and eating a slice of dry bread, almost too tired to eat, she lay down on her mattress and pulled an itchy grey blanket over herself to keep the chill off her body. Tears of dismay trickled down her face as she thought about the harrowing scenes she had witnessed that day and wondered if Joe, Charles or Thomas had been hurt like that and perhaps lying in a hospital somewhere or worse than that, dead. She shuddered at the thought.

The following day the rigmarole of it all started over again as Sarah worked hard taking orders from Sister and the other nurses, helping desperately ill men, many of them on the brink of death.

The days felt endless and without really realising, Sarah had been working flat out for three days with very few breaks and very few hours sleep.

`Sarah, Dr Gregory is outside, he says he has a message for you. Can you please go to him,' Sister said, holding an armful of bandages and balancing some tubes of cream on top of the bandages.

Sarah walked outside to find Dr. Gregory sitting on a bench sipping coffee from an old mug that looked to be his personal mug, worn from many years' use.

`Dr. Gregory, Sister says you have a message for me,' Sarah asked nervously. She had hardly spoken to Dr. Gregory since she had started working at the hospital. The doctors had very little to do with nurses and she couldn't imagine what sort of message he could possibly have for her.

`Yes, Sarah. Your mother has called for you to return home as soon as possible. It's important.' He had overheard the conversation between the nurse who took the call and Lady Whittington. It didn't sound good and he offered to give the message personally to Sarah. He liked Sarah. She was a great asset to the hospital.

`Did she say why I have to return?' Sarah asked looking puzzled at the doctor. She was so tired she felt dazed and wondered for a moment if she was actually dreaming all this.

`No. She didn't say but she did sound rather anxious according to the nurse who took the message. Look - I'm on a ten minute break, I'll run you home quickly,' he offered feeling sorry for her.

`Thank you Doctor.'

Sarah arrived at Whittington Manor to find her mother nervously pacing up and down at the entrance of the house. Dr. Gregory had dropped her at the gate and sped off back to the hospital.

`Mama, whatever is the matter?' Sarah called out running frantically towards her. When she reached her side Laura stared at her, trying desperately to find the right words. Her bottom lip quivered as fresh tears appeared in her eyes.

`We have received a telegram... I'm afraid it's bad news.' She took a deep breath. `Charles has been killed,' she let out a sob as if she had been holding it back and just couldn't control it any longer. Sarah threw her hand over her mouth, staring at her mother in disbelief. She flung her arms around her and they stood for a while, both crying and holding on to each other.

`I must see papa,' Sarah said eventually, pulling away from her mother and walking towards the front door.

`No, wait!... Sarah there's more I need to tell you.' Laura was still shaking as she reached out for Sarah to come back to her. `When your father received the news about Charles, he suffered a severe stroke. He is very ill, Sarah.'

Sarah looked panic stricken. The news was getting worse by the minute. `Well, where is he? Can I see him?' Her head was spinning. First Charles and now her father seriously ill.

`He is with the doctor at the moment. Let's wait until the doctor has finished,' Laura replied softly, as she put her arm around her and they walked inside together.

Annie appeared suddenly in front of them. `Come inside you two, I've got a fresh pot of tea waiting for you.' She would have done anything to take away their pain. She stopped and stared at them both and then stood with her arms open wide, as if she knew precisely what Sarah needed. Annie knew Sarah better than Laura did. Sarah flung herself into Annie's arms. The past three days of exhaustion built up inside of her, the terrible news of her brother, now her father so ill and the constant worry of Joe, was too much to bear as she sobbed on Annie's shoulder. `There, there,' she said smoothing her hair and looking at Laura over her shoulder.

Sarah and Laura sat in silence waiting for the doctor to finish upstairs. The loud ticking of the old grandfather clock from the far side of the room seemed deafening. The drawing-room door was wide open and finally, foot steps could be heard coming down the stairs. The doctor walked in the drawing-room. He was close to retirement age with a neatly trimmed white beard that matched his thinning hair. His spectacles were perched on the end of his nose. He had been the family doctor for nearly thirty years and had delivered all three of the Whittington Children. He looked tired as he stood in front of them and his dark brown narrow eyes were sorrowful.

`Lady Whittington. Miss Whittington,' he addressed them both in a low deep voice.

`I'm afraid Lord Whittington has suffered a terrible stroke and quite frankly it is remarkable that he actually survived it.' Laura's hands were shaking so much her cup rattled uncontrollably in its saucer and she had to place it on the table in front of her.

`His heart is very weak and I really don't think' he paused and looked mournfully at the, both.

`You really don't think what, Doctor?' Laura asked, her eyes full of dread.

`I think we should prepare ourselves for the worst.'

Laura let out a sob and Sarah buried her head in her hands.

'I'm sorry to give you this awful news, especially after your terrible loss' He said feeling awkward and not wanting to go into detail about Charles's death. 'I shall be back in the morning but if there is any change please call me,' he insisted as he walked out of the door.

'Thank you Doctor' Laura replied in a low whisper from where she was sitting, too devastated to see him out of the house.

Sarah gently turned the bedroom door handle. Papa' she whispered quietly as she approached his bed. The curtains were drawn and the room was dark with just a dim light shining in from the moon outside which managed to filter its way in through the parting of the curtains. 'Sarah' he groaned as she sat down next to him.

It pained her to see him so frail, her father who was always so full of life, so strong and so passionate about life. 'I love you Papa,' she whispered as she picked up his large heavy hand and kissed it. His bristly hairs on the back of his hand prickled her lips.

He felt her warm tears on his hand. 'Don't cry my dear,' he said in a weak and hoarse voice. There was a moment of silence and then he began to speak. 'I regret so many things in my life, Sarah,' he paused to catch his breath.

Sarah looked puzzled at him. 'Why should you have anything to regret?'

'I should have found a way to keep your brother at home.' A tear rolled down his pale cheek. 'Papa... Stop it! No one could have stopped him from going away. He had to go, he had no choice.' She sniffed as she brushed the tears from her eyes. But she knew just as he did that with his power and contacts he could have found a way to keep him at home.

'I regret making you cry too. I made you cry too often,' he continued sorrowfully.

'You were being a father and I am young and strong willed,' she said, recognising her faults and feeling remorseful.

'So you don't hate me then?' he said in a soft whisper as a frail smile appeared on his lips.

'Papa, I could never hate you... I love you.' He nodded his head, too tired to speak anymore. He closed his eyes and as he drifted off to sleep, Sarah sat for a while holding his hand before quietly creeping out of his room and closing the door quietly behind her.

Sarah promised her mother she would stay home while her father was ill. She called to let the hospital know and as much as she hated to let them down in their hour of need, her loyalties laid with her mother and father. She wanted to be there for them and especially for her father.

The following morning Laura was relieved to see that her husband looked a little brighter. He had more colour in his cheeks and he was sitting up reading a book. `The doctor will be here soon, William,' she said, drawing back the curtains.

`Laura, after he has gone can you please arrange for Edward Hamilton, my solicitor to come and see me,' he said slowly, between taking long drawn out breaths. `What do you need to see a solicitor for?' Laura was looking pale and withdrawn. She hadn't even had time to grieve for her son and now her husband was desperately ill, but she had to be strong, she had to continue the fight.

`There are some things I need to change in my will, now that,' he paused and looked down.

`I know. You don't have to say anything more, but do you have to do it today?

`Well, given the seriousness of my condition I think it's best to do it now,' He coughed and gave a small groan from the pain in his body.

`Now stop speaking like that William. You are going to get better. You are a fighter, you can't give up.' She sat on the edge of the bed and holding his hand tightly in her own she kissed his hand and held it up to her face. `I need you.' She looked into his tired eyes. The man she had loved and cherished for so many years, the man who had given her three wonderful children, one of which they had now lost, taken away from them with such tragedy but together they could share the pain. Only as parents could they comfort each other, understand one another and know how it really felt. She needed him to be strong so that they could grieve together.

`You're a good woman Laura,' he whispered. She kissed his cheek before walking out of the bedroom.

Eight

A bright red, shining and new MG sports car drove up the long gravel driveway and pulled up outside of the entrance of Whittington Manor. Edward Hamilton reached over to the passenger seat and picked up his black leather brief case and then stepped out of the car. He stood for a moment looking at the impressive manor as if admiring it before walking up the steps and knocking the big brass door knocker. A few minutes later the old butler opened the front door.

`I'm Mr Hamilton. I'm here to see Lord Whittington,' he sounded irritated that he should have to speak to the butler. Time was of the essence. He had three other engagements booked for the same afternoon and if it wasn't for the fact that it was Lord Whittington himself requesting to see him and that this appointment sounded interesting and perhaps indeed lucrative if he played his cards right, he would without a doubt have refused this last minute appointment.

The old doddery butler invited him in and led him up the sweeping staircase to Lord Whittington's room, located on the left hand side, five doors down.

Lord Whittington sat propped up with a number of white plump comfortable cushions, wearing a navy blue robe edged in white and holding a large piece of paper and a gold pen in his hand.

`Edward, thank you for coming at such short notice,' he coughed to clear his throat.

`No problem at all my Lord. I am so sorry to hear about Charles and to learn that you are so ill,' Edward replied standing tall. He was wearing a smart grey tailor-made suit and a pale blue tie that matched the colour of his eyes. Edward Hamilton was not considered as handsome, but better described as charismatic, and for his twenty five years he was certainly very astute.

`Edward, I need to make some changes to my will, now that' he stopped in mid flow struggling to bring himself to say *now that Charles has died.*

`I understand' Edward said sensitively. `I believe that Charles has left his estate to you.' Edward said, propping his briefcase on the chair nearby and opening it fully to find the will.

`I have made some changes to my will and I have added Charles's estate too. He went through it all with me before he went away,' Lord Whittington spoke, in a low and passive voice, passing the paper over for Edward to read. Edward closed his briefcase and placed it on the floor then sat down to study the paper.

`My Lord, if I may be so bold, I would like to make some comments on your changes. Please forgive me. I am merely acting as both your solicitor and trusted friend. You were a good friend of my father's,' he cleared his throat with a nervous cough.

`You have stated that the largest amount of your estate is go to Thomas, including Whittington Manor, is this correct My Lord?'

`Yes, that's correct.'

`If I'm not mistaken, Thomas joined the Navy before the war, wishing to pursue a life long career at sea, am I right?' He waited for Lord Whittington's reply, as if he was cross examining him on a prosecution stand in court.

`Yes, he joined the Navy to pursue a career,' he replied, his eye brows meeting in the middle to create a deep frown.

Edward ran his fingers through his perfectly groomed fair hair, acting mystified. `Well if he is at sea, what would he possibly do with Whittington Manor whilst he is away for months on end?'

`Well, one would hope he would find himself a wife and make a home for his wife and children here.' Lord Whittington didn't understanding where any of this was leading to, or what business it was of Edward's.

`I know that he won't inherit the house until his mother has died and one would hope he would be married by then, however, I can't help thinking that perhaps Sarah would benefit far more from inheriting the house. After all, this is her home and should something happen to Laura sooner than one would expect, what would happen to the poor girl?' he asked with a look of concern.

`Well, I have left a very generous amount of money to her, and I'm quite sure Thomas wouldn't see his sister out on the street, besides I'm certain she will be married in a few years time.'

`I clearly see your reasons for leaving the house to Thomas, with him being the eldest, and carrying on with the Whittington name, but my lord, I have seen it on so many tragic occasions when the youngest has been overlooked. There are many possibilities to consider, such as a terrible feud between brother and sister or the girl's husband dies leaving no money and only debts and Sarah could then be left homeless and penniless. I am sure you would hate for something so awful to happen.' Edward said, pursing his lips and raising his eye brows.

`Well, that's absurd! Edward. With respect, my daughter will not be left homeless or penniless for that matter' he said sounding irritated.

`My Lord, we never know what the future holds for any of us, and we must always look at various scenarios when writing a will, each child must be well provided for. Of course this is not my business, but as a friend, I sincerely believe that Sarah would have more use for such a beautiful house as Whittington Manor than her brother would.'

Lord Whittington sat staring anxiously at him, a few pearls of sweat were forming on his forehead.

`Should Sarah have the misfortune of not marrying, she would at least have a roof over her head, and if she does marry, she and her husband could live here and make a home for themselves.' Edward added with a soft sensitive tone to his voice.

There were a few moments of silence, neither man speaking a single word.

`I... I clearly haven't considered this thoroughly,' Lord Whittington said rubbing his forehead and feeling uncomfortable. He felt hot and his hands were clammy. Edward had sewn seeds of doubt in his mind. Had he really done the right thing leaving Whittington Manor to Thomas? Edward did have a point. Thomas was always at sea and had never shown any interest in the house. Suddenly he remembered the argument with Sarah regarding Joe Lambert. Images of that evening flashed in his mind. If she was determined to marry the boy, he certainly couldn't provide for her in the way she was used to, and it would be up to him as her father, to make sure his only daughter was well provided for. He didn't know this Joe Lambert and it seemed logical he would only be interested in Sarah's inheritance, being a poor land work, but there was very little he could do to protect his daughter. He would have to trust her judgment and hope that Laura would be there to guide her, if he wasn't. He stared at Edward, absently, who was continuing to read the rest of his will.

`Edward, please give me back the will. I would like to make some changes, Sarah may also need more money as well as Whittington Manor,' he said, with Joe Lambert still very much in mind.

`Very wise' Edward handed back the paper looking pleased with himself.

`I shall state clearly that her inheritance will be held in trust until she turns twenty one, when she will be of suitable age. She will have a small sum of money in a bank account that I have opened for her, which will tide her over in an emergency if necessary.'

He finished writing and handed the paper back to Edward.

`I quite agree, that is very sensible, My Lord, young girls can be somewhat frivolous with money,' Edward placed the paper back in his briefcase and closed it tightly.

`Will there be anything else, my Lord?' he asked smiling at him.

`No, that will be all. Edward' he paused for breath again starting to feel tired. The conversation had carried on far longer than he had anticipated and he was feeling very weak. `Thank you for your concern and your care about my family. It is much appreciated.' Edward nodded and gave a fleeting smile, showing a row of perfect white teeth. `If there is anything else you need just call me.' With that he shook Lord Whittington's hand and left the room, closing the door behind him. He stood for a second and grinned with amusement and then continued back down the long winding staircase.

Sarah was standing at the bottom of the stairs. When he reached the bottom, he stopped and looked into her eyes. `You must be Sarah?' He had never seen her before, Lord Whittington had only been his client for a year and on the odd occasion her father had needed to see him he had always visited Edward at his office in Fareham.

`Yes, I'm Sarah.' she replied gracefully. Her eyes were a little swollen from both tiredness and crying but he could still see how beautiful she was. Her auburn hair was placed in a bun and wispy curls hung down in ringlets almost to her shoulders. She was more than beautiful she was exquisite.

`I'm Edward Hamilton, your father's solicitor,' he held out his hand for her to shake it.

`It's a pleasure to meet you' she politely accepted his hand shake and taking the back of her hand to his lips, he kissed it. She quickly withdrew her hand looking embarrassed and shaken by the whole experience.

`The pleasure is all mine, I can assure you,' he smiled charmingly at her and then carried on walking to the front door. Stunning as well as rich, now that's a bonus he mused as he walked to his car.

As he got into his sports car and drove down the drive way, he passed the sign next to the old oak tree that read `Whittington Manor.' `Hamilton Manor' has a much better ring.' He smiled to himself and turned the corner.

On the tenth of June 1940 Lord Whittington sadly passed away with both Laura and Sarah at his bedside. Many mourners turned out in their droves to attend the service held on the grounds of Whittington Manor. The Howlett family had sent their condolences but were unable to attend the funeral, as the Admiral was not in good health himself and would not have been able to cope with the journey.

When the sad sombre day was over and Lord Whittington was laid to rest at the family vault in Whittington Manor's estate, Laura said goodbye to the last of the mourners.

`Darling, I'm going to have a lie down now.' She looked weary with eyes full of anguish.

`Alright, Mama,' Sarah kissed her gently on the cheek. There was nothing she could say or do, each of them equally lost in their own grief.

Sarah wondered through the grounds of the manor, between the many shrubs and plants that were neatly pruned. Some in full blossom and other just buds starting to peep through. Lost in thought she wandered to an area of the garden she used to play in when she was a child. She sat down on an old wooden bench with a brass plate, speckled with rust. It read in *"Memory of Albert Whittington 1817 – 1897"*. It was her grandfather's bench. She sat staring at the roses in front of her. They were out in full blossom... yellow, white and red, they were a riot of wonderful colours. There were times in the winter as a child, when she would have stood and stared at those same rose bushes, looking at their sorry state with no petals or leaves, just bare twigs as if they were dead, and much to her amazement by spring there would be new shoots and magically the roses would reappear. She would clap her hands in glee and run to tell Annie the roses had come alive again. Why couldn't people be like roses? Why did they have to die? Why couldn't we come back to life, just as a rose, year after year? She thought, not noticing she was crying again.

She was startled by footsteps approaching her. She looked up and saw Edward Hamilton standing in front of her. He was dressed in a black suit and black tie holding a small cream envelope. He spoke in a low and gentle voice. `I'm so sorry for your loss, Sarah.'

Sarah sniffed and dabbed her eyes with her handkerchief. `Thank you.'

`I know what it is like to lose one's father, my father died a year ago.' He looked at her sympathetically. She gave a nod, fighting hard to hold back her tears.

`Your father was a good man and a close friend of my father's. If you ever need to talk I would be happy to listen.' He was trying to make eye contact with her but she continued to sit staring at the rose bushes.

`Thank you' she said again not wanting to look at him or talk to him, she was too tired and too broken. All she wanted was to be left alone. Sensing this, Edward passed her the envelope. `Your father left this letter in my trust. It was his wishes that you read it in private.' Sarah looked puzzled as she accepted the small cream envelope.

`I shall leave you in peace now.' He turned and walked away from her. Sarah sat staring at the envelope for a moment. Seeing her father's handwriting brought fresh waves of sorrow.

Slowly she peeled it open and pulled out a letter neatly folded in two. She carefully unfolded it and begun to read.

My Dearest Sarah

I have not always found it easy to express my feelings, and writing, perhaps, is the best way. There are men fighting in this wretched war as I write this letter. Men standing shoulder to shoulder fighting for their country, losing their lives just as your brother did. It pains me to think that those young men are much loved sons, brothers or husbands from all walks of life. My dear Sarah, you are quite right, love is far more important than money. Money is merely a symbol used to make life more comfortable. I only ever had your best interests at heart and I only wanted to protect you, which won't be easy now. I want you to remember something - be sure to marry for love, respect and sincerity. Sarah you will always have my blessing but please grant me two wishes, and that is 1) once married, you shall both live in Whittington Manor and continue with the Whittington name and 2) that my grandchildren are to be raised here. I want Whittington Manor to remain a happy and loving home as it has been for so many years. As you will soon learn your share of my estate will be yours on your twenty-first birthday, however I have opened a bank account in your name and have deposited some money in it for you, enough to tide you over should you need it. Use it wisely. The bank account details are shown below. All that remains for me to say is stay safe, may you have a long and healthy life. Be happy my darling.

All my love

Papa xx
P.S Please look after your mother for me.

`Oh Papa!' Clutching his letter close to her chest she sobbed uncontrollably.

*****

Audrey's shrieks of excitement could be heard all down Portsdown Road when Tommy Lambert walked through the front door of `The Laurels'. He was home on leave for a long weekend. `Oh 'ow I've missed you' she hugged him so tightly. `Let's 'ave a look at you, good and proper.' She pushed him away from her, as she eyed him closely up and down.

`Nice uniform eh' Tommy said stretching out his arms and giving a pose as if he was having his photo taken.

`Never mind the uniform, you're all skin 'n bone, you need feeding up my boy.'

`Leave the lad alone, Audrey. Come here' Frank placed a firm arm around his son and drew him in tightly to his chest.

`Ello Dad' Tommy said after getting his breath back from his father's tight grip. The all familiar cheeky grin lit up his face as they walked into the lounge together.

`Oh it's you back again is it?' Maureen said, with a smirk on her face, secretly happy to see her brother live and well.

`Ave you missed me, Sis?'.... `Ave you.... 'ave you? He sat next to her on the sofa nudging her in the side.

`Sort of' she hated to admit it.

`You know something, believe it or not, there were actually times when I missed you too' he said with a cheeky grin. It was normally when I felt like shouting at someone or annoying someone, you know those things that you are good for.'

`Oh Tommy, stop it!' Audrey said trying not to laugh. `You've only been 'ome two minutes. She sat down in the arm chair opposite and Frank sat in the other.

`So what's new, Mum? You 'eard from our Joe?' he asked, with a more sombre expression on his face.

`Your brother is fine. He said in his last letter he will be home on leave soon.'

`Good, he can give me a hand... leaving me to do all the work back here' Frank joked, grinning at them both.

`I suspect he would much rather give you a hand than what he's doing every day out there' Audrey pointed out, playing with a strand of hair hanging down from the side of her face as she sat staring at Tommy from her arm chair.

73

`Ere our Joe's gone 'n got himself a posh girl, all hoity toighty she is' Maureen piped up with excitement, like it was the hottest gossip to date.

`Oh yeah, who's that then?' Tommy rubbed his hands enjoying the gossip about his brother. It was a far cry for being stuck at sea in the thick of war.

`She's a nice girl actually' Audrey said in her defence.

`Her name's Sarah Whittington and she comes from that big 'ouse called Whittington Manor, you know that big white one, just outside of Portchester, going towards Fareham,' Maureen explained as Tommy looked at her with a puzzled expression trying to place where the house was.

`Oh yeah I know...'ow did our Joe land himself a girl like that?' Tommy looked over at his mother in amusement. Joe was always the quiet one, he couldn't imagine him chatting anyone up, least of all some posh girl from that big house.

`Actually, Audrey, I read something in this morning's newspaper I meant to tell you about' Frank said. He looked a little sheepish.

`Oh and what's that?'

`I read that Lord Whittington died on the 10th of June and his eldest son had also died a few days earlier at war. I know I should of told you and I'm sorry, but I forgot with Tommy come back n'all.'

`Oh good gawd... the poor child' Audrey placed her hand over her mouth in dismay. She sat for a moment looking shell-shocked. Maureen looked down at her slippers feeling remorseful. She wished she had not made fun of her now.

`She must be going through 'ell right now,' Audrey said at last.

`It's this bleeding war init. His son dying like that must of been what caused him to have a heart attack, I should think,' Frank felt sorry for Lord Whittington, even though he had never met the man. He couldn't even imagine how it must feel to loose a son at war and he hoped to God he would never find out.

`Joe comin' home will be the best thing that could 'appen to Sarah right now' Audrey said getting up out of her arm chair. `Anyow, I'm gunno get the washing in and put the tea on. I've made you, your favourite tea cake, Tommy' she smiled broadly at him and then walked out of the room. It was so good to have him home safe and sound, even if it was just for a weekend, she thought still smiling to herself as she began to potter around the kitchen.

Nine

`As I am sure most of you know, the Germans have now invaded France, therefore we can assume that it's only a matter of a short time before the air-raids can be expected.' Sister said, addressing her staff in the canteen and holding a cup of steaming hot watered down vegetable soup. `We should start to prepare for as many casualties as possible. We can expect both civilian and military,' she continued to prepare them. `As from today, Sarah I would like you to work in casualty with Cynthia and gain as much experience as you can.' She smiled fondly at her. She was happy to have her back at work and felt so sorry for the poor girl after losing both her brother and father in the space of a few days.

`I'm glad you will be working with me, I've missed you Sarah,' Cynthia said as they finished their tea before making their way down to casualty. How are you feeling now?'

`Oh I don't know - empty, tearful.'

`Well it is to be expected but they say time is a great healer. It was a good year or so before I could come to terms with my father's death' Cynthia said, placing her empty cup down on the side.

`I didn't know your father had died. How did he die?'

`He died of pneumonia, he was already in weak health…Anyway, have you heard from Joe lately?' Cynthia asked, changing the subject as they started to make their way down the long corridor that led to casualty.

`I received a letter about two weeks ago, saying he was expecting to be home on leave soon.' Sarah suddenly looked brighter. The thought of Joe coming home was the only bit of good news she had to cling on to.

`Oh that's wonderful news Sarah, that's exactly what you need.'

`*He* is exactly what I need, I can't wait to see him, Cynthia. I'm missing him like mad everyday.'

They walked into casualty. There was an elderly lady with white curly hair sitting in the waiting-room. She had a nasty gash on her leg, blood was streaming down from it and there was a small puddle by the side of her puffy looking foot. She had fallen over in her back garden and gashed it on a piece of timber. The girls went about attending her wound.

To Sarah's surprise the day passed fairly quickly and by 4pm her shift had ended. After saying goodbye to Cynthia and the other nurses on duty, she walked out of the main entrance door. The sun was shining brightly and there was a warm breeze blowing. She squinted from the sunlight as she walked down the steps, passing a lady with a baby and two elderly gentlemen who appeared to be on their way to visit a patient. As she reached the bottom step she stumbled and bumped straight into a soldier who was standing in her way.

She looked up feeling flustered and silly for bumping straight into him. `Sorry!' She was in the shade now and focused straight into the soldier's face. `Oh my God... Joe!' She screeched in delight as she flung her arms around his neck.

`Ello Sarie' he was beaming from ear to ear as he picked her up, and spun her around joining her excitement. It was a few moments before they got their breath back and could talk.

`Oh look at you, you look so handsome,' she stood admiring his Khaki uniform.

`Never mind about me... look at you. You're a nurse, I'm so proud of you, Sarie.

`I'm not a qualified nurse.' Sarah replied. `Who cares? You are still a nurse.' His smile faded and his expression turned solemn. `My parents told me about your brother and your Dad, I'm so sorry,' Sarah's expression changed and her eyes clouded over with anguish.

`I should have been here for you.' He pulled her close, holding her in his arms.

`Well, you are now;' her voice was muffled in his jacket. She then pulled away and looked up at him. `How long are you here for?'

`Three days only...but hey, at least it's better than nothing' he said smiling ruefully.

`You fancy a walk up Portsdown Hill?'

`No, there is somewhere far more important we should go.' He frowned. `Oh and where's that?'

`My house. It's time for me to show you off' she said grinning at him, bursting with pride.

`But Sarie, do you think this is a good idea?... I mean.' She stopped him in mid flow and put her finger to his lips. `Trust me it's fine. I want you to meet my mother. It's time now. I love you Joe and you are not going to be a secret any more... Those times are over.'

As they walked up the long gravel path leading to the entrance of Whittington Manor, Joe was speechless. He was in awe of the magnificent house that stood before them. It was even more impressive up close. He began to feel nervous. He felt like he was off to meet the queen. As if she could sense it, Sarah turned and looked at him. `It will be fine, just be yourself. My mother is really quite nice when you get to know her,' she reassured him with a smile.

They walked through the huge white front door of the main entrance, and entered into an elegant open plan spacious foyer, painted in a soft tone of peach with a graceful high ceiling and an enormous crystal chandelier hanging above them, and straight ahead a long wide staircase with highly polished wooden banisters.

Annie was walking down the stairs. She had spotted them from one of the upstairs windows and was walking towards them smiling warmly.

`Nanny, this is Joe, and Joe this is Annie... although I call her Nanny, don't I Nanny?'

`You certainly do. `Ello Joe, pleased to meet you. Sarah's told me all about you.'

`Oh really' Joe looked surprised, he assumed Sarah hadn't told anyone about him.

`I know your mum and I've met your dad a few times 'n all'

`You know my mum and dad?' Joe looked genuinely astonished. Annie nodded at him.

`You ask your mum if she remembers Annie Philpot who used to live down Spring Drive, just off Autumn Grove... why we used to go to school together, although she were a bit younger than me mind... well a few years younger' Joe stood watching her with a bemused expression.

`Nanny, I would like Joe to meet mama, do you know where she is?' Sarah enquired politely not really wanting to interrupt her but she was too excited to wait any longer.

`Oh hark at me going on, your mum is in the second drawing-room, so I believe'

`Thank you, Nanny. It's this way Joe.' Sarah took Joe's arm and trotted off down a corridor towards the second drawing-room as they called it.

Before opening the door Sarah turned and looked at Joe. `It's best to address her as Lady Whittington and like I said… just be yourself.'

`Mama, I have someone I would like to introduce you to' Laura was sitting in Lord Whittington's favourite leather arm chair, gazing absentmindedly out of the window. She appeared to be startled when she looked up to see Joe standing in the doorway dressed in his khaki uniform. `Mama, may I present to you Joe Lambert' Sarah said proudly as Joe walked across the room to where Laura was sitting. She got up and stretched out her frail and delicate hand. `Pleased to meet you Joe, Sarah has told me *all* about you,' she said with a small smile and a trace of cynicism in her voice. He looked surprised to hear that Sarah had talked about him just as she had done to Annie. `It's a pleasure to meet you Lady Whittington' Joe replied respectfully. She watched him cautiously, remembering the day that her daughter had arrived home freezing cold and announcing she was engaged without a ring.

`Please sit down' Laura gestured towards the sofa in front of them. He sat down nervously and Sarah sat next to him, giving him a smile of encouragement.

`Joe is here for three days, isn't it a wonderful surprise, Mama?' she said, smiling radiantly at Laura and then glancing back at Joe, her eyes dancing with excitement.

`Yes, it certainly is a surprise,' she replied coolly. `It must be a relief for you to be home I suspect?' He could feel her eyes of steel pouring into his soul as he nodded and smiled politely.

`Would you like to stay and have some tea, Joe?' There was a tone of hostility to her voice. It was obvious that she was inviting him for tea out of politeness.

`Well… um' the thought of staying for tea with this woman gave him the shivers. She looked like an older version of Sarah but that was where the familiarity stopped. There was nothing warm or fun about her. It was clear to him that she didn't like him and he knew he shouldn't have come the moment he had walked in the room.

`Oh please stay Joe. It would be nice for Mama to get to know you' Sarah's eyes were pleading with him. His lips twitched as he forced a nervous smile and then looked back at Laura. `Thank you that would be very nice,' he replied, not wanting to upset Sarah.

`Well, that's settled. Now Sarah, please run along and find Annie, tell her to prepare tea for us all. In the meantime Joe and I can have a little chat'

Laura smiled at him in an unnerving way. He felt like a small boy who was about to be told off. He had an overwhelming desire to run out of the room and beg Sarah not to leave him alone with her but instead he remained seated.

As soon as Sarah had closed the door behind her, Laura sat forward in her chair and glared at him. `As I am sure you know, this family has been through a terrible time recently and Sarah has suffered a great deal. My daughter is obviously very taken with you but she is young and vulnerable.' Joe sat watching her anxiously, his cheeks turning scarlet. He felt like he was about to face punishment, perhaps a prison sentence or even hanging. It really was like a meeting with the queen.

`I respect that you don't have an easy time at the moment... fighting in this dreadful war, but quite frankly that is not my concern. I will get straight to the point, Joe.' She shuffled restlessly in her seat. `I am uncertain of your intentions towards my daughter,' she narrowed her hazel eyes suspiciously at him.

`I can tell you Lady Whittington that my intentions are totally honourable. I love your daughter.' His cheeks coloured deeper and he started to feel hot under the collar.

`You love my daughter?' she repeated with a hoot, as she pushed back a lock of auburn hair with tiny threads of silver from her face. `I am sorry Joe but I am not convinced of that. As you know Sarah will be a very wealthy young lady one day, and with you coming from' she stopped for a second trying to find the most suitable words to describe what she wanted to say. `Well, shall we say a less fortunate background... you can see my concern can't you?' Joe looked insulted. His green eyes grew wide. She had gone too far now. She maybe Lady Whittington but how dare she think he was after Sarah's money and speak down to him like that? He stood up and walked to the window, glancing out at the view of the perfect blossoming gardens and then turned to face her with anger in his eyes.

`I love Sarah with all my heart. I love everything about her, she is beautiful inside and out and if she was from the slums of Portsmouth I would still love her.' He spoke in a low and precise voice trying to tame down his accent although it was very apparent. `You see I am not interested in money and fortune and neither are my family. I have been brought up with strong morals and in a loving 'ome, and I wouldn't say that that was a *less fortunate background*.' He was looking deep into her narrow hazel eyes and she stared back at him, listening to his every word.

`I loved Sarah from the first moment I clapped eyes on her and I had no idea who she even was then but it didn't make a jot of difference when I did find out.' Their eyes were still locked as if challenging one another. Laura said nothing, she was observing him closely.

`Let me tell you something' he continued. My parents welcomed her with open arms, but it took until now before Sarah could bring me to meet you and now I know why.' He stepped away from her and folded his arms. Laura felt awkward. She could see that he meant every word he was saying. His eyes were sincere and so was his anger but she still found it hard to agree or accept her daughter's relationship with him. All said and done, he was still a common land worker. She could only hope in time with a bit of help from the war it would all fizzle out.

`I needed to be sure' she said softly as he continued to glare at her. It was clear that he was genuine and Sarah's happiness was all that mattered. It was easier to go along with it for now, she decided. `Joe, please sit down' Laura insisted, pointing to the leather sofa he had previously been sitting on. He stood hesitantly for a moment before doing as he was told.

`I apologise if I offended you but I was simply looking after Sarah's welfare. It may appear that I have misjudged your intentions... but.' Before she had a chance to say anything further, they were interrupted by Sarah who walked into the room holding a paper rolled in a tube.

`Nanny is on her way with the tea and Mama I brought this to show you' she said handing over the portrait that Joe had drawn of her almost a year ago.

`Joe drew it' she added as she smiled proudly at him. Laura rolled it open and then looked directly at Joe. `Joe you are a very talented young man, that's a most beautiful drawing. Do you enjoy drawing?' she enquired, raising her eyebrows.

`I do' he replied, feeling a littler calmer now.

`You know, you are very good, you should seek out galleries in this area. I am sure there are many who would be happy to display and sell your work.' There was no hostility in her voice anymore and when she smiled she reminded him of Sarah.

`Maybe after the war' he replied shyly. Annie entered the room carrying a tray with an elegant china tea set and freshly made Victoria sponge cake. She placed the tray on the table in front of them and began serving.

`So, Sarah tells me you live in Portchester.' Laura said, trying to keep the conversation flowing.

`Yes, that's right in Portsdown Road.'

`His family are from Portsmouth. Nanny knows Joe's mother... don't you Nanny?'

`Oh is this right Annie? Do you know Joe's mother?' Laura asked with surprise. Annie looked nervously at her, not really wanting to get involved. She guessed that Lady Whittington would not be best pleased her daughter was courting a land worker.

`Yes, I do my Lady. She is very nice... may I say.' She answered in honesty out of respect for the boy's mother. Laura looked impressed. She thought highly of Annie's opinion. There had been many times when Laura had confided in Annie and asked her advice with various matters. She was more like an old friend than a house keeper. Her call of duty went far beyond what was expected of her.

`Well, it's nice to hear that,' she said as she sipped her tea, looking more relaxed.

It was almost two hours later before Joe noticed the time on the big grandfather clock. `I really should be going. It's difficult to walk down some of the streets in the dark, especially ones with pot 'oles' he said with a smile.

`Oh I know. These blackouts are horrid and so many accidents are caused from them. Cars simply can't see where they are going.' Laura said. Despite his low-class accent he was rather charming in his own way and she could see her daughter's attraction, but there was no denying he really wasn't suitable for marriage.

Audrey had queued for over half an hour the day before at the butchers, hoping that Mr Peacock wouldn't run out of meat before it was her turn to reach the counter and much to her delight she had a choice of a whole chicken or a small joint of beef. The beef looked a little scraggy and fatty in places so she opted for the chicken. You know what you've got with chicken, no fatty bits on it she decided, feeling pleased with her choice as Mr Peacock wrapped it up in paper for her.

Audrey wanted this Sunday lunch to be special for two reasons, one because Joe was home and second because Sarah was coming for lunch. She made crispy roast potatoes, carrots and runner beans that Frank had picked from the allotment that morning.

`That was a lovely dinner, Audrey. Would you like me to help you clear the table?' Sarah offered eagerly. There was nothing she loved more than to spend time with the Lamberts. They were so easy to speak to, always happy even though they had very little to give other than their love and friendship of course, which is something they gave unconditionally. Sarah was in awe of them all and their attitude in general towards life.

`You'll do no such thing... you're a guest and besides... I expect our Joe wants to take you for a nice walk after that big dinner.' Audrey picked up the plates and trotted off to the kitchen. She liked Sarah, and was glad Joe had found a nice girl. She was different but nevertheless she was still a nice girl.

`Yeah, your sister'll give your mum a hand. You go and enjoy yourselves.' Frank said, as Maureen gave a groan and glared at her father.

Sarah and Joe went for a stroll up Portsdown Hill. They hadn't been there since Joe had returned on leave. On Saturday they had had a picnic in Portchester Castle that Annie had prepared for them after Sarah finished working at the hospital. She had only gone in for a couple of hours in the morning and Sister had told her to spend the afternoon with Joe. `Time is precious, you should spend all the time you can together' she had said, thinking how terrible it had been that Sarah had lost her father and brother.

The sun was setting as they reached the top of the hill and the sky was a beautiful tone of peach and orange. A black bird was sitting in a tree nearby singing to its heart's content and there was a soft aroma of lavender in the air.

`Oh Joe' Sarah turned to him with tears brimming her eyes. `Why do you have to go again? Why is life so unfair?'

`Because life is unfair sweetheart and there ain't nothing we can do about it. We just gotta keep strong and keep our chin up.' He held her close to him.

`You know I spend every day and night worrying about you when you are away. Wondering what you are doing, seeing those soldiers that came back from Dunkirk and after Charles...'

`Shush! now stop that, you can't think like that. I can look after meself, you need to concentrate on you.' He stroked her long silky hair, she was wearing it loose and he held a lock of auburn hair to his face as he inhaled the sweet perfumed scent.

`Joe, I wish we were married. I want so much to be your wife.' The ache in her heart was unbearable.

`And I want you to be my wife too, but being married won't change me 'avin to go away.'

`I know but perhaps it would feel easier knowing we were married,' she said, stroking the arm of his jacket as she pursed her lips.

`Trust me Sarah, you wouldn't feel any different. We both love each other and we have to bide our time until this bloody war is over, then we'll get married... I promise,' he kissed the tip of her nose. `Besides there's no time to get married now, I'm off tomorrow morning.' Although he knew it wasn't only the fact that he was going away that would have stopped them from getting married, it was extremely unlikely Lady Whittington would have agreed to them marrying. `I'll be back you'll see, and you won't get rid of me that easy then.' He grinned at her and his eyes twinkled.

`I love you, Joe Lambert.' She offered her lips to him and he kissed them, savouring the last kiss for a very long time.

They sat down on the grass and watched the sun setting over Portsmouth. It was a peaceful summer's evening and apart from the barrage balloons looming in the distance, it was hard to believe there was actually a war going on. It was also hard to believe that it was only a matter of hours before he would be gone again, and for how long this time? Neither of them knew the answer to that question.

Ten

As predicted the dreaded air-raids began only two days after Joe had left. Portsmouth was hit the worst as everyone had feared. The Germans had dropped a large number of explosive bombs including oil bombs on the city and especially around Portsmouth dock yard. Houses were burnt to the ground and debris strewn all over the streets and pavements. The dust and acrid smell of explosives hung in the warm summer air. There were people wondering aimlessly in the streets looking shell-shocked, many had lost their homes and loved ones. Church halls and schools became the communal places to gather for people who had lost their homes. There they could find a mattress and food while the authorities would try to find somewhere else for them to live.

Sarah worked long hours as more and more civilians were rushed to hospital as a result of the brutal air-raids. On the 27th of August the raids spread further hitting Vospers boat yard, Portsdown school and worst of all Portsdown Road. The hospital shook from the vibration of the impact and as casualties poured in to Queen Alexandra Hospital all Sarah could think about was her mother, Annie, Audrey, Frank, Maureen and little Nancy.

`Portsdown Road's been hit' an old man cried anxiously with blood gashing from his forehead as he came flying through the doors of casualty. Sarah ran over to attend to him.

`Do you know which part of the street has been hit?' she asked nervously as she frantically cleaned up his wound.

`No, it's difficult to see it's all a mess up there. Why d'you know anyone there?' he winced as Sarah dabbed alcohol onto his open wound.

`Yes, my fiancé's family.'

He noticed that her eyes were wide from fear and he patted her hand in sympathy then winced again with the second dab of alcohol.

`Audrey!' Frank shouted frantically as he ran up Portsdown Road. The street was a mass of dust and rubble and it was hard to see where there had ever been a pavement. There were empty shells instead of houses as the residents slowly started filtering back to the street. Their cries of distress and woe could be heard from afar, many of them returning to find they no longer had a home.

The closer Frank came to The Laurel's the quicker his heart raced and then he stopped in his tracks, his heart still continued to thud and the sweat on his forehead dripped down the sides of his face. He stared ahead of him, his face emotionless and then gave a sigh of relief when he saw that from Phyllis Grimshaw's house upwards the houses were still intact, untouched by the bomb that had caused so much devastation down the lower part of the road.

A new wave of panic came over him. What if Audrey and Maureen weren't at home? What if they had been out at the time?

In the distance he saw two figures making their way through the thick grey smoke. It was hard to see who they were. They were almost like an apparition. One of the figures was carrying something and as they drew closer he could see the shape of a small child.

`Thank God.' It was Audrey and with her was Maureen carrying Nancy in her arms.

`Audrey! Maureen!' he shouted out with sheer relief, tears streaming down his face as he ran towards them.

`Oh Frank... it was terrible' Audrey was shaking violently as she reached out for him.

`Dad has the house been hit?' Maureen asked, desperately trying to look behind him to see if she could see their home.

`The house is fine... where were you, Audrey?' He wiped his tears from his eyes.

`We took Nancy out for a walk. The siren went off and we made a quick dash for the shelter down London Road, it wasn't even properly dark yet.'

She was still shaking as Frank placed his arm around her and took Nancy in his other arm as they walked through the garden gate.

Frank fumbled in his pocket to find the house keys. Audrey glanced next door and noticed Phyllis sitting crouched, cowering in the doorway of her house like a frightened mouse. She nudged Frank and nodded her head in the direction of Phyllis. `Take Maureen and Nancy in, I better go and check on her.' Audrey said dusting herself down and walking back up the garden path.

`Phyllis. Are you alright my love?' Phyllis looked as white as a sheet. Two of her curlers had come loose where she had been holding onto her head while crouching down in terror.

She reached out for Audrey, relieved to see a familiar face. `It was terrible Audrey, I thought I was gunno die.'

`Look at you... you're shaking like a leaf. Now you comin' with me and 'ave a nice cup of tea.' She helped her to her feet and slid her arm inside Phyllis's as they made their way back next door. She was so concerned for her, her own shock seemed to have subsided.

`Mum, Tabby was ere all the time, he was on the sofa' Maureen shouted out stroking the cat who was sitting next to her on the sofa wondering what all the fuss was about. Audrey walked through the lounge door still gripping tightly on to Phyllis.

`Never mind the cat...budge up Maureen and let Phyllis 'ave a seat'

`I've put the kettle on' Frank said looking concerned at Phyllis.

Phyllis sat down on the sofa and then burst into a hysterical fit of crying.

`There, there, you let it all out... You let it all out' Audrey repeated, sitting down beside her and rubbing her shoulder trying to comfort her. She glanced over at Maureen who was staring worriedly at Phyllis. `Maureen, make yourself useful and go and make some tea.'

Nancy was sitting on the carpet playing with her favourite rag doll that Audrey had made her for her first birthday, and when Phyllis started to cry, her big brown eyes welled up and she let out a huge wail.

`I'll take Nancy out the way' Frank said softly, picking her up and kissing her blond curly hair, before walking out of the room.

`I thought I was gunno die' Phyllis said again.

`What append to you Phyllis?...Were you at home?' Audrey asked in a low soothing voice.

`I was doin' some baking when the siren went off. Our Nelly is coming up with the baby tomorrow. I couldn't of left me cake, it would of burnt but then the sirens continued and' She let out a sob and grabbed her hanky from the front pocket of her floral pinafore.'

`And then what 'append?' Audrey was desperately trying to understand her.

`The noise was deafening and I got scared. So I put the cake on the kitchen side, even though it weren't cooked, and then I ran to the front door.' She turned to face Audrey, tears still pouring down her face. `As I come out the front gate, and a bloody great big plane swooped over the roof tops. It was dark grey and it came so close to me, I could see the Swartz sticker painted on the wing. I even saw the pilot with his big goggles.' Her eyes were wide with fear as she relived the experience, telling Audrey. `He flew up the other end of Portsdown Road and he dropped...' she sobbed again not being able to finish her sentence. `You mean he dropped the bomb? Audrey shivered and her hands were beginning to shake again. She put her arms around Phyllis to try and calm her down.

Maureen walked in the room holding two mugs of steaming hot tea `I put a bit of sugar in 'em' she said handing them each a mug.

Just then there was a loud knock at the door. `Oh get that Maureen will you love?'

`Yeah, don't worry I'll fetch the tea and open the door and anything else that's gotta be done round ere, Me Lady,' she mumbled as she opened the front door.

Audrey took Phyllis's tea from her and placed it on the table in front of her. She was shaking so much and it was far too hot for her to drink.

`You gotta visitor, Mum.'

`Sarah! Oh Sarah! 'Ow lovely to see you.' Audrey got up and rushed across the room to give her a hug.

`I came as soon as I could, I was so worried about you all,' Sarah looked relieved to see them all fit at well. Frank appeared in the front room holding Nancy's hand and in his other hand he was holding her rag doll. He had heard Sarah arrive and presumed it was safe to go back downstairs again. Hello Sarah, I thought I recognised your voice. Are you alright my love?'

`I'm very well, thank you Mr Lambert. I was worried about all of you.'

`Oh, we're all fine. Me and Maureen were taking little Nancy for a walk and then had to run into the shelter down London Road.' Audrey butted in. `Thank gawd the house is still standing.'

Sarah was looking at Phyllis sitting on the sofa. `That's Phyllis our neighbour. She's not too good' Audrey said following Sarah's gaze. Sarah walked over to where Phyllis was sitting. `Hello Phyllis, my name is Sarah, are you alright?' She bent down in front of her to look into her eyes.

`Sarah's a volunteer nurse' Audrey told Phyllis proudly, sitting back down next to her.

`I thought I was gunno die' she said again as her lip trembled and new tears welled up in her eyes.

`That's all she keeps saying... she thought she was gunno die' Audrey said in despair. Sarah asked her a few questions such as if she felt sick or had a headache and then felt her pulse. It was still racing. `She's had a terrible shock and she needs to be looked after. Does she have a husband or any family?'

`Her husband died in the first world war, she's lived alone for years. Her son's at war, he's in the army, he's been in the army for years. She has got a daughter who's s'posed to be coming up tomorrow,' Audrey explained trying to give a brief summary of Phyllis's family and history.

`I think she should stay with you until her daughter comes up and if she's not any better tomorrow, please bring her to the hospital to run some tests,' Sarah said gently.

`She can sleep in the boys' room,' Frank said, walking towards the sofa.

`I've given her a cup of tea with sugar' Maureen announced proudly wanting everyone to know that she had done her bit in helping Phyllis, even though she didn't like her. Nosy old bat was what she called her most of the time.

`Has she drunk it?' Sarah asked.

`It's there. Her 'ands were trembling too much.' Audrey pointed to the cup of tea sitting on the little coffee table in front of them. Sarah picked up the mug and held it to Phyllis's lips. `Phyllis, please drink some tea for me, just a little sip' Phyllis started to drink it, pausing between sips. Sarah sat with her until she had drunk most of the cup and then miraculously some colour started to appear in Phyllis's cheeks.

`I'm sure she will be fine, but like I said if you are worried about her, bring her into casualty tomorrow. I'm working all day tomorrow' Sarah said standing up straight. Audrey stood up next to her. `You're a good girl Sarah. My Joe picked a gooden when he picked you.'

`You make her sound like a potato... Picked a gooden.' Maureen chuckled and Sarah blushed.

`You want a cuppa before you go?' Audrey asked ignoring Maureen's silly comment.

`No thank you, I really need to get home and check my mother is alright.'

`But it's late now and dark, you want Frank to walk you back?'

`Thank you but it's alright, I'm walking back with another nurse from the hospital she is waiting outside for me.

`Like I said you are a good girl, always thinking of others. You come and see us soon my love,' Audrey shouted out to her as Frank saw her to the front door.

When Sarah arrived home she frowned as she saw the new red MG sports car parked at the entrance of the house. Much to her disapproval she found her mother talking to Edward Hamilton in the drawing-room.

Sarah burst into the room `Mama, are you alright? I came home as soon as I could,' `Why wouldn't I be darling? Oh Sarah you have met Edward Hamilton haven't you?'

`Yes, we've met' she replied coolly. Edward smiled at her, revealing his row of perfect white teeth. He was wearing a navy blue suit and a maroon coloured tie. He gently ran his fingers through his fair hair and looked back at Laura again. `Well I shall leave those papers with you then, my Lady, and if it's convenient for you, I will return later in the week to collect them.' He reached for his brief case that was placed on the table next to a handful of papers he was referring to. He closed it and picked it up.

`Yes, no problem Edward and thank you so much for coming to deliver them personally, especially at this hour.' She flashed him a gratifying smile.

`Not at all…Goodbye, Sarah' he said nodding in Sarah's direction. He had a look of amusement in his eyes as he turned and walked out of the room.

`What was all that about?' Sarah asked in astonishment.

`Oh just some legal papers of your father's that need signing. He dropped them off on his way home.' Laura said, putting them to one side and walking over to the armchair nearest the window where she had left her tapestry before Edward had arrived.

`That man is really something" Sarah said shaking her head from side to side. `Do you have any idea of the devastation caused today? You must have heard the siren and the bombs dropping, Mother? She looked exasperated as she walked across the room to where Laura was sitting.

`Well, yes of course I heard them. I was in the shelter,' she replied, picking up her tapestry and continuing to sew again.

`He must have driven through the chaos to get here. So while people were running for their lives and homes were being destroyed and the whole place in a state of emergency, Mr Hamilton decides it's a perfect time to drop off some papers for you to sign!'

`Oh Sarah, really, life goes on you know. Of course I am aware of what is happening out there, as I am sure Mr Hamilton is but he doesn't stop work because of it. You get too involved in it all with working at that hospital.' Laura narrowed her right eye as she threaded a needle with red wool.

`Mother there is a war going on for goodness sake. I am doing my duty, helping others, of course I get involved.' There were times when her mother really frustrated her, it was almost like she had shut herself off from the rest of the world since losing her husband and son. Sarah watched her from where she was standing. It was as if her life revolved around reading, tapestries and having tea with a few old cronies who were left in the neighbourhood and had not fled to the countryside, like the rest of them had.

Three days later Sarah returned home from the hospital to find Edward Hamilton's car parked at the entrance again. The weather was still warm and although the sun was starting to set, it was as warm as mid afternoon.

She found her mother in the back garden chatting and laughing with Edward. It was the first time she had seen her laugh since her father had died, but even so, she resented that it was Edward who was the one that was making her laugh, there was something about him she didn't like. She couldn't quite put her finger on it and she felt sure that he wasn't to be trusted.

The garden was in full bloom and there was a strong scent from the roses framing the archway of the patio leading into the garden. Edward sat on the long white wicker sofa next to her mother in the garden.

`Oh there you are, Mama' she said forcing a smile in Edward's direction.

`Oh Sarah, I've invited Edward to stay for dinner tonight to show my gratitude for all his hard work recently.'

Edward looked up at Sarah, shading his eyes with his hand from the sun. `Sarah, there is really no need for Laura… I mean your mother to thank me, but as she insists,' he glanced back at Laura and gave a small wry smile. `I would be delighted to have dinner with two charming young ladies.' He was so slimy, she almost felt sick. Since when had her mother become Laura and not Lady Whittington to him? She wondered as she stared at him, sitting next to her mother, making himself at home.

`Fine' she said abruptly and then walked back into the house.

`She's still grieving' Laura explained apologetically.

`It's only natural but I don't wish to intrude.'

`Intrude?…Nonsense! You are very welcome. In fact I enjoy your company.' Laura smiled broadly at him and he sat back in his seat looking relaxed and pleased with himself.

`Something smells lovely, what's for dinner, Nanny?' Sarah asked as she walked into the kitchen. Annie was standing at the stove stirring a thick rich tomato soup. `Tomato soup for starters followed by chicken pie.'

`You know that we have a guest staying for dinner?' Sarah said as she poured herself some orange juice.

`Yes, your mum told me Mr Hamilton's staying. I've laid an extra place.'

`Can you poison his slice of the pie?' Sarah closed the pantry door and turned to face Annie.

`Miss Sarah! What d'you go and say such an awful thing like that for?' Annie's face had an expression of horror.

`I was joking Nanny but I don't like him. I think he has a thing for Mama.'

`Don't be so daft, Miss Sarah, she's old enough to be his mother.' Annie scolded.

Sarah sat down at the table placing her head in her hands. Life was so tiresome without Joe. It was all such a struggle now that he was gone again. She was back to the endless worrying and sleepless nights again and the only thing to look forward to was a letter in the post.

Sarah said very little during dinner while Laura and Edward chatted animatedly and appeared to be getting on as if they had known each other for years.

`Laura, I can't believe you haven't been to the New Forest for nearly three years,' Edward said, wiping his face on his starched white linen serviette.

`I know… it's remarkable how time flies' Laura replied taking a sip of her wine.

`Well, I think it's time you went back. In fact I insist it's time you went back. So how about I pick you up next Sunday and we go for a picnic? I know a great little spot just perfect for picnics.' Sarah glared at them both. This was getting out of hand. Staying for dinner was one thing but taking her mother out on a date was disgraceful. She stood up from the table.

`I've heard more than enough. You are both despicable!' She threw her serviette onto the table and marched out of the dining-room.

`Sarah!" Laura called after her with a look of bewilderment.

`Edward, I sincerely apologise for my daughter's behaviour. Like I said, she is still in shock over her brother and her father's recent death.'

Edward looked uneasy. `Laura, with your permission would you allow me to speak to Sarah alone? I know what it's like to lose one's father and I feel if I could have a chance to speak to her alone, she wouldn't feel threatened by me. I only want to be friends with you both.' His lips turned into a gentle smile and Laura nodded in agreement.

`I will have a look where she is, I won't be a moment.'

She found Sarah reading a medical book. Laura peered through the door and then hurried back to the dining-room.

`Edward, she's in the second drawing-room, if you wish to speak to her. I will join you both in a little while, I'll give you time to talk.' She was grateful that he wanted to help. Sarah was becoming rather tiresome lately and not having her husband around to keep her in check made things difficult.

Edward walked into the drawing-room cautiously as Sarah continued to read, not even raising her head to acknowledge him.

`Sarah, I don't wish to intrude' He continued to walk towards her with caution. 'But I would like to apologise if I have upset you in anyway.' He sat down in the armchair opposite her. `I truly am sorry' he apologised again, not really knowing what he was sorry for, but it was clear to him that she had been offended with something he had said or done. `I know you have been through a difficult time recently.' She closed the book and carefully placed it down by the side of her and looked at him with glazed eyes.

`My father is not even cold in his grave and here you are pursuing my mother. How do you think that makes me feel?' Edward's eyes grew wide with shock. Is that what she really thought? That he was after her mother? It was so ridiculous it was almost amusing.

`Sarah, I can assure you, I am not pursuing your mother. We are merely friends.'

`Friends? Is that what you call it?'

`Yes, Sarah, we are friends. My father was a good friend of your father's. I liked Lord Whittington a great deal. I feel that I owe it to him to look out for you and your mother.' He stood up and walked towards the window, he looked pensive as he stared out at the extensive gardens and ran his fingers through his fair hair again.

`We don't want your pity' Sarah snapped, looking as though she was about to cry. He turned to face her and spoke in a soft tone.

`My friendship is not out of pity but out of respect for your father.'

`So why were you asking my mother to go on a picnic with you? Don't you think it was a little presumptuous? She's old enough to be your mother, for goodness sake!' She looked at him in disgust.

`I have no romantic interests in your mother, only friendship and to prove it, I would like to invite you with us next Sunday.'

`I am not interested in going on a sordid picnic with you and my mother.'

`Why do you have so much hatred towards me Sarah? What have I done to you? I want to be friends with you and your mother… Is that so bad?' He walked towards her and stood in front of her looking down with his blue sorrowful eyes.

Perhaps she had over reacted a little. She looked at him and felt a wave of guilt wash over her. She had behaved a little childish. She missed Joe dreadfully not to mention her father and even Charles although they had not been that close but she did miss having him around. Edward was about the same age as him, which probably explained why her mother liked to have him around so much. The world felt a cruel place and she wanted to lash out at someone, anyone. Why couldn't life be like it was before? Why were there so many changes? She knew she shouldn't have taken her anger out on Edward. He could see her expression softening and he asked her again.

`Will you please come with us to the New Forest next Sunday?' She wavered for a moment and then a small smile appeared on her face.

`Alright. Maybe I have been a trifle unfair to you.'

`Sarah, I only want to be your friend," he reiterated sitting back down in the armchair in front of her. She nodded accepting his invitation to go on a picnic with him and her mother.

*****

`Mama, are you nearly ready? Edward will be here soon,' Sarah called out from the bottom of the staircase. Laura appeared at the top of the stairs dressed in black as she had been since the day Lord Whittington had died. She looked weary again. `I'm not going Sarah, I have a dreadful headache. I called Edward about twenty-minutes ago to explain.'

`But Nanny has prepared the picnic now.'

`I know my dear, so you must go and enjoy yourself,' Laura said, stroking her forehead. Sarah looked alarmed. `I'm to go on a picnic *alone* with *him*?'

`Sarah, my dear don't look so worried. Edward is a respectable young man and I'm sure you will have a lovely time. Now if you don't mind, I'm going to have a lay down now.'

`But, Mama!' It was bad enough having to go on this silly picnic at all but with Edward, *alone*. It wasn't right to go on picnics with strange men, she was engaged for goodness sake. No, there had to be a way out of it. Just then her thoughts were interrupted by the beeping horn of Edward's bright red MG as he pulled up outside the entrance of the house.

Sarah opened the door and stepped out into the sunshine. She was wearing beige corduroy trousers and a pale pink short sleeved blouse with a beige cardigan draped over her shoulders.

`Hello Sarah, you look very summary today. We are almost matching' Edward said, pointing to his trousers as he got out of his car. He was wearing beige trousers the same shade as Sarah's.

`Edward, Mama is not coming' Sarah said.

`Yes, I know, she called me. Why do you think I turned up in this' he said smiling and pointing to his car. `It wouldn't be big enough for the three of us now would it? I would have had to bring my other car if your mother was coming.'

`Edward I don't think it's a good idea we go alone. I just' - she attempted to try and excuse herself.

`Nonsense, I don't bite. I'm a perfect gentleman and besides I'm really looking forward to going on a picnic.' He pouted his lips like a small child. At that moment Annie appeared with a brown wicker picnic basket and a red and navy blue checked blanket draped over the top of it. She handed it to Edward. `You've got chicken, pate and cheese sandwiches in there, plus other goodies' she informed them excitely.

`And I've got drinks and fruit, so we will have a banquet' Edward pointed to a small identical brown wicker basket in the boot of his car. Sarah sighed. Getting out of this was going to be too difficult and perhaps it would be nice to get away for a few hours, it wasn't that bad she decided.

`Thanks, Nanny.' She got into the passenger seat of Edward's red sports car.

`So the New Forest, here we come' he said as he started the engine. Annie waved them goodbye from the entrance of the house as the engine of the MG revved and sped off down the gravel path out of Whittington Manor.

The journey was pleasant and Sarah enjoyed the feel of the summer wind breezing through her hair as they drove with the open top roof down. They spoke very little during the journey but they both appeared relaxed and were enjoying the drive.

`If we park here, we need to walk about five minutes to the spot I want to take you to' Edward informed her as he turned off the engine.

Sarah followed him curiously through the trees carrying the small picnic basket and the folded blanket while Edward carried the larger basket packed with food that Annie had prepared for them. It felt like they were getting further and further away from the car and the woodland became suddenly thicker. She began to feel nervous. She didn't even know this man and here she was far from civilisation following him like a lost puppy dog. Her mother's words were the only thing she could draw comfort from `Edward is a respectable young man and I'm sure you will have a lovely time.' Her words kept ringing in her ears and she hoped that she was right.

All of a sudden her fear subsided as they arrived at a small clearing. Sarah gasped. It was beautiful. It looked like something out of an idyllic painting. The stream sparkled like crystals in the sunlight. It was surrounded by mature trees and a patch of lush green grass edged with daisies, bluebells and many other wonderful wild flowers.

`Edward this is unbelievable... it's magnificent.' She looked around her in amazement.

`I know. I found it years ago and not many people know about it' he boasted, as he inhaled the fresh summer air. They laid out the picnic blanket and placed the baskets downs by the side of them.

`Apple juice or orange juice?' Edward asked as he took two cups out of the basket.

`Orange please' Sarah replied, whilst peeking inside the basket full of Annie's goodies. There were chicken pieces, scotch eggs, little sausages, cheeses and an assortment of sandwiches cut into triangles.

`It's so nice not to be working and to be able to relax like this' Edward said, stretching his legs in front of him. Sarah watched him closely. She was suddenly curious about him. `Do you enjoy your work?' He paused before answering, as if giving the question great consideration.

`Yes, I suppose I do. My father was a solicitor all his life and he encouraged me to study law. I was lucky enough to work with him and learn the tricks of the trade before he died.'

Sarah vaguely remembered her father talking about William Hamilton, although she never paid much attention to his conversations that referred to business. She offered Edward a selection of sandwiches. He picked out a pate sandwich and thanked her.

`Do you have any brothers or sisters?' Sarah enquired. He seemed only to ever speak about his father.

`No – my mother died when I was five years old. She died of a lung infection, not that I remember of course.' He took a bite of his sandwich. `And your father never remarried?'

`No... although he almost did about ten years ago. He was madly in love but I'm afraid she broke his heart'. `She left him for another man.' He added.

`How sad' Sarah said.

`I don't think he ever got over her. He became bitter when it came to love after that.' Edward looked at her and smiled wryly. `He told me – always trust your head and never your heart. You must never marry for love or your heart will get broken'.

`Well, I'm afraid I don't agree with him' she said with indignation.

`So why haven't you been called up for service?' she asked, changing the subject not wanting to discuss the matter any further.

`I was made exempt from duties. Haven't you noticed the way I walk?' he had a look of surprise on his face.

`No why?' Sarah looked puzzled.

`I was in a car accident four years ago and I damaged my hip. I have a limp when I walk and I can't run very fast or play sports anymore' he added.

`I'm sorry to hear that. Were you alone in the car?'

`Yes - fortunately.'

`But if you wanted to join up, couldn't they find you a desk job, something like book keeping maybe?' She took a sip of her drink, her eyes still fixed on him as she studied him with interest.

`They didn't ask and I didn't volunteer. My father worked hard to build up his business and in a way I am happy to be here looking after it, now that he is not around any more to do it himself. Going away would have meant closing the business. Besides I'm a solicitor and I'm needed here to do my job.'

Sarah nodded. `So did you play sports before your accident?' she had noticed the forlorn look in his eyes when he said he couldn't run or play sports anymore.

`I used to play tennis. I even have trophies' he boasted proudly and then sighed wistfully.

`It must be awful for you... not being able to play any more.'

He looked uncomfortable with the conversation and decided to change the subject.

`Anyway - enough of me. What made you become a volunteer nurse?'

`I've always been interested in medicine. I've read medical books since I was about twelve. I find nursing very rewarding.' She leaned back and put her face up to the sun, it felt good on her skin and it reminded her of when she used to have picnics with Joe at Portchester Castle.

`But it must be quite gruesome, I mean…all those soldiers who have terribly gory wounds?' Edward wrinkled his nose at the image he had in his mind. He hated blood and gore in fact he hated getting his hands dirty full stop. He was far too clean cut for all that.

`No not really. I enjoy being a nurse. I only wish those men didn't have to suffer.' Her mind wandered off as she remembered all the soldiers she had helped treat who had come back from Dunkirk. It would be a memory that would stick with her for the rest of her life. And then her thoughts drifted back to Charles and then to Joe again. She wondered what he was doing at that precise moment. For sure he wasn't sitting having a picnic and she suddenly felt guilty.

`Did I say something wrong?' Edward asked as he watched her expression turn solemn.

`No. I was just thinking of Joe.' Edward frowned. `Who's Joe?' he asked casually as he helped himself to another sandwich.

`Joe is my fiancé.' She missed him so much her heart yearned for him day and night, just mentioning his name almost brought her to tears. Edward dropped his sandwich down his trousers and looked at her in astonishment.

`Fiancé? Laura had never mentioned anything to him about Sarah being engaged, and neither had Lord Whittington for that matter, which was even more bizarre given the fact they talked about his will and Sarah in great detail before he died.

`I had no idea you were engaged. You don't wear a ring' he pointed out as he closely observed her fingers, before rescuing the remains of the chicken paste sandwich that had slid down his trousers.

`No, that's because Joe proposed to me a few hours before he left to go to war. We decided to wait until the war is over before buying a ring and making it official'.

`I see' Edward said, still looking astonished. He brushed the remaining crumbs from his lap. `And what does Joe do, I mean what did he do, rather, before the war?'

`Do? What do you mean what did he do?' Sarah looked blank.

`I mean what's his profession?'

Sarah looked away from him so that he couldn't see her exasperation. He was starting to sound like her father had when she had told him she was engaged.

`Is it important what he does?' she replied with an edge of irritation in her voice.

`No, I was just curious.' He sheepishly, took a sip of his drink.

`Well if you must know, he works on the land with his father' Edward nearly choked on his drink and it took all his power not to laugh out loud. No wonder the Whittingtons hadn't said anything. There would be no way on earth they would allow their daughter to marry a land worker. He took another sip of his drink, trying to contain his amusement. He looked at the running stream rushing and rippling across the pebbles and sat staring lost in thought for a moment. She couldn't win whatever way it turned out. If this Joe died at war she wouldn't be able to marry him, and if he came back, she wouldn't be *allowed* to marry him, so whichever way one looked at the situation it was destined to be doomed, so the boy was clearly of no threat.

He turned to face her again. `Come on let's throw some pebbles in the stream' he said trying to lighten her mood and take her mind off Joe. Sarah took off her shoes and dangled her toes in the crystal clear water. It was warm from the heat of the sun shining on it.

`Want to play *ask me a question*?' Edward asked jovially.

`What's that?'

`It's something I used to play with my friends when I was a young boy. We each throw a pebble into the water and the one who throws it the furthest has to ask a question.'

`What kind of question?'

`Any question you want. So here it goes... after three. Are you ready? One, two, three' Edward threw the furthest, his pebble almost reaching the other side of the stream.

`What's your favourite colour?' he asked turning to face Sarah, taking the game very seriously.

`Red' she replied with amusement and they threw the pebbles again. This time Sarah won, although she was convinced he had let her win.

`Do you play a musical instrument?' She giggled at the serious expression upon his face.

`I tried to play the piano when I was young but I just couldn't grasp it. I was so bad that my father was really embarrassed and he told my tutor not to bother anymore.' He pulled a face as if he was very upset about it all. Sarah laughed at him.

`I bet you can play the piano,' he said, pretending to be jealous.

`Actually I can' she boasted.

`How well?' Come on how well? He teased.

`Um you are not allowed to ask me that would make it two questions. You have to throw the pebble first.' She teased him back. This time he threw it so hard it ended up on the grass the other side of the stream.

`My... my you really wanted to ask me that question, didn't you?' He looked at her and laughed.

`Alright - how well can you play the piano?' He jutted his chin out and turned his head at a slight angle as if in preparation to hear her answer.

`Fairly well' she answered grinning at him.

`You probably mean brilliantly.' At that moment there was a crash of thunder in the back ground. They had been so busy talking they hadn't noticed the heavy rain clouds that were forming above them.

Edward looked up at the threatening sky. `I think we should get the picnic baskets into the car and put my roof down, before it rains'.

As soon as they had finished packing the picnic the heavens opened on them as they ran as quickly as they could to the car. It was only then that Sarah noticed Edward had difficulties in running, it was more of a hop than a run, and she remembered their conversation about his accident

He frantically put the roof down, throwing the baskets in the boot of the car and then jumping into the drivers' seat as quickly as he possibly could. Sarah jumped in the passenger seat next to him. They sat in their seats for a few seconds panting, trying to regain their breath and a moment later Edward turned and looked at Sarah. She was as soaked as he was. Her auburn curls stuck flat to her head, large rain drops trickled down her face. Her blouse had turned see-through and clung to her perfectly formed small breasts, showing her protruding nipples. Edward ran his eyes swiftly over her body. She's beautiful, like a sweet ripe peach almost ready for picking he thought. Reaching over to her he helped her put on her cardigan to keep herself warm. Oblivious to what he was thinking, Sarah looked at him and laughed. `Your hair!' A large piece of fair hair was sticking up on end, almost like it was glued in an upright position. It was normally combed so immaculately Sarah found it very amusing. Using the palm of his hand, he quickly flattened his hair into place.

By the time they arrived back at Whittington Manor the storm had suppressed and the sunshine had appeared again. Edward jumped out of the car and ran around to the passenger seat to open the door for Sarah.

`Thank you for today, Edward. I had a wonderful time.' She held her hand up accepting his offer for him to help her out of the car.

`So did I,' he was still holding her hand as they stood next to the car.

`It's good to have friends, Sarah, especially with the madness the world is in right now.

`I agree. As well as missing Joe, I miss Emma dreadfully, she confessed. Emma is my best friend. She went to live in Devon for the duration.'

`Well, I'm sure I am not as pretty as Emma and possibly a *tiny* bit older' he said holding his thumb and forefinger slightly apart as if to emphasise the word tiny. `But I would be happy to be your friend, if you would allow me to.' Sarah smiled at him, she couldn't help but like him, he was very charming, yet she still felt so guilty about going on a picnic with him. No matter how hard she tried it was like a knot in her stomach, a constant ache that just wouldn't go away. It wasn't fair to Joe. She was sure he wouldn't have approved of this afternoon. As if Edward could read her thoughts he quickly added `I'm not trying to replace Joe, I only want to be your friend. I promise I have no other intentions other than friendship.' He smiled at her as she watched him closely, trying to decide if he really meant what he said. Could they be just friends? Could it work? If he really meant it, then there was no reason for her to feel guilty and life was very lonely without Joe and Emma.

`Let's go out again sometime soon and have fun like we did today?' He pushed encouragingly like a little boy who had just found a new friend to go out to play with. Sarah smiled at him. `Alright. But just as friends, you know I'm engaged to be married.'

`Just friends' he repeated, smiling back at her. Friends was good enough for now.

Eleven

The air-raids continued relentlessly on Portsmouth for the rest of the year, and Portchester also suffered regular random bombings, mainly on Vospers Boat Yard, Portsdown School and around Portsdown Hill. By January and February of 1941 the concentration was also on other cities such as Plymouth, Swansea and Bristol and all along the south coast. Night after night the sirens sounded as people scurried frantically to their nearest shelter to listen to the evil snarl of German bombers overhead. And if that wasn't enough, the war news was bad abroad too. Malta had been attacked day and night due to its strategic position in the Mediterranean.

In other parts of the world it was just as bad. Italy had taken over vital ports of Sumaliland, Tobruk and Libya, as well as Greece and Albania. The war seemed endless.

Audrey and Frank sat at the kitchen table discussing the day's news. Frank enjoyed Sunday mornings when he didn't have to go to work. It was the one morning a week he could relax and read the newspaper, not that he enjoyed reading the news these days. It was all so depressing.

`Well, if there is anything good to say about reading this stuff, it's certainly good for me geography,' he said.

`Yeah, you're right there. I've never heard of Tobruk and Sumali whatsit' Audrey said.

`Where are they?'

`Africa…apparently. We never learnt about any of those places at school. Mind you, I s'pose there was nothing much to learn about, until now of course,' Frank peered over the top of his paper at Audrey to see if she was still listening to him.

She looked deep in thought. `I don't understand 'ow this has all got so out of hand. I mean what the 'ell has Africa gotta do with it all?' Audrey put her elbow on the table and rested her face in the palms of her hands.

`Well, it's to do with Italy really. Cause Italy is on 'itler's side' Frank began to explain.

`They've got lots of places in Africa you see and so `ave we, so we got to defend ourselves against them, if you know what I mean?' It sill didn't make any sense to Audrey. The whole war didn't make any sense to her. `You see it's like the Japs, they might join in too, cause they don't like the Americans being in the South Pacific,' he continued making the explanation even more complicated for Audrey to comprehend. `Oh that's enough Frank, it's too much information for me brain. I'm gunno nip round to see Ethel Chadwell. She wants to borrow me baking tin. She's making a cake for her son who's comin' ome on leave tomorrow. I'll be back soon and don't forget to keep an ear out for little'un,' asleep upstairs.' She pointed her finger to upstairs where baby Nancy was sleeping. She got up off her chair and walked out of the kitchen. Frank shrugged his shoulders and then went back to reading the newspaper.

Sarah, Cynthia and the rest of the medical staff at Queen Alexandra Hospital were rushed off their feet as more soldiers were ferried in on stretchers from the overspill of the other hospitals in the Portsmouth area that day. Haslar and The Royal were choc full and even St James', which was a mental hospital, were now taking in casualties. Yet, despite her endless chores and mundane tasks, Sarah still managed time to give a comforting word or two to the wounded men. Some of them, tried to flirt with her, as they recovered and got their strength back, but it never bothered her, she was just happy to see them on the mend and she chuckled at their compliments and funny comments. It was rewarding to see some of them leave after arriving in such a terrible state but it was devastating to see some of them never recover. She had pulled so many blankets over the agonizing faces of men who had died there in her ward.

`You can take your tea break now and with a bit of luck you can finish on time, if we don't get any more come in' Sister said, looking satisfied that everything was under control on the ward at last.

`Alright. Thank you Sister.'

Sarah walked into the canteen and found Cynthia on a break, she hardly saw her these days, they were working on different wards and had been for many months.

`Hello stranger.'

`Sarah! What a surprise, we seem to be like ships passing in the night these days.' Sarah sat down next to her, helping herself to a watery cup of tea.

`I don't know why I drink this stuff,' Sarah complained, wrinkling her nose.

`How's Joe? Have you heard from him lately?' Cynthia was always keen to hear Sarah's news, she liked her very much and still felt sorry for her after losing her father and brother the year before.

`Well, actually I'm starting to get a little worried as this is the longest it's ever been without a letter from him. The last letter I received was over a month ago.' She looked at Cynthia her eyes wide with worry.

`It's probably a delay in the post. We often go weeks without hearing from our Tim, and then all of a sudden they all arrive at the same time.' Tim was Cynthia's brother, he was in the Navy.

`Yes, you are probably right,' Sarah sighed wistfully. `The same happened, with Thomas my brother. Although, he is not a big writer and often the reason we don't get a letter is because he hasn't written, but I know Joe writes to me at least once a week.'

`Have you asked his mother if she has had a letter recently? She lives up the road from here doesn't she?' Cynthia remembered Sarah saying something about Joe living nearby.

`Yes, she lives in Portsdown Road but I don't like to keep bothering her, she must be worried enough without me adding to it.' Sarah looked sad as she stared down at her watery tea.

`You'll get a letter soon, don't you worry.' Cynthia gave her a reassuring tap on the arm.

It was two weeks later when finally Sarah received a number of letters from Joe, they had arrived all at the same time. She was thrilled when Annie handed them to her. `I thought you'd be happy' Annie said as she watched Sarah flick through the pile beaming with excitement.

`I'm so relieved, Nanny. I was getting very worried'

`Well, it must of been the post. Oh I almost forgot. Your mum got a letter today too. Guess who from?'

`Who?'

`Thomas, and he's fit and well' Annie said smiling broadly at her.

`Oh that is good news. Mama will be delighted.'

Sarah took the pile of letters up to her bedroom. After closing the door behind her, she sat down on her bed and opened each letter in date order. Just as she was finishing reading the last one, she could hear her mother calling her from downstairs. She wiped away her tears and carefully placed the letters into the shoe box she still kept under her bed and went downstairs.

`Ah, there you are. You have a visitor waiting for you in the main drawing-room'

`Who Mama?'

`Well, go in and you will see' Laura said pointing to the door of the drawing-room.

`Edward, what a nice surprise. Shouldn't you be at work?' It was almost lunch time, an unusual time of the day for him to visit.

`I could say the same to you' he said with a grin and raising his eyebrows.

Sarah pushed a lock of hair behind her ear and smiled at him. I've taken a day off today.'

`Well, I'm on a long lunch break and I thought which one of my friends would I most like to go to lunch with today, and guess what? I picked you' he said still grinning at her.

`Aren't I the lucky one?'

`I know a lovely little restaurant just outside of Fareham.'

She hesitated for a moment wondering if she should go, still wrestling with the guilt of spending time with another man. That nagging feeling just wouldn't go and even more so after just reading a month's worth of letters from Joe. She sighed. It was only lunch not a date as such, besides he was a perfect gentleman. `That would be lovely. I will just get my coat' She accepted his invitation quickly before she could change her mind. After finding her coat, she went to find her mother, who was in the kitchen chatting with Annie, about Thomas's letter. Laura was so delighted to hear he was fit and well. Annie could hardly get a word in edge ways as Laura read out every little detail of the letter including the part where he explained he was so sorry he couldn't make it back for his father's funeral. Laura wiped away a tear and Annie patted her hand in comfort.

`Mama,' Sarah interrupted, Edward is taking me out for lunch.'

`Wonderful darling, you have a good time.' Laura looked momentarily surprised and then as equally thrilled at the news.

`I'm so thankful Annie, now that she's spending time with Edward. He's a lovely young man' Laura said after Sarah had left the room.

`Yes, he is but she's still hankering after that lad, Joe. You should `ave seen her face when I gave her all those letters this morning. I've not seen her that happy in ages.'

`Oh, Annie, it's just a phase. Anyone can see she is much better suited to

Edward.' Annie nodded, although she wasn't convinced. She was well aware of how much Sarah loved Joe.

`That was delicious,' Sarah had polished off a plate of homemade beef stew. Edward smiled at her. `You seem happier than you did when I saw you last week.'

`I received six letters from Joe this morning.' Her eyes danced with excitement.

It wasn't quite the explanation Edward was wanting to hear. `I told you they would be in the post, didn't I?' He wiped his mouth on his serviette after finishing a mouth watering fish pie topped with creamy mashed potatoes.

`So is he coming home on leave?' Edward shifted in his seat apprehensively. He hoped he would never come back, but if he did, he would just have to be patient.

`No, he didn't say anything about coming home. He always makes light of everything but I know he's having a tough time out there.' Sarah's eyes clouded over, talking about Joe made her ache for him even more as always and she was so desperate for the war to end and for him to come home to her.

Edward looked relieved at the news. So Joe wasn't coming home on leave for the foreseeable future. `Well it must be tough for all of those men out there. It's not an easy job, is it? Anyway…how about dessert?' He rapidly changed the topic of conversation. He had found out what he needed to know, Joe wasn't coming back well not just yet. He waved to the waiter beckoning him over for the dessert menu. He tried not to show the irritation he felt whenever Sarah spoke about Joe. His job right now was to be the good friend with a sympathetic ear and it was working a treat so far.

`Edward, my goodness, I am going to be as fat as a house.'

`Rubbish! There's nothing of you'. They ordered two small vanilla ice creams and chatted easily about a number of topics. Sarah's knowledge impressed Edward. She would make a good wife one day. She was very well read, attractive, and more importantly she was rich or at least she would be as soon as soon as she turned twenty-one and that was worth everything to him. No one was going to get in the way of him getting his hands on her fortune and especially some hopeless loser of a land worker. It was all going to take some time but he was prepared to wait and in the end it would all be worthwhile.

Twelve

On the 1st of January 1942 Great Britain, the United States, China and the Soviet Union – plus twenty two other countries joined force in becoming the `United Nations' to fight against the Axis. This union was made up four-fifths of the world's population and with this great force it brought new hope, although the enemy was still attacking on all fronts. Japan had taken the Malayan capital, Kuala Lumpur, and even Singapore was also under threat.

Sarah had not seen Joe for almost two years and neither had she heard from him in months. Despite everyone around her, reassuring her, that it was most probably the postal delays again, she still became increasingly worried.

As she left the hospital after finishing her shift, she hesitated at the bottom of the entrance steps, debating to turn left to go and see Audrey. She had seen Audrey only a week ago and she hated to worry her again, so she decided to turn right and go home instead. As she began walking down the road, she stopped in her tracks, hearing her name being called out from afar. She turned around and squinted to see a figure running towards her, and a moment later she recognised who it was. It was Maureen.

By the time Maureen reached her she was panting and out of breath from running.

`What's the matter, Maureen? Is your mother alright?'

`Mum asked me to tell you' – She stopped to get her breath, bending forward and still panting.

`It's alright, Maureen, get your breath then tell me'

`We gotta a telegram…. it's about our Joe.' Sarah's heart skipped and she had an uneasy feeling in the pit of her stomach.

`He's missin' Maureen blurted out, standing up straight now.

`Missing, what do you mean? Missing where?'

`We dunno, it just said he was missin' in action. Look, I gotta go… me mum is in a bit of a state'

Sarah stared at her in disbelief. The colour from her cheeks had completely drained.

`Wait a minute...shall I come with you?' She rushed after Maureen trying to catch up with her quick pace.

`No. It's not a good idea. Seeing you might make it worse, if you know what I mean?' Sarah nodded.

`Maureen, if you get any more news, you will tell me, won't you?'

`I will.' Before Sarah could say anything more she was gone, running as quickly as she could down the hill. Sarah stood in a daze watching her retreating back fade away in the distance. None of it made sense. What did they mean he was missing? He couldn't just disappear into thin air, unless... She turned and started to make her way home. A sudden flush of panic came over her. What if he had been captured by the Germans and was being tortured? What if he was dead and they just hadn't found his body yet? She suddenly noticed tears were streaming down her face. A passer-by, a young woman, threw a sympathetic glance her way and quickly turned the next corner. Sarah began to feel sick. She was shaking violently and reached out for the nearest lamp post. She clung onto it, her head spinning and her heart racing. This couldn't have happened. Joe couldn't be gone... not Joe, oh God not Joe. She forced herself away from the lamp post. She had to get a grip. He wasn't dead, he was missing. Not dead just missing she said over and over again as she continued her journey home.

Audrey was sitting at the kitchen table with Phyllis. Phyllis had only popped in to give Audrey a slice of tea cake she had left over from when Nelly had come to stay. She didn't have much of a sweet tooth and being on her own it would have only gone to waste.

`Oh...Phyllis, where is he?' Audrey eyes full of sheer desperation.

`Well.... if they say he's missin', he could of escaped somewhere, you never know.' Phyllis patted Audrey's hand. She hated to see her in this state. Audrey had been so good to her after the incident where she had found her shell-shocked, cowering in her doorway scared to death after the bombing that day. She would be forever thankful to her.

`Or he could be in a prison of war camp somewhere, being tortured by the Nazis – or worse than that he could be –'She let out a sob and put her head in her hands.

`Now you listen to me Audrey Lambert, you can't go talkin' like that...dyou ere me. If he was – well you know, they would 'ave told you in that telegram.'

`Not if they haven't found him yet, they wouldn't 'ave' Audrey dabbed her eyes and blew her nose on her handkerchief.

`Who's to say he isn't hiding out somewhere safe – and you'd be worrying yourself silly for no reason,' Phyllis said, giving a reassuring tap on her hand.

`Where's safe? There's nowhere safe in the middle of a war, Phyllis'

`Does Frank know?' Phyllis asked ignoring her last statement.

`I've sent Maureen to tell him. She was s'posed to be working with him this morning but she was off with a bad tummy. I sent her to tell Sarah too.'

`Listen, Audrey – you gotta keep strong and keep believin' he'll be alright - And until you get a telegram saying otherwise, he's still alive.'

*****

The next few weeks Sarah drifted in and out of feeling distraught, sick from worry, then bouts of positive thinking and feeling sure Joe was alive somewhere. Every time a new influx of soldiers were admitted to hospital, she would search there faces looking for Joe's familiar twinkling green eyes. There were rows and rows of men stretched out and each time she dressed their wounds her thoughts drifted back to Joe. It was hard to concentrate on anything any more. She hated the thought of him in a hospital somewhere in the world, fighting for his life, just like all those soldiers she was treating. Images of him badly wounded tormented her constantly.

She noticed at one end of the ward there were two soldiers talking to each other. They were in the same regiment and had recently arrived from France. One had a broken leg and a fractured arm and the other had a burn wound to the right side of his face and a broken arm.

Despite their injuries they managed to chat and looked to be having quite a discussion. As Sarah moved closer to where they were, busily dressing a wound of a soldier who had an injury to his foot, she could pick up snippets of their conversation. They were talking about a battle that had taken place in France and it sounded horrific. She shivered as she listened to them.

`I can't believe those bastards got Hawkins and Lambert' the man with the broken leg rubbed his tired eyes and yawned.

Sarah dropped the bandage she was holding and froze as if she had just seen a ghost, the colour rapidly draining from her.

`I liked Lambert. Wasn't he from round 'ere?' The soldier with the burn on the side of his face turned to look at his friend.

He was yawning again. I dunno, I don't remember'

It couldn't be Joe, they were talking about, surely, Sarah turned to face them. Just then a nurse came and asked her for help right up the other end of the ward. She was needed to help lift a man into his bed, who only had one leg. She rushed away reluctantly, wishing she could have just found out if they were talking about Joe. It must have been her imagination, after all Lambert is quite a popular name and living near Portsmouth there were most probably hundreds of soldiers who had the name Lambert.

Further duties kept her busy for at least two hours before she had some free time to return to the two gossiping soldiers.

`How are you feeling?' she asked the man with the burn as she approached his bedside.

`Better for seeing you my darling,' he and his friend glanced at each other and grinned.

`I overheard you talking earlier and I would like to ask you a question' she directed the question at the man with the burn.

`You can ask me anything you want.'

`You were talking about someone, by the name of Lambert and I wondered…well if he was,' she paused for a second before plucking up the courage to continue her question. `If his name was Joe Lambert?'

The two men exchanged a knowing look.

`Yes, his name was Joe Lambert. Why did you know him?' Sarah noticed that he was talking in the past tense and the knot in her stomach tightened. `What happened to him?' Her eyes grew wide with fear, not really wanting to hear the man's answer.

`So you did know him?' he asked again.

`Yes, I'm his fiancé' she replied.

`Well, if you are his fiancé, you must know what happened to him. Surely you got a telegram to say he had been' – He stopped what he was saying and looked back at his friend.

`Please - What happened to him?' There was panic in her voice. The other man with the broken leg looked mournful. He beckoned her closer to his bedside. His face was covered in bruises and cuts, his deep brown eyes looked tired. He felt uneasy telling her what he knew but he felt he should anyway. If she really was Lambert's girl, she had a right to know.

`We were in a battle and the Jerries were slaughtering us.' He began. `Many of our boys got killed during that attack. Me and Harry…well we got away' he glanced over at his friend with the burn wound and broken arm. `Lambert, well he was with us, - he was in our unit you see.' Sarah stood at the edge of his bed listening to his every word, her eyes fixed on his, full of dread for what she was about to hear next. `I turned back before we fled and he was behind us. I called out to him to run but there was a Jerry right on his tail and it was too late' he gave a sigh.

`What do you mean it was too late?' she leaned closer to him.

`He was shot. - He fell into a ditch right behind us.'

`Couldn't you have got him out?' Was he alive?' Her eyes brimming with tears.

`The Jerries were coming after us, there were hundreds of them. We couldn't `ave gone back for him.' He looked down at his leg remembering how he broke it.

`But he wasn't dead though?' There was still a shred of hope in her voice.

`He wouldn't have survived. He was clutching his chest when he fell. He was shot down just like Hawkins who was running right next to him, – they got them both. I'm sorry.' There was an edge to his voice as if he was about to cry. He turned away from her with embarrassment.

`Thank you.' She nodded gratefully at both soldiers and found herself walking aimlessly out of the ward. She made her way out of the main entrance and on to the street. Her head was spinning and her chest was tight. She clung onto the railings next to the outside steps, stumbling her way down them until reaching the bottom. A woman brushed by her, rushing into casualty with a young baby in her arms but Sarah didn't even notice her. She walked away from the hospital in a zombie-like fashion. She suddenly became very hot and a film of sweat appeared on her forehead. Her stomach churned and she dashed to the side of the kerb not knowing if she was going to be sick but a moment later it subsided. Tears were streaming down her face as she stumbled down the road not even noticing that it was raining. Oh Joe, God no…not Joe.

For the next few days Sarah locked herself in her bedroom reading Joe's letters over and over again, and staring at his photo that she had taken on top of Portsdown Hill. It was the only photo she had of him and she was so thankful that she had taken it.

The scene that the soldier had painted in her head tortured her endlessly. The images were even worse when she closed her eyes. She lay on her bed staring up at the ceiling. The room had become noticeably colder and grew dark. She moved her head to the side and stared at the corner of the bedroom. A black shadow passed the door and seemed to disappear through the wall. The temperature suddenly plummeted. Her heart was beginning to race. There was strange sensation in the room. She reached out for the bedside lamp but there was an unknown force stopping her. She tried to scream but nothing came out just a pathetic whimper, it was if she was paralysed from fear.

`Sarie are you there?' Suddenly Joe was standing in front of her. He looked tall and handsome in his uniform. It was like a spotlight beaming on him in the dark cold room.

`Joe – they told me you were dead.' Sarah got up out of bed, opened her arms and reached out for him. The closer she came to him, he seemed to back away.

`Why are you walking away from me Joe? Why are you going away?' her voice was desperate.

`You must go Sarie, they are coming for me.' You can't be seen here with me. An eerie grey mist appeared around him. There were gun shots sounding from somewhere beyond. Her bedroom was not a room anymore it was like she was standing on wasteland, even a field perhaps. She looked down at the feel of wet grass soaking into her bare feet. In despair she started to run towards him, reaching for him into the mist that surrounded her. `Joe don't go, don't leave me here I need you Joe... Joe... Joe' Just then, through the mist she could see a figure walking towards her again. She put her arms out in front of her stumbling forward into the thick mist. `Sarah' she heard her name being called again but it wasn't Joe's voice. It was familiar and she stopped to listen to it. `Sarah you must go back it's too dangerous here.' There were voices in the background, crying men and the sounds of gun fire grew louder and louder. The clammy cold air sent chills down her spine. There was a sensation of evilness in the mist. It was as if it was reaching out for her. She was having difficulties breathing. `Go Sarah – Go Sarah' The familiar voice shouted out above the torturing cries from beyond. Not having to be told again she turned and ran, clutching her chest. She could feel someone or something running behind her. Whatever it was it gaining on her, almost at her heels. Joe help me! She screamed as loud as she could. The voices, the mist, the feeling of being chased suddenly disappeared. She opened her eyes. Her heart was pumping under her ribs and her night dress clung to her hot sweaty body. She stared around the bedroom. `Oh Joe – Come back to me - Joe!'

`I'm so worried about her, Annie. Do you think I should phone for the doctor?' Laura said, sitting at the kitchen with Annie one afternoon. She woke up screaming again last night and she hasn't been out of her room in days.

`I don't think the doctor will `ave anything for a broken heart. They say time is a great healer and that's what we'll `ave to give her – plenty of time.'

`I had hoped the infatuation with the boy had worn off with him being away, I didn't know that she was still so besotted.'

`I think the word is *love* not *besotted*' Annie said softly.

`I don't know, Annie. Love is a bit extreme – I mean, she hardly knew the boy, not really,'

`She knew him long enough to fall in love. She wouldn't be in this state if she didn't love him – and the way she talked about him to me, well you could just tell.' The look in Laura's eyes showed this was not what she wanted to hear. `As sad as it is, I still don't think he was suitable for her. She would be much better off with Edward. Perhaps it was a blessing in disguise.' Annie looked startled. Her initial reaction was to disagree but then thought better of it and nodded her head instead, after all it wasn't her place to interfere.

Finally, after two long weeks of refusing to come out of her room, Sarah put on a brave face and went downstairs to see Edward who was waiting for her in the main drawing-room. He had given a message to Laura, to tell Sarah that he wasn't going home until she came downstairs to see him.

He was horrified by the way she looked. Her eyes were sunken and she had deep black lines around them. She had lost weight and was deathly pale.

`Oh Sarah I'm so sorry to hear your awful news.' Edward stood up from the sofa and walked towards her. She looked broken, too broken to even cry any more. He took her into his arms and he hugged her tightly.

`Why don't we go for a walk? The fresh air will do you good' he said, taking her two hands in to his own.

She accepted with a nod. She needed to speak to someone and it felt like Edward was her only friend. Cynthia she hardly saw, they were always working on opposite shifts and never had time off at the same time and with Emma in Devon and now Joe... The world felt a lonely place.

They walked aimlessly for over an hour through country roads and over wasteland and fields. The wind was cold and sharp and the trees stood bare with just their ugly branches sticking out like dead twigs. The sky looked grey and dismal which fitted Sarah's mood.

`Edward, do you think there could be any chance he is still alive? What if those soldiers had got it wrong? She respected Edward's opinion. He was so clever and in many ways she admired him. He had become a good and trusted friend and good friends were not easy to find.

`Sarah, No – not for a moment would I believe he is still alive, after the way you explained what happened to him. If he wasn't already dead, and if he had got up out of that ditch, the Germans would have killed him anyway – that's for sure.'

`That's what I fear. I just feel so…oh I don't know… just so' he stopped and leaned closer to her, pushing her grey scarf back over her shoulder that had come lose in the wind.

`You are grieving. It's normal, but you have to stop going over it in your mind, or else it will drive you mad.'

`I know. You are right.'

They walked down a small path lined with bare looking trees, its leaves long gone from the force of the wind.

`Do you think I should tell Audrey, his mother?' She was sure they hadn't received a telegram to say he had died otherwise Maureen would have come to tell her.

`If you want my honest opinion' Edward said as he kicked a stone out of his way. `I don't think you should. It could be very distressing for her, look at the state you are in. This is her son we are talking about. Sometimes the less you know the better it is. Would you have liked to know in detail how Charles had died?' He said turning to look at her.

`No, I suppose not, but she is still thinking he is missing and could come home one day.' Sarah said sounding worried and guilty at the same time.

`He won't come home and in time she will get used to the idea that he is dead. Rather that than you telling her some dreadful story about her son who was shot down in a ditch by the Germans.'

`But I can't visit her, knowing what I know' Sarah ran her hands nervously through her hair.

Edward softly pulled her arm towards him, forcing her to stop in her tracks and face him. `Listen to me Sarah, you mustn't visit her. You must keep away from that family. It's for their own good.' For a moment she saw a flash of anxiousness in his eyes. Realising his desperation he softened his expression with a small smile.

`You are probably right – in fact I know you are right.' Her pursed lips turned into a warm smile of gratitude.

`I always am. I'm a solicitor' He grinned.

`Oh – Edward, I don't know what I would do without you. I feel so lonely and I'm thankful I have you. You are a good friend.'

`And so are you, Miss Whittington,' He took her hand in his own and squeezed it tightly. The wind whistled as they turned a sharp corner and took a short-cut down a country lane back towards Whittington Manor.

Thirteen

March 1943

`Sarah, I've said it before and I really mean it, - I believe in you, I think you could be an excellent nurse. With all your experience and the knowledge you have now, you should train and become a qualified nurse. That is what you want isn't it? Dr. Gregory passed Sarah a cup of tea in the canteen. They walked across the room and sat down in a quiet corner, away from prying ears.

Sarah hesitated before answering him. There was an expression on her face that Dr. Gregory had never seen before. It was almost wistful. `I would prefer to train as a doctor' she replied softly, surprising herself by what she had just said. She had never told anyone before not even Dr. Gregory that she wanted to be a doctor. He looked equally as surprised she did, and then he smiled broadly at her. `I think you would make an excellent physician. Why mess around with nursing when you could go straight to the top.' He gave a chuckle.

`Where would I have to go to train?' Although she hated to leave her mother and of course Edward, she had no ties, she wasn't married and she was young, Joe wasn't coming back so what would stop her?

`Well, there are a number of places you could go, but I do have a friend that runs a medical school in Scotland. I can't promise anything, but I could put in a good word for you, although, I warn you, it may take some time before I get an answer. He's notoriously slow at answering my letters.'

Sarah's eyes grew wide with excitement. `Oh – Dr. Gregory, that would be wonderful – Thank you.' Even if it was in Scotland, the thought of training to be a doctor was just too good an opportunity to miss.

`I know, with so many men at war, they would be slightly more open to the idea of a female training at their school and with my reference that should help.' He tapped her arm and then placed his empty cup on the table before leaving the canteen.

Sarah sat in a daze for a moment, then realising Dr. Gregory was walking out of the canteen, she ran after him. `Dr. Gregory, I just wanted to say –

114

thank you.' Her step quickened to match his speed. `My pleasure, but like I said I can't promise, but you are in with a good chance.' He smiled at her and then disappeared through the door that led down to surgery. Sarah stood for a moment looking at the closed door trying to absorb her conversation with Dr Gregory. She decided not to tell anyone just yet. Her mother would only get upset, especially if she told her the school was in Scotland, and there was no point saying anything to Edward either, after all, she may not even be accepted. Like Dr. Gregory said, they might be more open to the idea of a girl training but then again female doctors were very few, probably because they were expected to get married. She shrugged her shoulders as she turned to walk in the opposite direction. There was no chance of that now. She wasn't getting married any more and the only way forward was to work hard, build a career - become a top doctor. She smiled at the idea.

`Penny for them.' A voice startled her. She turned to see Grace, a nurse, standing next to her. She was a chubby girl with black curly hair always bubbly and Sarah liked to work with her. `Sorry, Grace, I was miles away.'

`We are needed in casualty apparently.' Grace informed her with a friendly grin as they both walked off in that direction.

It was later that same week, when Sarah received a letter from Emma. She sat in the drawing-room reading, chuckling to herself every now and again at Emma's humorous remarks. Devon hadn't changed her one bit. She was still as funny as ever. She could imagine her saying the words she was reading. Her voice would be engraved in her memory for ever. She missed her so much. Suddenly Sarah gave an almighty gasp and put her hand to her mouth. Laura looked up from her book, peering over the top of her spectacles in surprise. `What are you looking so shocked about?'

`It's Emma, Mama. She's got engaged – to Daniel Worthington.

`Really? Well, I'm delighted for her. He's a lovely young man, according to Florence.' Laura said approvingly.

`We are invited to their engagement party. It's in April and it sounds rather lavish.' Sarah continued to read on. `It will be held at the Royal Devonshire Hotel, and there are approximately two hundred guests invited. I had no idea they knew so many people in Devon.' Sarah said raising her eye brows with surprise.

`Well, I suppose many of the guests will travel from various corners of the country. The Howletts are well-known and well respected by all accounts.

`Can we go, Mama – Please?' She put emphases on the word please.

`I will have to give it some consideration. As much as I would love to go, I'm not up to socialising any more. I do hate to attend these functions as the lonely widow. It was different when your father was alive.' There was a look of sadness in her eyes. She missed him terribly. Social functions were always fun with William, but not now, she felt too old, like a misfit of society.

`You are not a lonely widow and you should go, Mama. We should both go – she's my best friend.'

`Well it's not until April so we still have some time to think about it.' Laura pushed her spectacles back up her nose and carried on with her book. Sarah sighed, she knew better than to push her mother, she would have to work on her with some gentle coercion if she was going to be able to persuade her.

*****

It was the end of March when Edward took Laura by surprise. `Edward, what a lovely surprise, but I'm afraid Sarah is working at the hospital.' She looked apologetically at him.

`Well actually, Laura – it's you I have come to see. I wanted to talk to you about Sarah,' he said looking a little sheepish.

Laura made a hand gesture for Edward to sit down on the sofa behind him. She sat down in her favourite arm chair opposite him, both hands resting on the arms of the chair. She looked intrigued. `Of course – now what would you like to tell me.'

He sat perched nervously on the end of the sofa. He took a deep breath. `Sarah, is the most extraordinary young women I have ever met. She is intelligent, intellectual, and a wonderfully warm and caring character and mature beyond her years.' He paused for a moment and after plucking up the courage, he then continued. `I have fallen in love with your daughter and I would like your permission to ask for her hand in marriage.'

There was a moment's silence while his words registered. Laura sat staring at him, her face showing no real expression other than amazement. He was concerned that she wasn't opposed to the idea. Perhaps he should have waited longer. He had waited as long as he thought appropriate but it was time to step things up a notch or two. He never meant to fall in love with Sarah, in fact, if he was honest, he still wasn't certain he was in love with her but one thing was for sure, they had become very close and he admired her in so many ways, and he also enjoyed her company, although that wasn't reason enough to get married, but her inheritance certainly was reason. Much to his relief Laura's expression changed and the answer he had hoped for was glowing in her eyes. `I'm delighted for you. I think you and Sarah would be wonderful for each other.' He was the answer to everything she had wished for, for Sarah. He was charming, exquisitely polite, well-educated and had a good job. It was clear to see that the two of them had become good friends over the last couple of years and that was always a good solid base for a successful marriage. Sarah was now old enough, at the age of twenty, she herself was married and it was the perfect age for starting a family too. In fact, she couldn't have picked a better match for her daughter if she had tried.

Edward looked relieved as his face broke into a smile.

`Do you think Sarah suspects your intentions?' Laura asked candidly. She had no idea if he had wooed her daughter, kissed her or even hinted that marriage was on his mind.

`No, I haven't mentioned it to her. I'm waiting for the right moment.' Laura suddenly sat up straight. `I think I might have an idea that could help you' she said with a small wry smile, her eyes dancing mischievously. Edward leaned forward with interest.

`How would you like to take a trip to Devon?'

`Devon? Oh – you mean Emma Howlett's engagement party.

`Sarah has told you about it then?'

`Yes she told me all about it.'

`Did she tell you that I wasn't keen on going?'

`Yes, she did mention that you felt uncomfortable about going.'

`Sarah would love to go and I think it would be wonderful if you took her to see her best friend and attend the engagement party. Besides it might prompt Sarah into thinking about getting married, herself.'

Edward looked pensive for a moment, mulling it over. Perhaps she was right. `What a marvellous idea – I would be delighted to take Sarah to Devon' he replied.

`Well, that's settled and I think this is cause for a celebration.' She gave a chuckle as she rang the little brass bell next to her on the table for the butler to come. A moment later when James the butler appeared, she asked for a bottle of champagne and two glasses.

`Don't you think champagne is a little premature? I still have to ask her yet. What if she says no? Edward suddenly looked concerned. He still hadn't made a back up plan if she was to say no. It hadn't even occurred to him until that moment that she might say no and if she did he would have to come up with a very good plan to win her over.

`She's a sensible girl and she is very fond of you. I see no reason why she wouldn't agree to marry you,' Laura assured him. James arrived and handed them each a glass of champagne. Lord Whittington had kept a remarkable cellar and the vintage was excellent.

`I hope she agrees.' He still looked uneasy about drinking champagne and celebrating so soon.

`Well, that's up to you to convince her' Laura reminded him. You will have a wonderful time in Devon and I am sure you will find the right moment to ask her.

Laura held up her glass and waited for him to join her. `To my daughter and my new son-in-law to be' she toasted, smiling broadly at him. Edward exchanged her smile and took a sip.

`Would you like to stay for dinner this evening, Edward?' She pulled a funny face after taking the first sip of her champagne. She had not drank champagne for quite some time.

`I would be delighted to' Edward replied, looking pleased and trying not to laugh at her expression.

`Hopefully we won't have to spend most of the evening in the air-raid shelter' she said pursing her lips, remembering the last time he had stayed for dinner.

`I don't know – it wasn't all that bad. We played cards and chess, it was quite entertaining.' They laughed at the memory. It had been a funny evening.

Edward arrived for dinner at 7pm looking casual but smart. He wore a dark pair of grey tailor-made trousers, a white shirt and a pale blue cashmere jumper resting over his shirt. Sarah arrived only a few moments after Edward. She had just got back from the hospital and was still wearing her uniform. She had no idea that he would be there and had come in the back entrance after taking a short cut home and hadn't noticed his MG parked out the front.

`I had a fantastic day' she said, bursting into the main drawing-room. Her beaming smile changed to a shy awkward smile, feeling embarrassed for entering the room with such gust. `I'm so sorry, Edward I didn't know you were here.'

`Your mother has kindly invited me to stay for dinner' he replied as he smiled back at her. Looking in her eyes, he suddenly felt a little strange. It was as if she was already his wife. He was starting to feel strong emotions towards her, feelings of tenderness and he longed to kiss her and take her in his arms. Of course it wasn't the right time to show his emotions - not yet anyway.

`So why did you have such a fantastic day?' Edward asked in amusement as Laura carefully observed them both, thinking what a lovely couple they made.

Sarah gave a short laugh. `They let me watch how to sew up a really huge and nasty wound. It was quite remarkable' she said with a look of awe.

`Oh Sarah – really. You make me feel quite ill and I'm sure Edward doesn't want to hear such ghastly stories.' Laura shook her head in exasperation.

Edward laughed. `I've heard worse' he said smiling at Sarah.

`You'll have to stop doing that someday.' Laura said cryptically. `One day you will be married and have children and you won't be able to hang around that hospital watching them sew up wounds any more.'

`Why not?' Sarah joked. Her face then turned more sombre. `Anyway, I'm not getting married *now*.' She wanted to say now Joe was gone but she still found it hard to say his name. He was the only man she wanted to marry and he was gone and wasn't coming back to her. The idea of marrying another man had never even entered her head. Her life was nursing now and if she was very lucky, one day she would be a doctor.

`I don't want to hear you speak like that' Laura sounded annoyed. Sarah was going to marry Edward. She just knew it and she could hardly wait. It would be like a new chapter in their lives after all the misery of the past few years. Sarah was going to make a wonderful wife and mother and she was bursting from happiness just thinking about it. `Is that a blood stain?' Laura asked pointing to the bottom of Sarah's uniform.

Sarah shrugged her shoulders. `It could be.'

`Oh – go and get changed and wash your hands' she scolded her. `We'll be having dinner soon so don't be long' she shouted out after her as Sarah left the room to go and get changed.

As soon as they were seated at the dinner table Laura exchanged knowing glances with Edward.

`Edward has something to ask you?' she said, and for a moment Edward had a sudden look of panic in his eyes before remembering that Laura was referring to the trip to Devon and not his proposal.

`Something to ask me?' She frowned.

`Yes I do. With your permission, I would like to escort you to Devon to Emma's engagement party,' he announced.

`Oh my goodness - really?' Sarah's eyes lit up with delight. `So are we are all going?' she asked looking across the table at Laura.

`Your mother doesn't feel comfortable about going and it wouldn't be right for you to travel alone on the train, so I offered to take you' Edward explained saving Laura the trouble. `Edward, you really are such a good friend. I can't believe you would actually do that for me. You are such a remarkable man.' She leaned over and kissed him on his cheek. He looked slightly embarrassed in front of her mother. Laura sat watching them both with a smile of contentment. She couldn't wait for them to go and come back with the news that they were engaged, it was all so exciting.

`That's what friends are for. Anyway, apart from me of course, Emma is your best friend and it's important you attend her engagement party. And if you promise to be good, I might even take you to the wedding.' He grinned at her. She was positively beaming at the idea.

Over dinner they talked about the engagement party and going to Devon. Sarah was so excited. Laura was relieved that she hadn't let her daughter down and extremely happy to know that she would be with Edward and what going to Devon really meant.

They enjoyed a wonderful evening and for the first time for as long as they could remember there were no air-raids and they weren't forced to spend the evening in the shelter. It was also the first time since Joe had died that Sarah felt happy and relaxed again. The all familiar anguished look that appeared so often, seemed to be fading. It was as if she had come to terms with his death and accepted it was time to put it behind her and try and build a new life.

`Would you like to have a night cap in the drawing-room' Laura asked her son-in-law to be. There was a clear fondness in her tone.

Edward glanced at his watch. It wasn't too late but he wondered if he would be out staying his welcome, although looking at both women he soon realised he wouldn't be. `Oh please, Edward. It's been such a wonderful evening – you must stay for one last drink' Sarah pleaded.

`I will stay a little longer, only on one condition.' His eyes were challenging.

`Anything, you name it. I owe you now' She still couldn't believe he was taking her to see Emma.

`You don't owe me anything, but I will stay if you play the piano,' - remembering their conversation in the New Forest during their game of asking questions. He had only ever heard her play once before and she had stopped when he had walked in the room and had refused to continue. She was shy about playing in front of anyone. Although Mrs Hopkins was one of the best tutors anyone could ever wish for, but she was very critical and there were times when Sarah hated to play, the lessons were sometimes tiresome and gruelling.

`Alright - as it is you I will play' It would have been unfair to deny him of his request after he announced at dinner that he was taking her to Devon.

`She is a wonderful pianist' Laura said, smiling proudly at her. `Her father loved it when she played `Nocturne' by Chopin. That was his favourite. She refused to play in front of us, so he used to stand outside the door and listen whenever she played. It never failed to bring a tear to his eye' Laura's eyes became sad and she thought of her husband.

`I don't want to make anyone sad, it's just I would love to hear you play.'

`No one's sad, silly – Come on,' she took his arm in her own and they walked out of the dining-room and towards the second drawing-room with Laura following behind them.

James the butler arrived with three brandies as Sarah sat down at the piano ready to play. She began to play one of her favourite pieces by Beethoven - `Fur Elise.'

`My goodness, Sarah – you really are very talented' Edward clapped in amazement.

`Those piano lessons certainly paid off my dear' Laura complimented her. `Can you please play Nocturne for me? - For Papa? She pleaded, putting her two hands together in prayer position. Sarah looked at her sad eyes and then back at Edward, who nodded encouragingly. With out a word she began to play. After a few notes she had completely forgotten that her mother and Edward were in the room. It was if she was in a trance as she played with sheer passion straight from her heart, with fond memories of her father, Charles and then Joe.

Laura's tears cascaded down her cheeks remembering her husband and how he loved that tune so much. When she closed her eyes, images of him sitting in his favourite arm chair, smoking his pipe flashed before her. It was as if she could feel his presence in the room.

Edward was speechless, utterly moved by Sarah's performance. A sudden rush of guilt came over him for pursuing her for the wrong intentions. Yet, despite those initial wrong intentions, he had to admit that Sarah Whittington was truly and undeniably a talented and remarkable young woman. He watched her with admiration.

Fourteen

Audrey stepped off the bus in Portchester, she had just got back from Portsmouth after visiting her sister and the rest of her family. She turned the corner in to the top end of Portdown Road and saw Rose Gladstone busy cleaning her front windows.

`Ello Rose – How d'you get 'em so clean? You should offer your services as a window cleaner.' Audrey chuckled. Rose, turned to see where the voice was coming from. She pushed a stray lock of bright auburn hair from her right eye. Her freckly complexion was pale, her dark brown eyes danced with humour. She was a cheerful soul and always happy to stop for a chat.

`Ello, Audrey.' She gave a short throaty laugh. `I don't `ave enough time to clean other peoples' windows, - got enough work of me own to do,' She walked towards the garden gate where Audrey was standing, wiping her wet hands on a yellow tea cloth. `Where's your little Nancy today?' she asked. She liked Nancy; she reminded her of her own granddaughter who lived down King George Road.

`She's with her mum - Maureen ain't working today.' Audrey added. I've just got back from Pompey actually. I don't like to take her there, it's too dangerous.'

`They've been hit badly, so I've heard. I've not been there for a while now, mind' Rose said propping an elbow up on the garden gate.

`You wouldn't recognise the place, Rose. Many of the shops are nothing more than burnt-out shells. The guildhall is completely gutted – it's so sad, it really is. Audrey shivered remembering the images she had witnessed that day. It was as if the Germans had intended to blast the heart out of the city by destroying its centre. It had been bombed time and time again, houses flattened, roads obliterated by vast craters. The fires raged day and night at the dockyard, whilst the fire fighters struggled to keep the flames at bay.

`I heard the railway station is a mess too.' Rose often got snippets of information from her daughter's neighbour who visited Portsmouth quite regularly to visit family.

`Yes, it's a mess but the dockyard is worse. It's been hit so many times there's hardly anything left of it.' Audrey said with a look of despair.

`So how's your family over there coping with it all?' Rose asked removing a weed that was growing out the moss covered wall next to the gate.

`They're fine. My sister is so stubborn. I've asked her countless times to come and stay with us, but she won't. I worry about them all the time.' Audrey sighed.

`Ello Audrey – Ello Rose. At that moment Phyllis appeared in her normal dress code of pink floral pinafore, curlers and slippers. She had spotted the two women having a chat from her front-room window and couldn't resist the opportunity to join in and see if there was any new gossip to be heard.

`Audrey's just been saying what a mess Pompey is' Rose said updating her on what she had missed so far.

`Of course - you said you were going today. Was it bad there?'

`Yes, very – it's a big mess' Audrey's face was solemn.

`I saw your Colin was home last week' Phyllis said to Rose. There wasn't much that escaped Phyllis's attention.

`Yes, he was. It was so lovely to see him.' She was smiling broadly and then her smile quickly faded when she saw the sad look in Audrey's eyes.

`Still no news?' Rose asked Audrey.

`No – nothing. I don't think we will 'ere anything until this flaming war is over' she said, fighting back her tears and with a trace of anger in her voice. `I just keep 'opin that one day when this stupid war is over, they will find him alive and well.' Rose and Phyllis nodded simultaneously.

`At least Tommy is fine.' Audrey sniffed trying to look a little more cheerful if not for her sake but at least for the others. She did her best to put on a brave face especially in front of the neighbours.

`Well that's something to be thankful for' Rose said with a warm smile.

`Have you heard from that young girl – what was her name? The one that helped me when the street got bombed a couple of years ago. Phyllis was frantically trying to remember her name.

`You mean our Joe's girlfriend, Sarah?' Audrey said.

`Yes, Sarah. That's her name.' Phyllis looked relieved to be reminded of it. Her memory wasn't like it used to be these days. It was so annoying remembering things, especially names they were the worst to remember.

`No – not seen her since our Maureen told her our Joe was missing. I don't blame her though. I mean – you can't expect a young, pretty girl, well educated n'all to wait around forever.'

Phyllis and Rose nodded in agreement.

`D'you think she's still working at the Q.A?' Phyllis asked feeling pleased that at least she had remembered that much about her.

`I dunno – maybe.' Audrey shrugged her shoulders.

`Perhaps she's fallen in love with someone else now, maybe one of them soldiers' Phyllis said. Rose pursed her lips. She could see the topic of conversation was not easy for Audrey. `Well – it's like Audrey said, you can't expect the girl to wait around for him. It's not like they were married or anything. Anyow, I best be getting back to me windows.'

`Yeah I best be off too.' Audrey gave a wave to Rose as she walked away' Cheerio Rose'

`Yeah cheerio,' Phyllis joined in the chorus of cheerios as she walked back down the road with Audrey.

*****

Sarah and Edward arrived back at Whittington Manor in fine spirits after spending a wonderful, relaxing few days in Devon together. Sarah was delighted to see Emma after so long and was thrilled for her that she had got engaged to such a lovely man. Daniel was positively charming and very handsome. Edward appeared to enjoy himself too and got along very well with many of the guests at the party. He was extremely polite and enchanting, and everyone enjoyed his company. Emma had dropped hints on more than one occasion about how well suited they both were, although the hints were in vain as Sarah brushed off the comments and made it quite clear that her relationship with Edward was strictly friends.

Yet, despite the fact they both had a very enjoyable time, much to Edward's disappointment, he still couldn't find the right moment to ask the question he so much wanted to ask Sarah. They had been constantly surrounded by people, the whole time they were in Devon, so he decided to wait until they got back to Portchester.

`Mama – we're back,' Sarah shouted out as she got out of Edward's sports car. Laura had been pacing up and down, nervously waiting for them to return. She could hardly wait to hear the news that Edward had proposed to Sarah. She was sure that he must have bought the ring already and she was most probably wearing it.

`Hello, Darling. Did you both have a good time?' She kissed her daughter on the cheek and glanced over Sarah's shoulder, trying to catch Edward's eye but he was still busy taking Sarah's case out of the car. James the butler was waiting eagerly to take the case inside.

`Oh – Mama it was truly magnificent' she said pulling away from her mother so she could look into her eyes. `You should have seen the party – it was like a fairytale, the way the hotel had been lit up and the dresses – oh my goodness…

`It sounds fabulous my dear, and did *you* and *Edward* enjoy yourselves?' she asked, glancing a second time at Edward, searching his face for an answer as he walked up the steps to join them. He shook his head discreetly.

`Well – of course we did, Mama, didn't we Edward?'

`Yes, it was very enjoyable.' He nodded his head in agreement.

`I must see Annie, quickly.' Sarah ran inside leaving Laura and Edward alone standing on the entrance steps. There was a sudden look of disappointment on Laura's face. She was silently praying that Edward hadn't had second thoughts. `I thought I would be hugging my new son-in-law.' She sounded disappointed.

`I'm sorry, Laura, we just didn't have a single moment to ourselves, but I've decided to take Sarah out to dinner tomorrow evening. I know a very special, romantic restaurant near Fareham and I shall ask her then.' He flashed a reassuring smile at her.

`Well – I've waited this long, so one more day won't hurt, I suppose' and with a fond smile Laura linked arms with him as they both walked inside to find Sarah.

`Mama, Edward has asked me out to dinner tomorrow night. He says we are going to a very special restaurant.' She frowned. `I don't know what to wear?' Sarah and Laura stood on the gravel drive way, waving goodbye to Edward, as he drove away. He reached the bottom of the path and tooted his horn waving his hand as the car disappeared around the corner. Laura put an arm around her daughter. `I will help you choose something to wear. I think you should wear something special.' She grinned knowingly.

`Why?' Sarah narrowed her eyes with suspicion.

`Because it's a special restaurant – didn't you say?'

`Well – that's what he said. I can't imagine why he wants to go out for dinner with me so soon after spending four days with me in Devon. One would think he would have had enough of my company by now.' They walked up the steps and inside the house.

Edward and Sarah arrived at the restaurant at seven-thirty sharp. They were shown to a quiet table in the corner, romantically lit with a single candle in the centre of it. The restaurant was chic and elegant and Sarah felt very adult and special as she sat down in front of Edward and took off her cream shawl that matched her beautiful cream and soft pink laced dress.

The waiter asked if she would like an aperitif and she nervously declined. Her mother had warned her not to drink too much, except for a little wine with her dinner. It wouldn't create a good impression she had said to her daughter. Edward ordered a scotch which startled Sarah. She had never seen him drink hard liquor before, apart from the occasional brandy after dinner. Perhaps he was nervous too but she couldn't imagine why, since they had been such good friends for so long now.

`Are you sure you wouldn't like an aperitif?' Edward offered, when his scotch arrived.

`No, I'm fine' and then she giggled. `I had strict instructions from Mama, not to drink too much and embarrass you.' There was nothing they couldn't say to each other. They must have discussed thousands of different topics during the last couple of years and they never ran out of things to talk about. `Embarrass me? What are you going to do, dance on the tables?' They were still laughing at the idea when the waiter arrived. They both ordered succulent duck and homemade baked Alaska for dessert.

The evening was going to plan so far and it was after dinner that Edward ordered a bottle of the finest champagne on the menu. The waiter brought the bottle to the table and opened it for them. Sarah smiled as she tasted the champagne. She was happy she had taken her mother's advice and only had one glass of wine with her dinner. Edward had more to drink than she had but he was still sober, he needed to calm his nerves before he said what he wanted to say. She hadn't the faintest inkling of what he was planning to say to her, she was a picture of innocence as she sat sipping her champagne in front of him.

`I would like to make a toast. To you – Miss Whittington and the most wonderful friend you have become,' he complimented her with a fond smile.

`And to you too Mr Hamilton' she held up her glass to toast him back. `The most wonderful friend anyone could ever wish for.'

`We always have so much fun, don't we?' Sarah giggled. The champagne was giving her a buzz and she felt relaxed and happy.

`We do in deed, which is why I have something to ask you.' She looked blankly at him.

He cleared his voice ready to make his speech. He had rehearsed the lines he was about to say what seemed a thousand times these past few weeks. `Sarah, somewhere along the way, during our beautiful friendship, I'... He paused a moment before continuing. She was still smiling at him, waiting for what he was going to say next. `I fell in love with you,' he said, reaching across the table to touch her hand. `I think we have a lot of fun together. You are beautiful and I have never met a woman that makes me feel the way you do. I can't stay single forever and for those reasons I would like to ask you if you would do me the great honour of being my wife – Sarah, will you marry me?' Sarah sat staring at him in utter amazement. Her mouth was slightly open and her eyes were wide.

`Are you serious?' she asked eventually, after catching her breath.

`Deadly.' he replied with a grin.

`Edward, I had no idea you felt that way about me.'

`I've loved you for a long time, Sarah.'

`But why didn't you say something?' He couldn't tell if she was angry or happy but most of all she looked shocked.

`I thought I should wait, especially after Joe' he said. She nodded. That was typical of him, he was always so thoughtful, and it was one of the things she loved about him.

`Are you angry with me, Sarah?' He asked gingerly.

`Angry? No - of course not. I'm very flattered.' She reached out and touched his hand.

`I know you don't feel the same about me, as you did Joe.' He hated the look in her eyes every time she talked about him. It filled him with jealousy and he was just thankful that in recent weeks she had hardly mentioned him. `But I know you love me in your own way. We are good friends and being friends is always good for a marriage,' he said trying to convince her, as he had himself on so many occasions. He felt sure that the marriage would work. As well as the money and owning Whittington Manor it helped a lot if they could be good friends and being attracted to her was also another bonus.

`Does my mother know?' that would explain why she had been so keen on her going to Devon with him and all the advice she had given her about this evening.

`Yes, I asked her permission and she said yes.' Sarah nodded her head.

`Sarah, do you want sometime to think about it?' She sighed and looked at him. This had come as such a shock. It had never occurred to her that she would be anything more than friends with Edward and then there was the possibility of her being accepted at medical school in Scotland, not to mention Joe. She still carried a persistent guilty feeling, like she was turning her back on him, even though the soldier at the hospital had no doubt that Joe was dead, nevertheless she still felt like she was betraying him, in an odd sort of way. There was suddenly so much to consider.

`I'm not saying no, but I do need to think about this. I'm sorry Edward, I can't give you the answer you want to hear right now.' She bit into her bottom lip nervously, regretting that she wasn't jumping for joy, just as she had been when Joe had proposed to her. There had been no fancy restaurant. Not even a ring but there was something far more apparent. Love. Love was the one thing she didn't really feel for Edward, well not in the sense she knew she should. A love one would have for a friend perhaps, or a brother. Yet, would she ever find that someone special again? And if the answer was no, would she want to spend the rest of her life alone, with no husband to love or to love her and no children to love and cherish? She looked so confused and torn and Edward suddenly felt sorry he had put her in such an awkward situation.

`Whatever happens, we are still friends and we always will be but I can assure you one thing.' He stretched his hand across the table and gently stroked the side of her face. `I will look after you and will be a good husband to you that is if you decide to marry me of course.'

When they arrived back at Whittington Manor, Edward declined Sarah's invitation for a night cap. She could see in his eyes the look of disappointment, although he refused to admit it. There was definitely an air of tension between them both.

`Sarah, you are back – Where's Edward?' Laura asked, looking behind to see if he was following her in.

`He's gone home, Mama. He was tired and so am I.'

`Did the evening go well?' Laura asked, fishing for information. Surely, he must have asked her. There couldn't be a better way of proposing, than over dinner in a beautiful romantic restaurant.

`Yes, mama, we had a lovely evening and if you are referring to whether he asked me to marry him or not, then the answer is yes, he did propose.' She flopped down on the sofa looking weary.

`And?' Laura stared at her anxiously, her eyes dancing back and forth.

`I said I would think about it.'

`Oh my goodness, Sarah! What is the matter with you?' She threw her hand up in the air in an angry gesture. He is charming, well-educated has a good job' She looked at her daughter in disbelief. How she could not say yes and yet say yes to that common land worker who couldn't even afford to buy her a ring. Despair was written all over her face.

`Mama, I didn't say no, I just have a lot to think about. He took me by surprise.'

`A lot to think about? What on earth is there to think about? He's perfect in every way'

Sarah sighed. There was no point even beginning to tell her about the possible chance of her going to medical school in Scotland or the fact that she still so desperately missed Joe. Edward was a friend and a good friend at that, but the spark and the chemistry she had shared with Joe just wasn't there.

`I'm going to bed, Mama, it's been a long day and I'm working at the hospital tomorrow.'

`That wretched hospital - that's what's stopping you, isn't it? If your father was alive...' she shouted after her as Sarah walked out of the room, not wanting to listen to her mother any longer.

It had been over a month since the night Edward had proposed to Sarah and she had only seen him once during that time. It wasn't that Edward had given up on her - far from it, there was too much at stake for that. Whatever it took he was going to marry her but he decided to give her space to think. If he kept his distance he was sure Sarah would miss him and come to her senses, and his plan was beginning to work. So much so that Sarah confided in Cynthia how she was feeling during a tea break one afternoon in the hospital canteen.

`I thought I didn't love him but I'm beginning to think I do after all' Sarah said, looking confused at Cynthia.

`Do you miss him when you're not with him?' Cynthia asked trying to analyse the situation.

`Yes - I do. This past month has been terrible. I've only seen him once. It's like he doesn't want to see me any more, I couldn't bear to lose him.'

`Sounds very much like love to me.' Cynthia grinned. Tell me - So why did you want to think about his proposal?' She couldn't understand why

Sarah had hesitated, after all her and Edward had been good friends for a long time now.

`I was shocked at first, and then I kept thinking about Joe and other things.' She stopped what she was saying. She was supposed to keep it quiet about Dr. Gregory helping her to get into medical school.

`Other things?' Cynthia raised an eye brow.

Sarah moved closer to her. `Do you promise, - if I tell you something, that you won't tell a soul?' She spoke in a soft whisper.

Cynthia looked intrigued. `Yes. I promise. Now come on spill the beans'

`Dr. Gregory is helping me to get a place in a medical school in Scotland. It's not certain that I would get accepted and I'm still waiting to hear, but if I do get accepted, then how could I possibly marry Edward?'

Cynthia had a look of shock on her face. `You want to be a Doctor?'

`Yes, well at least I thought I did until now.' She sounded confused again.

`Sarah, you have to think about this sensibly. It's a big commitment to become a doctor.

You will not only be giving up the opportunity to be married but to have a family of your own too. There would be no time for a husband or children' Cynthia pointed out. `Can you imagine being a spinster all your life – no husband to love, or to love you? No children in your life – could you live without that?'

Sarah fell silent. The very same questions had been haunting her ever since Edward had proposed to her, yet hearing it from Cynthia forced her to be true to herself.

Sarah's face suddenly lit up, her hazel eyes dancing with excitement. `Cynthia, thank you so much.'

Cynthia frowned. `What for?'

`To help me make up my mind. Of course I don't want to live my life as a lonely spinster, even though I would love to be a doctor, but the sacrifices are too high a price to pay. I couldn't imagine a life without children.' She gave a wistful sigh. `I didn't really realise it until now but I want so much to have children and I couldn't possibly turn Edward down. He's a good man and more than that he's my dearest friend.'

`Well that's all the more reason to marry him' Cynthia confirmed.

`He's not Joe, but I do love him – in a different sort of way'

`Sarah, the kind of love that you had with Joe was special and I know how much you loved him, but he's gone now and he wouldn't want you to spend the rest of your life mourning him.' She patted Sarah's hand. 'I've only met Edward a couple of times but he looks a decent kind of man and you have a wonderful friendship, I don't think you should give that up, I certainly wouldn't.' There was a touch of sadness to her voice.

'Cynthia, I would like to ask you something.' She gave a chuckle and then continued.

'Will you be my chief bridesmaid?'

'I would be delighted to.' Cynthia beamed with delight as they hugged each other tightly.

'Now all I have to do is call Edward after work and meet him somewhere, so I can sort this mess out' Sarah said with a smile as she stood up ready to go back to work.

Sarah arrived home just as it was starting to get dark. She had no sooner stepped foot in the front door when the air-raid siren began to sound. The whining siren they had all become used to, became louder and louder. Siren or no siren I'm going to call Edward.' She had promised herself she would speak to him today. She rushed to the telephone in the hall way.

Annie suddenly appeared at her side, as if from nowhere. 'What are you doing, Miss Sarah? You gotta go to the shelter – there's no time for phone calls now.'

'Nanny, I will be there in a moment. Go on, - you go. I promise I'll be there in a moment.'

Annie shook her head in despair. 'Make sure you do' she called out as she rushed back down the long hallway that led through the kitchen and out to the air-raid shelter.

Sarah dialled Edward's office number. She knew he would most probably still be there. He spent more time at work than at home. Luxurious as his flat was, situated in heart of Fareham, he was still living alone and he didn't like to be home.

Edward hesitated. The phone was ringing. He had his coat in one hand and keys to the office in the other. The siren was loud and he knew he only had minutes to get to the shelter at the end of the road. He turned his back to the phone but something inside made him stop. 'Oh for goodness sake' he ran to the phone and answered it abruptly. 'Yes'

`Edward, it's me – Sarah'

`Sarah, what are you doing calling me – the siren has just sounded.' He was shouting above the noise.

`I know and I'm just going. Edward can you please come and see me as soon as this raid is over. I have something I want to tell you.' There was seriousness to her voice which he couldn't quite work out. `Alright – now go, you are mad, Sarah, - calling me moments before a raid,' he said before hanging up the phone.

As she placed the receiver down, she smiled. It was all going to be alright now. She ran as quickly as she could through the house and out to the back where the air-raid shelter was. Just as she arrived in the shelter, the noise of the droning enemy planes above made her panic. Her heart was racing as she frantically ran down the steps and inside. The sirens she had got used to but she would never get used to the heavy enemy planes, with their droning engines, and evil snarl.

`You were just on time. You shouldn't leave it that late.' Annie chided.

`Where's mama?' Sarah asked nervously, noticing her mother wasn't there with them.

`It's alright, she's visitin' her friend – you know – Mrs Winters and I'm sure they 'ave shelters in that great big house of theirs.'

`But it's dark, she never goes out after dark' Sarah said, looking worried.

`Well, she was most probably on her way when the siren went off and then had to dash in their shelter.'

Their talking was disturbed by a violent shake and vibration of two planes flying low. There was a sudden almighty explosion that sounded in the distant as one of the planes dropped its load. A few minutes later there was another explosion but that one seemed to be even further away and Annie gave a sigh of relief.

`Where do you think that was? Sarah asked looking in the direction of James who was sitting at the wooden table and chairs that were placed to the right of the shelter. Her father and Charles had made it quite homely with oil lamps and candles. There was a long soft pink sofa with plump matching cushions in the lounge area. There was even a coffee table with some books and games to play. At the far end were two separate bedroom quarters that were always kept made up in case of emergency. There was a good stock of food, snacks, drinks, including wine and even champagne in the cupboards, although Sarah never understood why her father had kept champagne down there. It's not as if they were going to celebrate anything being stuck in an air-raid shelter while above them the Germans were busy dropping bombs and killing innocent people.

`Close to Portsmouth, I should think.' James the butler said, from where he was sitting.

`Sounded nearer Paulsgrove' Annie argued.

`Well wherever it is, I just hope it's not near where Mama is.' Sarah looked deeply concerned. Annie placed her arm around her. `She'll be fine you'll see.'

They were in the shelter for just over an hour before the all clear siren sounded. Which was extremely quick compared to the last few raids. Sarah flew inside the house leaving Annie and James straggling behind her.

Laura arrived back home exactly half an hour later. `I could have been home ages ago if it wasn't for that wretched siren' she moaned as she walked into the main drawing-room removing her head scarf.

`I was worried about you, Mama.' Sarah had been pacing nervously up and down, waiting for her to return home, not that her mother showed any gratitude for her concern. She had been distant towards her ever since Sarah had said that she wanted to think about Edward's proposal. `I'm quite capable of looking after myself. I'm going to get changed before dinner,' she snapped as she walked out of the room.

A few moments later Sarah heard the doorbell ring and Edward speaking to James, who then promptly showed him in.

`Edward.' She looked startled and anxious to see him even though she had asked him to come over and see her as soon as he could.

`Hello, Sarah' he sounded cool and a little reserved.

`I've missed you,' she said softly from where she was standing, close to the window. He didn't answer but stood observing her closely.

`I'm sorry, Edward – I never meant to upset you.'

`What makes you think I'm upset' he replied with a wry smile.

`I've hardly seen you this past month.' She walked towards him in the middle of the room.

`I was giving you some space – time to think.' He replied.

`I know – thank you. Edward, you are not angry with me are you?' He looked uneasy standing in front of her.

`No – like I said I was giving you space and if you must know it was hell. I missed you too.' He gently stroked the side of her face and his face softened into a smile.

`Edward, will you please ask me again?' she replied in barely a whisper, reaching for his hand that was touching her face. He took her hand and looked deep into her eyes. There was twinkle of amusement in his eyes. `I would get down on one knee, only - I probably wouldn't make it back up' he said grinning at her. She giggled at the idea. `Sarah, would you do me the great honour of being my wife?' he asked for the second time, still looking into her eyes but this time more sombrely.

`Yes – yes.' Tears flooded her eyes. Leaning closer to him she kissed him. It felt strange kissing him, yet at the same time it was sensual and the feelings she thought she didn't have for him seemed to stir as they continued to kiss passionately. Eventually, he stepped back to look at her. `Sarah, you have made me the happiest man in the world' and then suddenly remembering, he reached into his trouser pocket and brought out a small black velvet jewellery box with a tiny gold bow.

`I didn't give this to you at the restaurant because I could feel you were not ready but I brought it with me tonight just in case,' he added, as he handed her the box. He had hoped her serious tone on the phone was because she had decided to marry him and he had been right. She opened it carefully and gasped as she looked down at the most stunning white gold ring, set with three beautiful diamonds that sparkled and gleamed up at her.

`If you don't like it, I can change it.' he said with a sudden look of concern.

`Edward, it's beautiful.'

He took it out of the box and slid in on her finger.

`How did you know my size? It fits perfectly.' She held her hand up to admire it.

`I've had over two years to study your finger size, my darling' he replied, with a short laugh.

`Have I told you that I love?' He said grinning at her.

`I think you did, but you can say it again,' she replied primly with an enchanting smile.

`I love you, Sarah.'

`I love you too, Edward.'

Her eyes filled with tears and her bottom lip began to quiver. `My darling whatever is wrong?' surely she had not suddenly changed her mind or was thinking of that worthless land worker again.

`This is such a happy day and my father and Charles are not here to share it with me. Who is going to walk me down the aisle?' The tears continued to roll down her face.

`Shush, don't worry - we will figure it out.' He softly wiped away her tears and she looked up at him with a look of anguish.

At that moment Laura walked in the room, totally oblivious to what was going on, or even aware that Edward was there. She stopped in her tracks at the sight of Edward wiping Sarah's tears away, naturally presuming there was something wrong. Perhaps they had had an argument, or worse than that she had told him she won't marry him.

She looked extremely worried. She couldn't bear the thought of Sarah turning Edward down. He was perfect for her in every way. `Something wrong?' she asked gingerly.

`No - Nothing wrong, Mama' Sarah replied smiling up at Edward.

`Come on - put her out of her misery and tell your mother' Edward encouraged with a grin.

`Tell me what?' Laura frowned and walked towards them.

`We're engaged to be married, Mama' Sarah shrieked, bursting with excitement and with a beaming smile from ear to ear.

`Oh my goodness – you said yes.' Laura rubbed her hands together in delight and tears sprung to her eyes. `Congratulations to you both.' She kissed her daughter and then flung her arms around her new son-in-law and embraced him tightly.

`Look, Mama' Sarah was holding her hand in front of her mother's face to show off her ring as soon as Laura had finished hugging Edward.

`Oh Edward, you have exquisite taste,' she complimented him, admiring every detail of the ring.

`I know, that's why I'm marrying your daughter,' he replied with a smug grin and the three of them laughed.

`You must stay for dinner, we need to discuss the wedding plans' Laura insisted excitedly as she rang the bell for James to bring them a bottle of their finest champagne from the cellar.

Fifteen

For the next several weeks Laura was insanely busy with organising Sarah and Edward's wedding. She had to organise caterers, the florist, and musicians for the garden party, contact the dress makers, and book the church. Sarah had insisted she wanted to be married at St Mary's church in the grounds of Portchester Castle despite Laura trying to talk her out of it and telling her it simply wouldn't be big enough. Whatever Laura said, Sarah wouldn't listen she had been adamant that she only wanted a small wedding and it was to be at St Mary's. There were invitations to send out, and a million details to plan and organise. Laura had not been this happy since before her husband had died. At last she was busy and had something to do. A real purpose in life and she was determined to give Sarah the wedding of her dreams.

The wedding date was set for the 23rd of August, exactly one month after Emma and Daniel's wedding. Emma was thrilled at the news of Sarah getting married and had promised to be maid of honour just as Sarah would be at her own wedding.

Even though there was so much going on with all the wedding plans, Sarah still managed to work at the hospital as much as she could. `Sarah, have you got a moment?' Dr. Gregory said one morning just as she arrived on duty. `Yes, of course.' She followed him into his office. Neither of them sat down. He was smiling at her and had a letter in his hand.

`They've said yes. They've accepted your application' he announced, waving the letter excitedly in front of her. `You are going to make such a fine doctor' he continued and then stopped when he realised Sarah wasn't sharing his excitement.

Sarah was solemn. `Dr. Gregory, I'm so sorry but I can't go to Scotland. I can't be a doctor.'

`Nonsense, it's what they call cold feet, you will be fine. You are made to be a doctor, I'd stake my life on it,' He frowned as he searched her face for a flicker of enthusiasm or a even a small smile would do, but there was nothing, just sadness in her eyes.

`I can't go to Scotland or be a doctor...because I'm getting married,' she said, suddenly feeling guilty as if she was letting him down.

`I see' He looked surprised. `Are you sure about this? I mean – are you really ready to get married? This is a great opportunity, Sarah.' He hated to see her throw away this chance but he could understand it if she really was in love, although her eyes said otherwise. She didn't look like a girl who was madly in love and about to be married and he hoped she was making the right decision. It wouldn't be easy being married and being a doctor, he wasn't married for the same reasons, although he did know doctors that juggled their lives between work and home, but it was far more complicated for a woman to be expected to take on such a challenge.

`I love, Edward and it's what I want' she replied unconvincingly. There was a trace of hesitation in her voice still.

`Are you sure, Sarah? I know this is not my business but I do want what's best for you. Marriage is a huge commitment' he reminded her.

`I know it is and so is being a doctor,' she reminded him.` I am very grateful for all your help in getting me accepted at the school in Scotland, but I can't go through with it, I just can't' she looked terribly sad and Dr. Gregory was not convinced that she was doing the right thing. It would be such a shame. She was a talented young woman with a great future ahead of her. She would make an excellent doctor, he thought as he rubbed his chin pensively.

`I'll tell you what – I won't reply for another couple of weeks. You don't need to start until September.' He didn't want to burn her bridges just yet. He had a sneaky feeling or was it just wishful thinking that maybe just maybe she might not go through with the wedding.

The next few weeks were a whirlwind of dress fitting sessions and parties that had been hosted by her mother's friends or Edward's clients. Sarah was still working as many hours as she could especially as the air-raids continued relentlessly night after night. Elsewhere in the world the fighting was tense, especially in the Soviet Union as the battle of Kursk was taking place. It was the largest series of armoured clashes so far. The world was a strange place and the madness of it all was slowly getting to Sarah as she confessed to Edward one evening after just coming back from the air-raid shelter on the grounds of Whittington Manor.

`It's just all so mad!' They sat alone in the drawing-room. Her mother was in the second drawing-room doing her tapestry. She was considerate enough to leave the young couple alone as much as possible.

`What is?' Edward looked puzzled.

`Everything. I mean – I'm working in the hospital surrounded by devastation and people dying. We have just come back from being forced to run and hide in that stupid shelter,' She jerked her thumb behind her in the direction of the shelter, `away from bombs that were being dropped all around us, nearly killing us and probably, somewhere nearby, people were killed this evening, - and my mother is talking about what flowers I want in my bouquet or if I should wear my hair up or down. It's just madness!' She looked as though she were about to burst into tears. It was all getting to her now, the war, getting married, her mother's perpetual fussing , giving up the chance of being a doctor, which she had not told anyone about least of all her mother or Edward, and as much as she forced herself not to think of him, she still couldn't get Joe out of her mind. Day and night the feeling of betraying him nagged away at her.

`Sarah, life must go on, Darling. We can't keep our lives on hold because of one stupid man who wants to inflict pain and misery on the world.' Edward placed his arm around her and she flinched slightly.  He was starting to sound like her mother. ` If we give in, he would have won. Hitler or no Hitler, we are still getting married. You will feel better next week, when we are in Devon.' He kissed the top of her head and she sighed heavily.

Sixteen

By the time they arrived in Devon at Emma and Daniel's wedding, Sarah felt happier and more relaxed. She forced herself not to think about the medical school in Scotland or Joe. Her heart still ached for him but she had resided herself to probably feeling that way for the rest of her life. Life had to go on without him, whether she liked it or not.

`Emma, you look absolutely divine' Sarah exclaimed admiring her standing in front of the mirror. She was wearing a cream satin dress with a huge train. The wedding was held at the family home. The house was very similar to the Bowood House in Portchester except this one had twelve rooms instead of fourteen and the garden was much larger. There were acres of extensive gardens with just about every type of flower and plant available to an English garden. The house was decorated beautifully for the wedding, with white and pink carnations and matching pink and white ribbons tied in bows everywhere you looked. In the garden a marquee had been erected for over two hundred guests.

`I'm a bundle of nerves.' Emma confessed as Sarah kissed her cheek for luck.

`I'm nervous too and I'm the maid of honour, not the bride.' The girls giggled.

`God knows what I will be like on my wedding day.' Sarah fidgeted in front of the mirror her pink lace dress that had been chosen for her as maid of honour looked stunning but the lace was a little scratchy on her arm.

`It's not the day you need to be nervous about, it's the wedding night'. Emma said with a wink of her eye that Sarah just caught a glimpse of in the mirror.

`Oh Emma, you don't change do you. Mind you I've not thought about that. It's a bit scary.' She turned to face her giving one last scratch to her right arm.

`My friend who has just got married, I will introduce Celia to you at the party, - well, she said it was awful.'

`What was awful?' Sarah eyes were wide with wonder.

Emma raised her eyebrows. `You know – the first time her and her husband *did it*. She said it really hurt but then the second time it was better and then she said she got addicted to it and they've been at it like rabbits, non stop and guess what? She's pregnant now.' She added without pausing for breath.

`Really? - Oh my goodness!' Sarah blushed. She had wondered what her first time with Edward would be like. It was a scary thought. She also wondered how long it would take before she became pregnant. Maybe she would have a honeymoon baby if she was lucky.

Laura sat with Edward at the wedding ceremony with Florence the other side of her. She was busy making mental notes of things she had to prepare and organise for her own daughter's wedding.

The admiral interrupted the girls upstairs. `Are you ready my darling? You look exquisite' he said as he smiled at his daughter. He looked frail and his white hair was thinner than Sarah remembered but his blue eyes sparkled with pride. Sarah felt a wash of sadness as she thought of her own father and how much she wanted him to be there at her wedding to walk her down the aisle.

The wedding was fabulous and the reception was fun. Everyone enjoyed themselves immensely. Edward and Sarah danced until the early hours of the morning before retiring to their separate rooms in the house where they spent the night, before setting off home the following day. Even Laura enjoyed herself, despite her reservations about going to social events without her husband. Emma and Daniel went to a little country cottage in Cornwall for their honeymoon and when Sarah said goodbye to them, she knew the next time she would see them both would be at her own wedding and the reality of the big day was drawing nearer. There was exactly one month to go until the big day.

`Where are we going to live when we are married?' Sarah asked Edward a few days after their return from Devon. They were sitting alone in the garden at Whittington Manor. It was a warm evening as they sat watching the sunset. The flowers were in full bloom and there was a strong smell of honeysuckle in the air.

`My flat in Fareham, I suppose – Unless you think we should buy somewhere bigger?'

Sarah looked emotional. `It was my father's wishes for me to live here when I get married.' She said remembering the letter he had written to her before he had died. Although she knew that in his letter he was expecting her to marry Joe, but she also knew he would have approved far more of her marrying Edward. He could offer her far more than Joe could – well far more in materialistic terms, but she couldn't help but wonder how she would be feeling right now if it was Joe she was about to marry.

`And we will. Of course we will live here, in Whittington Manor, but not while your mother lives here. It is her home, not ours - unless' his voice drifted and then stopped, Sarah caught the tail end of what he was saying as she turned to face him. `Unless what?' She frowned at him.

`Unless, she wants to move into somewhere smaller.' Edward shrugged his shoulders.

`We can't just throw, Mama, out of her home' Sarah sounded horrified at the idea.

`I'm not suggesting we throw her out, and technically we couldn't as it is her home until she dies.'

Sarah pursed her lips. `Now you sound like a solicitor.'

Edward sighed. `I was thinking perhaps she might feel more comfortable in a smaller house or maybe in my flat, we could swap houses. Now there's an idea.' His eyes lit up and Sarah looked even more horrified. `I can't imagine Mama for one moment, considering leaving Whittington Manor to live in your flat. This is her home and this is where she shall stay, and I can't see why we can't move in with her?' She sounded indignant.

`Because we will be newly weds and I want you all for myself.' Edward nuzzled his head into her neck as they sat staring at the sunset again. Sarah was lost in thought. The idea of getting married was becoming more daunting by the day. The thought of living in Edward's flat in Fareham wasn't appealing and she was shocked by his suggestion of moving her mother out of Whittington Manor. Sometimes she felt she really didn't know him as well as she thought she did. Every now and again she saw a flash of something she didn't feel comfortable with, yet it was so brief, it was difficult to even remember what it was that she didn't like and she simply brushed it off as pre-wedding nerves.

`We will stay in my flat until your mother – well you know, and then we can move into Whittington Manor.' He continued. He sounded like he had it all worked out.

Sarah bolted forward and stood up in front of him, staring at him indignantly with her arms folded. `Until my mother dies? So we are waiting for her to die are we?'

`Don't be so absurd, Sarah. We are not waiting for anyone to die, - I was simply saying'

`*You* were simply saying what, Edward?' She was glaring at him now.

`I was simply saying that we won't move into Whittington Manor until your mother dies because this is her home. Let's not argue, darling.' He got up from his chair and stood in front of her. `I love you, Sarah.' He took her into his arms and she pushed away from him.

`I just don't feel comfortable living in your flat, it's not very homely. It lacks furniture and it's very cold.' She had only been there a couple of times and although when she first saw it she had liked it, it was on the second occasion she realised how sparse it was.

`Then we shall make it homely. We will go shopping together and have lots of fun. Buy lots and lots of furniture. Paint the place red – your favourite colour, every single room if you like. What do you say?' He cupped his hands around her face and smiled at her. She forced a smiled back at him. `You're impossible, Edward'

`But you love me?' She kissed him without answering his question.

The weeks leading up to their wedding Sarah became more and more overwhelmed, between fittings for her wedding dress, helping her mother with the wedding plans and working at the hospital as much as she possibly could. She hardly saw Edward alone during those weeks and it seemed the only time they met was at parties that were held in their honour. The rest of the time, he was either at work or socialising with friends who were taking him on drinking binges preparing him for the `serious life of marriage' as they put it. She had only met a few of his friends and the ones she had met she didn't like much. They drank and smoked far too much for her liking and when she told Edward so he laughed it off.

She knew this was a time she was supposed to enjoy, but things seemed to be all too much for her and she felt absolutely exhausted. She ended up crying one afternoon on the steps of the hospital as she confided in Cynthia.

`It's alright. They say everyone gets like this before their wedding. I remember my sister was the same. She became so short tempered, snapping at everyone, she was. It's supposed to be a wonderful time but in reality it's not at all. She had an awful time of it before her wedding.' Cynthia took Sarah's hand in her own and patted it gently.

`Really?' Sarah turned her sad hazel eyes to her. It was a huge relief to hear that someone else had equally felt the same way before their wedding. `I keep looking at Joe's photo. I still have it in a shoe box with all his letters. I can't help thinking it should have been Joe I was marrying,' she confessed, wiping the tears from her eyes.

`Joe's gone, Sarah. You have to move on or you will ruin the rest of your life. You love, Edward and he loves you. That's all that matters.' In Cynthia's mind it was all so straight forward.

`I know and I don't doubt for a moment his affections to me or that he won't be a good husband, it's just...' new tears appeared in her eyes. `It's just I miss Joe so much,' she sobbed.

`The feeling I used to get when he kissed me, the excitement and the butterflies in my stomach every time I looked at him...The way he talked, his twinkling green eyes – Oh Cynthia, why did he have to die? I loved him so much.' She looked so terribly sad, not at all like a bride to be and Cynthia felt so sorry for her, yet she still believed marrying Edward was the best thing she could do. `Oh Sarah, it's not fair – I know, but believe me, you have to go on or it will destroy you. You have a man who loves you and you have a chance to be happy. It may not be the same love, but that doesn't mean to say you won't be happy with Edward.'

Seventeen

The long awaited day arrived and Sarah was a bag of nerves as she finished dressing in her bedroom. `Oh my goodness' Laura exclaimed as she flung open the bedroom door to see her daughter standing in front of her. `You look incredible.' Sarah smiled back at her nervously. Laura rushed towards her and finished buttoning up the back of her dress. The French Organdie dress with a twenty-foot train and matching lace veil, looked divine.

`I wish Papa and Charles were here.' Sarah was struggling to hold back her tears, her emotions were running wild.

`So do I, my darling – So do I. They would have been so proud of you today and they would want you to have a wonderful day. They will be watching from wherever they are.' Laura said, trying to comfort her daughter as she finished doing up the last tiny white button.

`Do you really think they would have wanted me to marry Edward? She turned to face her mother. `Mama, am I doing the right thing marrying Edward?' She looked at her with so much sadness in her eyes.

`My darling of course they would have wanted you to marry Edward. He is a wonderful man. You are nervous that's all. I was a bag nerves when I married your father too and look how happy we were.' She sounded wistful remembering her own wedding day. As the brides mother she looked stunning, wearing an Emerald green satin dress and a hat with matching green flowers, even her shoes were the same Emerald green and her diamond necklace sparkled and reflected the same deep colour.

Just then the door burst open and took both Laura and Sarah by surprise. `Oh my God – Sarah' Emma stood staring at her from the bedroom doorway, her hand over her mouth in amazement. `You look absolutely gorgeous.' Sarah smiled back at her friend. If only she could be as happy and as excited at getting married as Emma had been, she thought feeling suddenly envious of her, but all she felt was nerves and even doubts which were beginning to frighten her.

At St Mary's church the guests were being seated and as Laura had predicted the church was packed. Edward stood at the alter looking handsome in his tuxedo, standing next to Eric his best man and old school friend who had been busy leading Edward astray the past couple of weeks with non-stop drinking and partying. Thankfully Sarah had not witnessed the state Edward had been in on some of those occasions, he was always so well behaved and the perfect gentleman when they were at parties together.

There were many important guests at the wedding who had been friends of the Whittingtons for years including Florence and the Admiral. Close to the front of the church sat a couple of dowagers, wearing huge hats with gaudy floral designs, matching their equally gaudy floral dresses. They were busy gossiping about everyone they could lay their eyes on.

Before Laura slipped into the church to take her place, she turned and looked at her daughter one last time. Sarah stood looking radiant, with her maid of honour and a row of bridesmaids dressed in soft peach, waiting behind her. Despite her cool and collective look, deep down inside she was petrified. *Keep calm, keep calm,* she told herself over and over again just wanting to get into the church and get on with the ceremony before she changed her mind.

Laura smiled lovingly at her and then took her in her arms and held her for a moment, being careful not to pull on her dress. `Be happy, my darling... Papa and I love you so much and he's here watching you and so is Charles, remember that when you walk down the aisle. You are not really alone.' She whispered into her ear and with tears streaming down her face, she rushed to take her place in the front row of the church.

As the sound of the organ began playing the `Bridal Chorus' by *Lohengrin,* Emma whispered into Sarah's ear `Are you ready?'

`Ready as I will ever be,' she replied, standing tall and pushing back her shoulders as they entered through the large wooden church doors.

Laura glanced up at Edward, her new son-in-law to be, and he smiled proudly at her. She knew more than anything, he was the right man for her daughter and was sure they would be eternally happy together.

The tension was enormous as slowly and solemnly Sarah walked down the aisle with no one at her side. The dowagers gasped as they watched her walking alone. `The poor child having to walk alone like that! How terrible it was for the Whittingtons. Poor Charles dying like that, and then Lord Whittington, well he was a lovely man.... pretty little thing isn't she?' and the whispering banter continued relentlessly.

There was no one to lead Sarah, protect her, or hand her over to the man she was about to marry, and so she came to him slowly and quietly with total dignity. Since there was no one to give her to Edward, she was giving herself to him. As she reached his side and the music stopped, she looked up at him and he gave her a reassuring smile. Standing next to him she looked into his blue eyes. It was right to move on, now that Joe was gone she had to let go. Edward was her friend and a good man, she would be safe with him and he would make her happy, she was sure of it.

The vicar began the service, their eyes fixed as they made their vows. Sarah realised with absolute certainty that she was doing the right thing and she suddenly felt ashamed that she had even had doubts about marrying Edward.

Edward slipped a narrow diamond band onto her finger and she a simple gold band on his. After the vicar proclaimed them man and wife, Edward gently lifted back her veil and feeling the emotions he never set out to have when he first met her, he kissed her tenderly. There was a chorus of `ahs' and then clapping from the guests. Turning to face them all, both of them beaming from ear to ear, they walked back down the aisle as Mr and Mrs Edward Hamilton.

Eighteen

By September 1943, the Allies had gained a sweet victory after the fall of Salerno, Calabria and Taranto in Italy, which followed their earlier successful invasion of Sicily forcing Benito Mussolini from power. Progress was starting to show in the long, relentless war but it was still far from over. It seemed everyone had a tragic story of some sort to tell. All around was devastation and heartache and the Lamberts were also caught up in their own terrible turmoil the war had inflicted on them so far.

`We were numb from the shock after seeing him like that, Phyllis. Me and Frank didn't speak a word all the way back from Portsmouth.' Audrey wiped away her tears, as she and Phyllis sat at the kitchen table drinking a cup of tea.

`Did he recognise you both?' Phyllis enquired feeling so sorry for her. She couldn't imagine what it must be like to see your son in such a bad way and she was so thankful her son was still fit and well.

`I dunno... he spent the whole time staring out of the window. He never said a word to us. I turned his wheelchair around and looked him in the eyes, but there was nothing there, just a broken empty shell,' she sobbed, dabbing her eyes with her hanky. `I don't know what they did to him Phyllis but it wasn't my Tommy... I mean it was, of course it was but...'

`I know what you mean.' Phyllis sat rubbing Audrey's hand trying to comfort her.

`Did they say what actually happened to him?' Audrey asked as she took a sip of her tea.

`Not much. Only that the ship was torpedoed and went down. There were only a handful of men that survived and our Tommy was the lucky one. Looking at him, you wouldn't have said that though.'

`At least he's alive and I'm sure he will start talking when he's good and ready.' Phyllis said. `How long will he be in a wheelchair for, Audrey?'

`Until his legs are better, so they say, but gawd knows `ow long that will take. They say he will heal physically but they ain't sure mentally. He's got...' she paused to blow her nose, the tears were still streaming down her face. `Some fancy name they gave it – like post traumatic disorder or something. Anyway, whatever it is, they don't know `ow long it's gunno be before he's better, if he ever gets better that is.'

`He'll get better, mark my words,' Frank said, appearing at the kitchen door overhearing their conversation. He had just got back from the allotment and was carrying potatoes and green beans he had picked.

`Ow can you be so sure? You saw the state of him, Frank,' Audrey retorted. She felt so helpless and full of anger at what had happened to Tommy, not to mention the burden she carried day and night worrying about Joe and where he was or even if he was still alive.

`I know - and he's in shock but in time we can bring him home and we'll get him back on his feet, you'll see. At least we got him back.' He placed the vegetables on the kitchen side.

Audrey sighed heavily. `Which is more than can be said for our Joe, I spose. If Tommy's in that state, gawd only knows what's `appened to Joe.' She wished she could share Frank's optimism.

`You can't go thinking like that, Audrey. He might be safe and well in a POW camp somewhere, or hiding out, you never know.' Phyllis pointed out, trying to offer some words of comfort.

`See - there you go, Phyllis is right that's exactly what I told you.' Frank threw a thankful glance Phyllis's way.

`Ere - I never told you, did I? I bumped into Mary from the cafe yesterday, and her father's back.' Phyllis said changing the topic of conversation in an attempt to cheer up Audrey. Her gleaming eyes showed just how much she enjoyed the chance to deliver some gossip.

`Who?.... Hans Hoffman? - is he back?' Frank looked up with surprise.

`Mary must be over the moon,' Audrey added looking equally surprised.

`She is but he doesn't look the same. I saw him briefly just after he arrived and he's got a scruffy beard now. He looked dirty, like an old tramp. His clothes were filthy, they were hanging off him,' Phyllis said wrinkling her nose.

`Poor bugger, I dunno why they had to take him away in the first place. He might 'ave been born in Germany but he's as English as the rest of us. He wouldn't hurt a fly, old Hans,' Frank poured himself a cup of tea from the pot, sitting with its tea cosy on in the middle of the table.

`Wonder what they did to him.' Phyllis sounded curious. `Don't bear thinking about.' Audrey shivered at the thought. `This bloody war, it's seems to be going on forever. `Ow many more people `ave got to suffer before it's all over?'

`I agree with you there.' Frank nodded taking a gulp of his tea.

Audrey looked up at the clock on the wall. `I best get the tea on, our Maureen and Nancy'll be home soon. They've gone up Castle Street to visit her friend.' She stood up and started pottering around the kitchen.

`Yeah, I best be off n'all. Phyllis got up from the table. `Don't forget, if there's anything I can do, and I mean anything, you just give me a yell,' she said as she walked out the kitchen.

The news of Hans Hoffman's return spread fast around Portchester. It was the first bit of good news in a very long time and was the main topic of conversation for several days that and the news that poor Tommy Lambert was in St James' mental hospital and had lost his mind.

*****

By early December Sarah and Edward's honeymoon in the romantic little hotel next to the New Forest felt so long ago and they spent very little time together in recent weeks. Sarah worked long hours at the hospital and Edward, although professing to be working hard himself, had been coming home later and later each night and on many occasions he had come home drunk. He brushed off all Sarah's delicate attempts to discuss why he was drinking so much and also her questions about when they were going to start decorating the flat and make it homely as he had promised her. In fact he hardly spoke to her at all and by Christmas Sarah looked pale and withdrawn.

Christmas Day with her mother at Whittington Manor was unusually quiet and the tension was unbearable between Sarah and Edward. After dinner he excused himself and said he had to visit a friend and would be back to collect Sarah before dark.

`Darling, what's wrong?' Laura asked her daughter as they sat alone in the drawing-room. Edward was still as charming as ever to her mother and Laura had no idea of his recent antics and bad behaviour towards her daughter.

`I'm fine, Mama, just a little tired.'

`I know you well enough to know when you are not telling the truth. Besides, I'm not blind. You and Edward hardly spoke a word to each other since you arrived this morning.

`Really, Mama I'm fine.' Sarah insisted and then finally began to cry and found herself sobbing in her mother's arms, admitting she wasn't fine at all, in fact she was desperately miserable.

`We used to be such good friends and now we hardly talk. He's started drinking and he spends very little time at home,' she sobbed.

`Well to be fair my darling you are hardly spend any time at home with all this hospital work you do. Have you spoken to him about why he's drinking?'

`I've tried to but he doesn't want to talk to me.'

`What you both need is to start a family. That will bring you closer and you would then have to give up working at that hospital. Really Sarah, you should be at home for Edward, he needs a wife to look after him,' Laura said indignantly.

Sarah put her head in her hands and gave a loud sob. Laura put her arm around her and rocked her like a baby. `Come on Sarah, it will all be alright. Marriage is not always a bed of roses, sometimes you have to work at it.'

Sarah looked up at her with an expression of desperation. `Mama, I'm pregnant.'

It took a few seconds for Sarah's words to sink in. `But that's wonderful news!' Her face was beaming with delight. `I'm going to be a grandmother.' That would explain her moods and tiredness. Her hormones were all over the place, she thought looking lovingly at her daughter. `I bet Edward is delighted, isn't he?' Then suddenly she wondered why Edward had not mentioned it today.

`He doesn't know yet.' Sarah confessed.

`Why ever not? This would solve all your problems. You must tell him. Please tell him tonight, Sarah.' Laura insisted. `Believe me, when he knows you are pregnant things will get better between the two of you and what a wonderful Christmas present for him, – for all of us!'

Despite every intention of telling Edward her news, Sarah was forced to wait another day. As soon as they arrived home he told her he had to go out again on an urgent business matter.

`But it's Christmas Day, Edward. No one expects you to work on Christmas Day.'

`Trust me, this is urgent and not something I want to talk about or I'll be late. Don't wait up, it could be late before I get back.' He gave her a peck on the cheek and reaching for his jacket, he dashed out of the front door.

Nineteen

Sarah hadn't worked at the hospital for over a week since Christmas, she was too unwell. She spent the whole time at home. Her breasts were tender, she felt dizzy and weak and the endless wrenching from being sick left her stomach feeling sore and tender.

Edward came home less and less and paid no attention to her. She still hadn't found the opportunity to tell him she was pregnant. On one particular night he didn't come home at all until the following afternoon, but Sarah felt too ill to worry about where he was or what he was doing, she was just angry that he had left her to fend for herself while feeling so terribly ill.

She was sitting curled up on the sofa in the lounge after waking from his clattering around. `What time did you get home last night?' She glared at him.

`I don't remember. I played bridge with a friend and we had a few drinks after our meeting.'

`Is that all you do? Pretend to be at meetings and get drunk? For the first time she turned on him with venom in her voice and he was startled by her tone.

`What on earth do you mean?' His innocent blue eyes were open wide. `I am earning a living, or would you prefer for me to be home with you everyday? Oh, I almost forgot... of course, you're not at home everyday are you? No you are married to that hospital of yours, pretending to be a nurse. I mean come on Sarah you are not even a trained nurse for God sake. It's all one big act isn't it?'

She walked over to where he was standing. `Well you obviously haven't noticed I've not even been at the hospital all week because I've felt too ill,' and with all her anger welling up inside of her she slapped him hard across the face. `I'm not the one pretending,' she said in a whisper.

He stared at her, totally bewildered by what she had just done and then his eyes became wild as if he was suddenly possessed by evil. `I don't accept being spoken to like that and neither do I accept being hit by anyone, least of all my own wife,' he snarled angrily.

`You deserved it,' she retorted.

`So, little miss `prim and proper' is on her high horse. You know you make me sick, - you spoilt little rich, bitch. It's a shame Daddy is not here to protect you any more, isn't it.' He looked at her with hatred in his eyes. A side of him she had never seen before and a side of him she didn't want to see again. How dare he speak to her in such a way? She raised her hand to slap him again but this time he grabbed her hand and then the other which she had raised in her defence. Gripping both of her hands he threw her almost to the other side of the room, not realising his own strength.

`Two can play this hitting game of yours,' he sneered as he walked towards her where she lay huddled in the corner of the room. He picked her up, forcing her to her feet. `You shouldn't have hit me, Sarah,' BIG MISTAKE he shouted, his mouth so close to her face she could smell the whisky on his breath and with all his force he slapped her hard across the side of her face. She screamed as she fell backwards, grabbing frantically at the bookshelf beside her, which consequently toppled and fell on top of her. She fell to the floor with a pile of books around her. Blood trickled from the back of her head which circled into a sticky pool by the side of her. She was unconscious.

`Sarah, Oh god.... Sarah.' In panic Edward tapped her face and shook her, trying desperately to wake her. There appeared to be more blood coming from the lower part of her body in the region of her abdomen. The bruising on her face was already flaring up in angry shades or purple and blue. He stared down at her full of fear. What had he done? He'd gone too far. He never meant to hurt her this badly. She had made him angry and he had lashed out. He was shocked at his own strength.

He dashed to the other side of the room and reached for the telephone to call for an ambulance. His hands were shaking violently and he could hardly speak when the operator answered the phone. All he could think of was that he had killed her. He glanced back at her from where he was standing, there was no movement. `My wife has had a terrible accident.' The operator asked him a question but he wasn't listening, his head was spinning. `Is she breathing?' the voice on the other end of the phone asked impatiently.

`I think she's dead,' he croaked, nearly dropping the phone from fear.

Twenty

Sarah woke up in hospital with Edward and her mother sitting either side of her. She had been unconscious for quite sometime and she looked dazed as she tried to focus. There were monitors beeping faintly in the background and there was a strong hospital sterile smell in the air.

`The baby?' She ran a desperate hand over her stomach.

`There's no baby, sweetheart. You've had a terrible accident and you've lost the baby,' Laura reached out for her wondering hand. `You're young, there will be lots more babies my darling.' Laura was doing her best to hide her own emotions. She too was feeling her daughter's pain but she had to be strong for her and for Edward as well. It was his baby too and he must be going through hell, she thought as she glanced mournfully over at him.

A tear trickled down Sarah's cheek, her memory was slowly coming back to her. She turned her head and looked at Edward, her eyes full of anguish as the images of him hitting her and her falling flashed in her mind like a terrible nightmare.

Realising, by the expression on her face that she was remembering what had happened, Edward jumped to his feet and stood over her bed. He looked remorseful. `I'm sorry, Sarah.'

`Are you? Are you really sorry, Edward?' There was bitterness in her tone. More tears began to cascade down her face. `You killed our baby!' Her voice was raised now.

`Now, come on. No one is to blame here. Edward tried to help you put that book back on the top shelf.' Laura quickly rushed to Edward's defence.

`What?' There was a monetarily confused look on Sarah's face as she stared at her mother. Her head was still hurting and she felt like she had done ten rounds in a boxing ring.

`Edward has told me all about it. You slipped on a chair when you tried to put a book back on the bookshelf.'

Edward quickly interrupted his mother-in-law. `It won't happen again, I promise you, Sarah. I will take better care of you.' He reached for her hand

and she pulled away from him. She was weak and too tired to fight any more. She turned her head away from him, not being able to stand the sight of him any longer. She stared absentmindedly into space, feeling numb from the pain. Whatever he had told her mother, it really didn't matter. Her baby was gone and he was the one responsible for it. He had killed their baby and nothing would change that fact.

It was a few days later when Sarah was discharged from hospital. She wanted to go back to Whittington Manor but her mother had insisted she went back to Edward. Things won't get better if you don't spend time together. You have to have time to grieve and pick up the pieces, she had told her. She was still feeling too weak to argue and without a fight, Sarah went back home with Edward.

`Sarah, I had no idea you were pregnant. Really, I am truly sorry.' Edward said, sitting down in his arm chair opposite her the day she returned from hospital.

`So it's alright to beat me if I'm not pregnant? Why don't you just finish the job? She threw an irritated glance his way.

`Don't be silly. It was an argument that got out of hand and it never would have if you had told me you were pregnant. Why didn't you tell me, Sarah?' His voice had become soft.

`Why didn't I tell you?' Her impatience was growing. `You've been constantly drunk for the past two months and you were never at home for me to talk to you. You've behaved appallingly and then to top it all...' she paused and tears appeared in her eyes.

`And to top it all? Come on you've started saying something, so finish it. There was annoyance in his tone.

`And then you killed our baby.' She spoke in barely a whisper before walking out of the room, leaving him watching her retreating back disappear behind the closed door.

The guilt she had inflicted on him was more than he could take. He poured himself a scotch, swigged it down, slammed the empty glass onto the coffee table and marched out of the front door.

Sarah sat staring out of the bedroom window. There were no tears any more, she was past crying. It was almost as if when the baby had died, a part of her had died too. She resented Edward more than ever. She would never forgive him. She had given up so much for him and wished more than ever that she had accepted the place at the medical school in Scotland but most of all she resented him because he wasn't Joe.

It was late afternoon when Edward came home, the door slammed behind him as he walked into the room. Sarah was reading a medical book and didn't spare a moment to look at him. He stood and stared at her wondering what had happened to the friendship they had once shared. She was his wife. It wasn't meant to be like this. They used to be such good friends and he couldn't understand why she had made him feel the way he did. He felt not worthy of her. She was a Whittington and had all the money and power he could dream of and yet, what was he? A mere solicitor who earned a salary that would be no more than the interest she was earning in the bank right now from her inheritance. It was imperative he took control of the situation and it was also imperative he took control of the money. He had come so far now and things had to get better between them.

`Sarah, how long are you going to continue ignoring me?' He sounded a little impatient.

`Shouldn't you be at work?' She replied indignantly, still reading.

`I don't have any work to go to anymore.' He slipped his door keys into his pocket and ran his fingers through his hair. He was hovering in the door way of the lounge.

She suddenly looked up at him, with a look of confusion. `I don't understand.'

`I sold the business, yesterday.' He said melancholy.

`Why? It was your father's business. You love being a solicitor, that's who you are.' She looked bewildered by his announcement.

`After what has happened to us, it made me realise that there is more to life than my work. The business was putting me under a lot of strain. In fact it was running into financial problems. I couldn't manage it like my father did. I was clinging onto a sinking ship.' Edward confessed as he walked across the room and sat down on the sofa next to her.

`So what are you going to do now?' She was more curios than interested. It didn't matter how bad things had got with his work, his actions were still unforgivable.

`Nothing, just be here for you I suppose.' He took her hand into his own and smiled at her.

She pulled her hand abruptly away from him. She couldn't bear him to touch her and just sitting next to him made her skin crawl. `You have to do something, Edward. You can't just sit around here all day long,' she pointed out rather coolly.

Her tone annoyed him. He was trying to make an effort. He was trying to be nice and was willing to look after her and be a better husband now. `I'm married to a Whittington. I can do whatever I want, it's not like we need the money is it?' he scorned.

`What do you mean?' Sarah frowned.

`Well, I sold the business for a fair price, considering it's problems, and next year you will turn twenty-one and get your inheritance, so money is not a problem in my life.' He grinned at her. `In fact, I will have plenty of money when you become twenty-one. Don't forget I was your father's solicitor and I know exactly how much money you are worth.' Sarah stared at him in disbelief, a wave of panic suddenly washing over her. So that was his reason for wanting to marry her? His so called friendship, his charm his proposal to her, it was all part of his evil plan to take her money? She felt sick to the core and so foolish for falling into his trap.

Twenty-one

It was March before Sarah could find the strength to put on a brave face and go back to work at the hospital. Dr. Gregory had been sympathetic and kind to her regarding her miscarriage and the nicer he was the more she wanted to cry. It was the same when she spoke to Cynthia and when Cynthia told her she had accepted a post at Haslar Hospital, the news hit Sarah badly. She felt so alone. The only way she could cope with her pain was to throw herself into her work, which is exactly what she did, working as many hours as they needed her. With the constant air-raids there were always plenty of casualties, not to mention the constant influx of seriously injured soldiers.

Her work was her escapism from her desperately sad and lonely marriage, and her relationship with Edward went from bad to worse. Despite his intentions of being a better husband and making things better with Sarah. He spent more and more time drinking himself into a stupor and had started gambling day and night. She objected a great deal to the condition he was in. It was only yesterday when he had arrived in at 1am, stumbling all over the place. He scarcely recognised her as he tried to focus on her blurred face.

`It's a wonder you don't end up killing yourself in that state,' she grimaced as he made his way unsteadily to their bedroom and collapsed unconsciously on the bed. She stood looking at him for a long time, with tears in her eyes before leaving the room to sleep in the guest room where she had taken up residency since getting out of hospital. As she lay in bed that night she felt an ache in her heart for the baby she had lost and the husband she had never really had and never would have. She knew that her marriage to Edward was nothing more than a sham, a life of emptiness and bitterness. Her thoughts drifted to Joe as she cried herself to sleep.

*****

`I've made your favourite cake for tea,' Audrey said as she fussed around Tommy who had been discharged from hospital six months after his rescue. He no longer needed a wheelchair and although he looked fit physically, he was still suffering from shock and still had not spoken a single word.

157

`Do you think he will ever talk again?' Audrey asked Frank in the kitchen while she made a fresh pot of tea to go with the cake she had made earlier that day.

`Yes, but he needs time to adapt, he's only just got home, Audrey. You heard what the doctors said.' `Give him time.' Audrey joined in chorus with Frank and they smiled at each other.

It was in fact two weeks later when Tommy finally spoke but his speaking came at a high price. The Lambert's were half way through their supper when the air-raid sounded one evening. They had been accustomed to pushing Tommy into the shelter, along with Maureen and little Nancy, but this particular night, Tommy was not willing to go. For some reason his eyes looked wild with fear.

Frank pushed him out into the garden in the direction of the shelter but he stopped and pulled away from Frank as hard as he could. They stood in the garden, the pouring rain lashing down on their faces. He refused point blank to move. It was as if something had triggered his memory, something dreadful, something very bad and he became paralysed with fear.

Frank tugged on his arm. `Come on lad. Let's get in the shelter.'

`I'm not going in there.' Tommy's voice was croaky. Frank stared at him, trying to suppress a smile. They were the first words he had spoken since he had been rescued at sea.

`Don't be daft, lad, now come on.' Frank insisted. Audrey was already in the shelter with Maureen and Nancy, waiting anxiously for them.

`I'm not going in there. I'm staying here,' he shouted against the noise of the siren and the pouring rain.

Audrey poked her head out of the shelter and shouted at them to hurry up. The noise of the siren and the droning of the enemy planes approaching were deafening and Frank began to panic.

`Get in there now!' he shouted frantically as he pushed him towards the shelter but Tommy fell to his knees as Frank looked back at him in desperation from the entrance of the shelter. He was soaked to the skin and it was as if the heavens had opened as the torrential rain poured relentlessly down on him.

With a sudden burst of anger Tommy held his fist to the sky. `It should have been me... It should have been me they killed,' he yelled with so much aggression in his voice. `Come on then, finish the job. Take me. Take me you Bastards!... Take me you Bastards! And his yelling turned to a heart-breaking sob as Frank ran back for him. He sat hugging him while he cried like a baby in his father's arms. Just then an enormous explosion sounded in the distance and Audrey came to the entrance of the shelter again. She screamed at the top of her voice. `Get him in here now, Frank, or you'll both die.'

A German plane was fast approaching as it flew as low as the chimney's of the row of houses in front of them. Panic-stricken Frank pulled Tommy through the rain. The lawn had turned to slushy mud as they stumbled and slid towards the shelter, and finally, still sobbing, Tommy stumbled down the steps of the shelter with Frank behind him. A horrific blast shook the shelter, followed by another only seconds later.

Tommy sat huddled up next to his parents, whimpering like a frightened injured child.

`Oh Tommy, what happened my darling? What happened?' Audrey placed a blanket around his shoulders and held him tightly in her arms. She couldn't bear to see him this way, her bubbly, always so cheerful and confident son, destroyed and broken; bearing no resemblances to the Tommy they had once known and loved so dearly.

Maureen sat at the back of the shelter with baby Nancy who was playing quietly with her building bricks. There was a definite sadness about Maureen since Tommy had come home. She missed him, the way he used to tease her and even the constant arguments. She hardly recognised her brother any more. Glancing over to where he was sitting, she brushed a tear from her eye.

Tommy's sobbing subsided after a while and he sat staring aimlessly in front of him. Frank bent down in front of him trying to look into his eyes. `Tommy do you want to tell us what happened to you at sea? It might help if you share it with us?' He gave a small hopeful smile but Tommy just sat and stared straight through him. Feeling despondent Frank got up and walked to the other side of the shelter to take a seat.

`You wouldn't understand, Dad. No one could.' Tommy said quietly, taking Frank and Audrey by surprise.

Frank got up and rushed towards him again. He knelt down next to him. `Try me, son.' He looked encouragingly at him. Tommy took a deep breath. Maureen looked up and stared over. Frank and Audrey watched him intently, waiting desperately to hear what they so much wanted to know.

`I can't, Dad. I just can't talk about it.' Tommy looked away from their anxious stares and the tears began to fall down his face once more.

`Leave it Frank, let him be.' Audrey pleaded, realising that whatever had happened to Tommy it was just far too traumatic for him to speak about.

That same night Sarah arrived home after working eleven hours at the hospital. Vosper's boat yard had been hit and in and around Portsdown Hill too. There had been quite a few casualties and she was shattered by the time she got home. She was still in her bloodstained uniform after one of the nurses had driven her back. She had contemplated sleeping the night at the hospital but decided to go home instead. She needed to get a good night's sleep.

Turning the key in the door she walked into the lounge and placed her bag on the coffee table. She gave a tired sigh making circular movements with her neck and then rubbing her tired shoulders to remove the stress. She was distracted by a strange noise and straining to hear what it was, she soon realised the sound was coming from the other side of the flat. As she walked towards the bedrooms the sound became louder and then it stopped. She hesitated for a moment, her hand resting on the bedroom door knob. She put her ear to the door and quietly opening it, she stood and watched in horror.

`Hello, darling may I present to you, Amy,' Edward was slurring his words and had a pathetic grin on his face. The pretty young girl next to him carried a look of embarrassment as she pulled the covers over her naked breasts.

`How dare you!' The anger in Sarah was reaching boiling point.

`Oh come on, Sarah... don't be like that, it's harmless fun,' He lay on top of the bed covers, completely naked. In disgust, she slammed the bedroom door behind her as hard as she could and rushed into her own bedroom. With tears streaming down her face, she reached up for a brown leather suitcase on top of the wardrobe. Placing it on the bed, she quickly packed her clothes, and then glancing at her watch, she realised it was far too late to make her way to Whittington Manor and decided she would have to wait until the morning. She would leave as soon as it was day light. She didn't want to spend another day under the same roof as Edward.

Reaching in to the back of the wardrobe, under an old blanket, she pulled out the shoe box she had kept safe, which contained Joe's letters and his photo. She sat on the bed and read a few, crying and wiping her eyes so as her tears wouldn't stain the letters and make the ink run. Hugging his photo she laid back on her pillow, broken hearted and weak with tiredness.

When she awoke she was appalled to see the time, it was already 11am and she couldn't believe she had slept that long. Memories of the night before came flooding back as she got up out of bed and saw her suitcase packed, next to the bedroom door. After getting dressed she walked into the kitchen to find Edward sitting at the kitchen table reading the newspaper. He had made himself some breakfast and the remains of an egg and some bread was sitting on a plate in front of him.

`Morning!' He glanced at her, picked up a mug of tea, took a gulp and then went back to his newspaper.

`How could you, Edward? How could you be so cruel?' She stood in the doorway staring at him in dismay.

`Sarah, for God sake!' He peered over the top of his paper. `We haven't had sex in months... what am I supposed to do? It was just sex, nothing more ...besides she never charges much.' He grinned at her and then folded up his paper and placed it on the table next to his cup of tea. Sarah looked mortified, hardly believing that this was the man she had married, the man she had believed to be her friend, the man she had trusted.

`You brought a tart into our home? A prostitute? You are repulsive!' She turned on her heel and walked out of the kitchen.'

`Would it have been alright if she was for free, then?' He called out after her, trying to provoke her further. She didn't react. She picked up her suitcase and walked out of the front door. Her life with Edward was over. She had taken more than she could bear and it was time to go home, where she belonged.

Arriving back at Whittington Manor, Sarah felt comfort at last. It was home and always had been. A wave of sadness came over her as she walked inside and thought of her father. He would never have let Edward treat her in such a way and even Charles wouldn't have for that matter. She placed her suitcase at the bottom of the stairs and walked towards the kitchen.

`Sarah, what a surprise!' Annie shrieked, turning around to see Sarah standing behind her. But the broken look in her eyes showed the sheer pain and sadness she was carrying. `Whatever is the matter?' Annie rushed towards her, taking her into her arms.

`I can't do it any more... I can't be married to him anymore,' she sobbed.

`Now you come and sit down and tell Nanny all about it.' Sarah walked towards the kitchen table and Annie pulled out a chair for her to sit on. `All marriages have their ups and downs, my dear,' She passed Sarah a clean hanky from her pinafore pocket.

Sarah accepted it and dabbed her eyes. `You don't understand, Nanny. It's far more than an argument. What's happened just can't be mended.' She hated Edward now, and there was no way she could forgive him for killing their baby, the endless nights of drinking, or the prostitutes, she couldn't put up with him any longer.

`Well, it will have to be mended, you are married, my darling. `Is it about the baby?' Annie asked softly, which made Sarah cry even more. `You'll have more babies you will see.'

`No, Nanny, there won't be more babies. He killed my baby... he killed it.' Her face crumpled up and her lip quivered.

`What do you mean he killed the baby?' Annie hated to see her in this state. She loved her as if she were her own daughter.

`He hit me and he pushed me into the bookshelf, which fell on top of me and killed the baby.'

Annie stared at her in horror, her mouth slightly open. `Why didn't you tell your Mum, Sarah?'

`She wouldn't have believed me. She thinks Edward is so wonderful. Last night was the last straw, though.' Sarah gave a sniff and dabbed her eyes again.

`Did he hit you again?' Annie asked eying her all over to see if she could see any marks or bruises.

`No, but he might as well have. He brought a prostitute into our home.' She let out a loud cry as Annie got up and took her into her arms and held her tightly. She too was crying as she rocked her up and down remembering how she had comforted her when she was a little girl. It broke her heart to see her this way.

Laura arrived home just before dark. She had been visiting an old friend and had spent the day in the country.

`Sarah, my darling, how lovely to see you. I had no idea you were coming to visit me today.' She said, as she rushed over and kissed her daughter on the cheek. Sarah was sitting in the main drawing-room, looking out of the window at the gardens. It had just finished raining and a blackbird was busy hopping about, digging its beak into the wet grass hoping to find a worm.

`You still look a little peaky, my dear. Can you stay for supper?' Laura took off her coat and rubbed the back of her neck. It had been a long journey and she was tired.

`Yes, I can stay for supper, Mama.' Sarah replied, thinking it best to tell her mother over supper that she had left Edward and had absolutely no intention of going back to him. She had no idea how she was going to break the news to her and she hated to bring shame on the Whittington name by divorcing Edward, but there was no way she could continue this masquerade any longer.

`Well, that's wonderful! Now, I'm going to get changed out of these clothes. I need to freshen up... it's been a long day. And when I come back we can have a nice chat and you can tell me all about what you and Edward have been up to.' She smiled lovingly at her daughter and disappeared out of the room.

Sarah turned back to the window. The blackbird was still there and she carried on watching it until it found a worm and flew off out of sight. She sighed. It was starting to get dark. Just then the dreaded noise of the air-raid siren sounded. She rolled her eyes and sighed again. `This war is so tiresome' she mumbled, rubbing her tired eyes.

`Annie, I suppose you know that Sarah is here?' She'll be staying for supper. Laura said as she walked into the kitchen to find Annie busy putting the top layer of pastry on the beef pie she was preparing for dinner.

`I know she'll be staying and a lot longer than supper I daresay,' Annie's eyes were red and swollen and she looked like she had been crying.

`What do you mean, Annie? Is there something the matter?' Laura looked concerned as she walked closer to get a better look at Annie.

`You mean Sarah hasn't told you yet?' She looked worriedly at her, not wanting to be the one to tell her how atrociously Edward had treated her daughter.

`Told me what?' Laura rose her voice over the sound of the siren

`We've got to get to the shelter. Is Sarah in the shelter already?' Annie turned the stove off and placed the pie to one side. It would have to wait now until they got back from the shelter. At least there were always plenty of snacks down there if it was going to be a long wait.

`I expect so - she's always the first when the siren goes off.' Laura looked agitated. Annie I need to know if there is something wrong with Sarah, please tell me quickly.'

`But the siren... We really must go' Annie rushed towards the kitchen door. At that moment the house began to shake as a plane flew extremely low, almost touching the roof. Annie's eyes grew wide with fear. As if the fear was contagious Laura ran towards her tripping over the kitchen chair. She fell to the floor, gripping her ankle in pain.

`Oh my Lady, are you alright?' Annie rushed to her. `I'm not sure I can move it Annie. It feels sprained.'

Sarah stood in the air-raid shelter pacing nervously up and down, wondering why her mother and Annie were taking so long. Before she had the chance to run back and find out there was an enormous roar of an explosion. The ground beneath her swelled and shook. The corrugated iron that formed the shelter rattled and shook as parts of it began to crack and crumble. She stood holding her breath for a moment. The shelter seemed to be caving in. The monotonous heavy vibrations of war planes flying above seemed to go on forever and when the sound of falling masonry and smashing glass ceased, there was a deathly silence. She moved to the entrance of the shelter, her heart pounding with fear.

The all clear siren sounded and she clambered frantically upstairs and outside. And in the cold grey light she stood and watched in terror. A pall of dust and filth hung about like fog, filling her mouth and nose with its grit and stench. The sky was thick with smoke and sneering flashes of red and orange flames were raging through an almost empty shell of Whittington Manor. Sarah felt a new wave of enormous dread and fear wash over her and as if someone had just turned the lights out. Everything went black as she fainted.

`Miss, can you hear me?... Miss...' She awoke in the back of an ambulance and coughed violently.

`That'll be all that smoke. You're lucky to be alive.' The paramedic was middle aged, bald with a little grey hair around the sides. He pushed his glasses back over his deep brown eyes. He had a daughter more or less the same age as her. He smiled warmly and checked her pulse. She looked disorientated as she gazed around the back of the ambulance and it drove off at full speed with its siren on.

`Mama!... Nanny! She sat up right her eyes glazed with fear. The inside of her chest felt like it had been rubbed down with sand paper and she had an uncomfortable pain just below her rib cage.

`Shush, it's alright.' He gently pushed her back on the pillow beneath her head and she felt a slight prick in her left arm as he gave her a sedative to calm her down. She felt like she was dreaming, it was all part of a terrible nightmare and she couldn't scream, run, or do anything. The only thing she could do was just lay helplessly drifting in and out of consciousness.

`Aren't you supposed to be this side of the bed?' Dr. Gregory gave a wry smile as she came to. Tears immediately sprang to her eyes as she looked up at him.

`My mother... Nanny... Are they alright?' she asked in a small voice with such desperation, but looking into Dr. Gregory's eyes, she knew the answer. She let out a huge wail and he held her hand tightly, holding back his own tears.

`They wouldn't have suffered.' He was struggling to find the right words. The poor girl had been through so much. `Your husband is on his way... We've managed to track him down.' You are lucky to be alive, you must remember that.' He patted her hand gently.

`Am I?' Why did they keep saying that? What was lucky about being alive, now that everyone she loved had gone?

Twenty-two

By October 1944 there was still no sign of the war ending. Although there was slow but sure progress being made in some countries. The allies had liberated Athens, captured Belgrade and also Aachen which was the first city to be taken in Germany.

Edward's efforts to be a good husband after Sarah returned from hospital had soon long vanished. He felt awkward around her and it was as if they were complete strangers. He shared none of her grief. In fact he was silently revelling in the idea of rebuilding Whittington Manor to his liking, not to mention all the other plans he had as soon as he could get his hands of Sarah's money. He just had to bide his time as the long wait was almost over with only five more months to go before her birthday, yet it wouldn't come soon enough as his recent gambling addiction was getting a little costly.

`Sarah, I don't like to ask you at such an awkward time, but I need to ask something of you.' He sat down opposite her, perched on the edge of the armchair.

She looked at him without saying a word. He had sensed a big change in her, a kind of compliance and acceptance of his appalling behaviour. It was as if when her mother and Annie had died she lost all her strength to fight him any more, she had resigned herself to a life sentence of misery being married to him. But Edward didn't question it he just took full advantage of the situation.

`I need some money, Sarah. I've got a tax bill from a while back that needs paying rather urgently,' He rubbed his chin nervously studying her face for an answer.

`How much is it for?' There was no expression to her face or her voice for that matter.

`One hundred pounds, but I could do with one hundred and fifty to cover other bills too.' He said cautiously.

`You are asking me to use the money my father has left me in an emergency?' she asked calmly, knowing full well there was no tax bill to pay, not for that amount anyway.

`Well, this is an emergency and it's not long until you have your inheritance money, then there won't be a problem any more.' He smiled ruefully.

`I wasn't aware that there was a problem.' Money was all he wanted from her, that was all she was good for now. She decided to give him the one hundred and fifty pounds, it was easier than fighting him. All she wanted was for him to leave her alone.

`Alright, - I will get it out of the bank and give it to you tomorrow.'

He looked both relieved and delighted at the same time. `Thank you.' He rubbed his hands together, as he walked out of the room.

It was November when Sarah decided to volunteer again at the hospital. She needed to occupy her mind and lose herself from her world of misery. She felt desperately lonely since her mother and Annie had died. Emma had written to her on a number of occasions, inviting her to go and stay with her and Daniel. She had given birth six months earlier to a baby boy and her letters were full of news about the baby they had named Phillip, which only depressed Sarah further. Working at the hospital was her escapism where she could forget about her own life and be amongst people who really needed her.

And in March her birthday came and went. She didn't want to make a fuss of it and still wasn't in the mood for celebrating. It seemed the whole day she couldn't get the images of Joe proposing to her, under the old oak tree, out of her mind. When she closed her eyes they were even more vivid. She could still remember the snow softly falling around them as he picked her up and twirled her around as they kissed with such passion and excitement. Today was the day they should have been married, if there had not be a war and if he had not died and left her alone in this cruel and bitter world. Instead she was married to Edward, the man she despised, loathed and wished more than anything that he would leave her or drink himself to death.

Edward was the only person who wanted to celebrate Sarah's birthday, but not with Sarah of course. He had his own party with his drinking partners which had lasted all day and night.

`Sarah, darling... Happy Birthday!' He was far from sober as she walked in the door late that night.

`I think you and I need a little chat - don't you?' he said pouring himself a large scotch from the drinks cabinet before flopping down in the arm chair in front of her. Her eyes were emotionless as she stared at him. There was nothing he could say or do to her that could hurt her any more.

`We need to get some money out of the bank... bills don't get paid on their own and I also thinks it's time we look into rebuilding Whittington Manor.' Sarah hadn't been back to the Manor since losing her mother and Annie. Most of it was a burnt out empty shell and the remaining part of the house that was still standing had been boarded up. She just couldn't bring herself to go there. The memories were far too raw.

`No, Edward bills don't get paid on their own that is why you should never have sold your business.' She said indignantly, stating the obvious.

`Why do I need to work, when I'm married to a Whittington? He slurred, taking another swig of his drink.

`I don't want to touch Whittington Manor... not yet... I'm not ready, Edward.' The anguish was written all over her face and even Edward couldn't fail to see it.

`Alright, we'll leave it for now... but the money... well that's important. I've opened a new bank account and I want you to transfer money in to it...£2,000 to start with.' He held his glass up in front of him as if surveying its contents and then he took another swig and took a deep breath after the burning sensation of the whisky hit the back of his throat.

`And what if I don't?' She pursed her lips and folded her arms. He had already spent her emergency fund and now his intentions were to work his way through her inheritance.

`Oh I think you will, my dear... after all, I'm your next of kin and should you have the misfortune of having a terrible accident, that money would be mine anyway.' He gave one of his evil grins; the ones that made Sarah shiver.

Are you threatening me?' She was determined to stand up to him this time. Enough was enough. Her parents wouldn't have wanted her to lose her inheritance.

`Threaten you, why of course not my dear... I'll give you the bank account details tomorrow and I expect the money in my account right away.' He sat forward and glared at her. Sarah stormed out of the room in disgust.

The next day she went to her bank and transferred the £2,000 to Edward's account to keep him off her back for now but she had no intention of paying him any more. He had gone too far and she had to take the matter in to her own hands now. Later that week she then visited a solicitor who she had checked out thoroughly, making sure he had no links to Edward.

Mr Shaw was an elderly gentlemen and his office was on the outskirts of Fareham.

He waved her into his office and pointed for her to sit down. How can I help you, Mrs Hamilton?' He had kind gentle brown eyes and his grey hair was thinning on top. Sarah sat down on the leather chair placed in front of his mahogany shiny desk. The office was furnished tastefully and with no expense spared. There was a strong smell of leather and on the far side of the office was a drinks cabinet displaying crystal glasses and a whisky decanter. His desk was covered with various files and papers and there were numerous photographs of his family.

`I've been left some money... my father died and he left it to me in trust until I turned twenty-one. My mother also passed away recently and I have inherited her estate plus the family home.' She pulled out a copy of her parent's will and handed it to him. There was a few moments silence when Mr Shaw read it in detail. `I see, so how can I help you?' He frowned at her, peering over the top of his reading spectacles that were halfway down his nose.

`I'm in a desperately unhappy marriage and my husband wants' she paused nervously. `Well... he wants my money, including my home... and' she paused again trying to find the right words.

`And you don't want him to have it.' Mr Shaw said finishing her sentence for her. He had seen so many young women like her come into his office asking him to help them. Most of them had only be married a short time and realised that had made a grave mistake. Adultery was the main cause of most of the break-ups.

`Yes, that's correct.' She answered fidgeting nervously on her seat.

`I suppose you have thought about divorcing him?'

`Yes, on many occasions. At first I wanted to divorce him, although I was afraid of bringing shame on the family name, but since I have no family left, other than a brother at sea whom I've not heard from in nearly five years, I suppose it doesn't really matter any more.' She sighed and her eyes were full on sadness.

`Would you like me to start a divorce application?' Mr Shaw asked sympathetically. She seemed a nice girl and so young to have been through such heartache. `Although I must tell you, he will still be entitled to at least half of your estate as part of the divorce settlement.' He added with a sigh.

`I have thought about that, which is why I need to think this through properly, but I would like to make a will, which is why I am here today.' Her sudden change in direction surprised Mr Shaw and he continued to listen to her with intent.

`I would like to leave my entire estate to my brother Thomas Whittington, and not to my husband.' She said primly.

`I see... well you are within your rights to do that however, your husband may well contest against the will. I presume you don't have any children?' Sarah nodded her head reluctantly. `And you say you haven't heard from your brother for nearly five years. Is he still alive?'

`I don't know if he is still alive, but I'd rather the money goes to him than my husband.'

`The point I'm trying to make Mrs Hamilton is... if your brother is no longer alive the money will automatically go to your husband anyway, who is of course, your next of kin.'

Sarah looked down at her hands resting on her lap. She stared at her wedding band, wondering why she was still wearing it. It meant nothing to her any more, all she felt was bitterness and emptiness. She looked back at Mr Shaw. `I know and I've thought about that too. I want to state in my will that if my brother is no longer alive when I die, I want my money to be left to a family that I care about deeply.' She sounded slightly wistful.

`A family?' Mr Shaw looked puzzled.

`Yes, the Lambert family. I was in love with their son once.' The truth of the matter was she still was but that was beside the point. `We were engaged to be married. Joe was killed and I know the family are not well off. I would rather they had my fortune then my drunkard husband who will squander the money away on drink and gambling.' She would have preferred anyone to have the money than Edward, but she knew the Lamberts were kind and decent people and would definitely make use of the money wisely.'

`Very well, Mrs Hamilton but I must still point out that your husband can contest your will and it is very likely he could still have a claim of some sort.' He hated to be the bearer of bad news and dash all her hopes of protecting her money but it was his job to tell her.

`Well, I'm willing to take that risk.' Sarah said indignantly.

`Mrs Hamilton, may I ask you a personal question?' He watched her with a frown on his face.

`Yes, Mr Shaw.' She sat forward with interest.

`Has your husband ever cheated on you...had another woman?'

Sarah stared at him as if staring right through him. Eventually she nodded without saying a word. She felt ashamed and even more ashamed that he had cheated on her with a prostitute. She was sure there must have been hundreds of women by now and he had only brought a prostitute back to their home because he had wanted to hurt her.

`If you are unhappy, you may want to think about a divorce, adultery is quite an easy case for us to win.' He looked sympathetically at her.

`Will he still have a claim on my money?'

`I'm not entirely sure, it will depend on how good a solicitor he gets himself.'

`He will probably represent himself, seeing as he was a solicitor, and knowing him he would probably worm himself out of it and end up with half my estate not to mention the family home.' Sarah was doing her best to fight back her tears just thinking about him drove her to distraction. But she wasn't ready to fight him just yet, not in that way anyway. There had to be another way. An easier way.

`Why don't you go away and have a think about it.' He sighed. He could see her torment.

Sarah sighed heavily. `It's the principle, Mr Shaw. I hope you understand. I just don't want him to take my money from me and more than anything my home.'

`I understand. Well if you would like to make your will and give it to me as soon as you are ready.' He stood up and escorted her to the door where they shook hands before she left his office.

Twenty-three

It was 1st April 1945 when Edward's drinking and gambling spiralled completely out of control. He was insisting on more and more money for which he squandered away night after night. He owed money to a number of very unsavoury character and had clearly got in with the wrong crowd. He drank so heavily he often didn't make it home, much to Sarah's relief, but when she found out he had been stealing her jewellery she finally lost her temper one night.

`What have you done with my jewellery?' He had stolen her mother's pearl necklace that she had given her before she died, plus a beautiful sapphire ring that her grandmother had left to her. Her jewellery was the only memories she had of her family. There was nothing left after losing everything in the house when it had been bombed.

`You weren't using it and I needed it.' He answered looking nonplus.

`What right do you have to take what's mine? It was precious to me.'

`Stop whining - you're giving me a headache. Precious – really... just some tatty jewels.' He said with a short laugh.

`Tatty Jewels?' She raised the glass vase that was standing decoratively near the window. It took all her strength not to throw at him. Instead she threw it on the floor next to him in a rage. He looked up at her with a bemused look and then started to laugh at her. `Oh - what's the matter? Spoilt little rich bitch has lost her jewellery. Never mind you can always buy some more with all that money you got stashed away. That money you keep hidden from me.' He added with aggression.

He took a swig of whisky, placed it on the coffee table and then without warning, he jumped up and grabbed her to the floor. She struggled to get away from him but he was over powering her. Ignoring her screams, he pulled up her dress and holding onto both of her arms with one hand, after hitting her hard across the face, he quickly unfastened his trousers. He ripped off her underwear and kicked her legs apart with his own and in an instant he was inside of her, pumping her violently and groaning at the same time. She shook her head from side to side and tried to fight him off but he only pressed her harder to the ground. Within moments it was all over as he released himself with a shout and another deep groan. He lifted himself off her, reached down for her wrists and then threw her to one side with such force that she sat cowering in a corner shaking from head to toe like a battered rag doll.

He fastened his trousers, finished his whisky then stormed out of the room. A few moments later she got up with her dress ripped and her underwear torn and hanging around her ankle. She ran into her bedroom and locked herself in. She then heard the thud of the front door bang as Edward left for another night of boozing and gambling.

She unlocked the door and after cleaning herself up and getting changed into fresh clothes she found some note paper and a pen and sat at her dresser to write a letter to Emma. Her hands were shaking with both rage and fear. Her tears cascaded down her face like a waterfall or misery. She began to write to the only friend she had left in the world. There would be no putting on a brave front any more, she was going to tell Emma everything, and agree to come and stay with her. In Devon she would have time to think and decide what to do next. She was interrupted by loud knocking at the front door. She placed the pen on top of the unfinished letter and ran out of the room to answer the door. She hesitated when she reached the door but the knocking was so persistent she opened it slowly.

`Is he here?' Two very frightening men stood watching her. The man who spoke to her filled the entire door frame with his muscular body. He was bald, clean shaven and was dressed in a long black trench coat. The other man was smaller with fair hair and a growth of at least two days' stubble.

`Is who here?' Sarah asked timidly.

`Santa Claus – Who do you think? - Your husband. The man was looking impatient with her as he tried to look into the room behind her.

`I heard him go out a little while ago,' Sarah replied.

`Why do I get the feeling you 'aint tellin' the truth? Get out me way!' He pushed her to one side as he walked inside with the other man in tow. They searched each room as Sarah stood shaking close to the front door. A moment later they appeared in front of her again.

`I apologise – you were telling the truth,' the large man confirmed as he glared at her. `You tell him from me, he's got twenty-four hours to pay up.'

`Who shall I say called?' She was doing her best to keep her composure and not show how scared she really was.

`You don't need my name, he knows who I am. Oh and if he doesn't pay up on time, I might just have to help myself to things that belong to him.' He grinned at her and took a lock of her auburn hair in his hand and inhaled her perfume.

They left the house and Sarah slammed the door behind them. She stood with her back to the door and took a deep breath. She noticed she was shaking all over and she walked into the lounge and sat down on the sofa. She had reached her limit and she broke down and cried uncontrollably. She felt so useless... so trapped with nowhere to run and no one to help her. More than ever she missed her parents and still after almost five years she still ached for Joe and wished he would come back for her and rescue her from the torturous life she was living.

Finally, she laid her head on the sofa cushion, closed her eyes and then fell into a deep sleep. She dreamt of Joe standing in the distance calling out to her. He was standing under the old oak tree, at the entrance of Whittington Manor, reaching out and she was running towards him, smiling and happy. She was at peace and in love, beaming with happiness. Suddenly her dream was broken by a tapping at the front door. She sat up and for a moment felt disorientated. She looked around her wondering why she had fallen asleep on the sofa and glanced at her watch. It was 7am. There was another tapping at the door and she walked towards it, worried it was the two men back again. Peering through the crack on the door whilst the chain was on the latch, she was startled to see two policemen standing there.

`Mrs Hamilton?'

`Yes'

`May we come in?'

`Of course.' Sarah opened the door and the policemen walked in, eyeing her cautiously.

`I'm afraid we have some bad news. There is no easy way of saying this but I'm afraid, Mrs Hamilton, that your husband has been murdered – his body was found on the grounds of Portchester castle a couple of hours ago.' Sarah flung her hand over her mouth and gasped. Tears sprung to her eyes but they weren't tears of grief as the police suspected but tears of relief.

`I know this must be a terrible shock for you Mrs Hamilton. Would you have any idea of who would do such a thing to your husband? Did he have any enemies?'

There was most probably a long list of people who didn't like Edward and would want him dead and then suddenly remembering the two men who had come calling that night, she told them about their visit.

`They were not nice characters and insisted on coming in and searching the flat. They were desperately trying to find him.'

`Did they say why they were looking for your husband?' The policeman, who hadn't spoken a word so far, took out his note pad and started making notes.

`Yes, they said he owed them money.' Sarah watched him write what she was saying.

`Do you know their names?' The other policeman asked.

`No.'

`Can you describe them?' She described them to the best of her memory but her head was spinning and her hands were shaking.

`Thank you Mrs Hamilton. We will be back in touch but if you think of anything more please contact me at the station. Oh and I'm very sorry for your loss.' The other policeman who had not said a word nodded his head and placed his note pad in his top pocket. They both nodded and left. Sarah stood staring out of the window then suddenly realising she was free from Edward, she began to laugh and then her laughter turned to tears then laughter again, almost hysterically. He was gone, it was all over. No more feeling scared or feeling of dread as he walked in the door, no more feeling humiliated as he ran around town with his long string of women, most of which were local prostitutes. The misery he had inflicted on her was finally over. She was so relieved she could shout it out of the widow. `I'm free' she laughed raising her hands above and giving a little dance of joy.

It was almost a week later when the police came calling again. `Mrs Hamilton, sorry to intrude however, I'm afraid we will need to search your home.'

`Why?' Sarah looked startled as she stared at the plain clothed inspector. He was a chubby man and his grey suit seemed to fit where it touched. He pushed a piece of grey hair back over his bald patch that had blown out of place in the wind.

`It's routine.... It may help us with our line of enquiries,' he said as he took a step closer to entering in the flat.

`Very well.' It was obvious she had no choice, so Sarah showed them in. There were two policemen in uniform that followed the inspector in and they each went off in various directions to search the property.

`Please take a seat.' Sarah pointed to the arm chair in front of the sofa for the inspector to sit down.

Claire Voet

He accepted her offer. `Thank you. This must be a very difficult time for you, Mrs Hamilton. Were you married long?' He observed her curiously. She looked a lot more relaxed than the last time he saw her, in fact she looked remarkably well, under the circumstances.

`It would have been two years this summer.' Two years too long she wanted to say but instead smiled politely at him.

`Were you happily married?'

She hesitated for a moment and then decided it best to tell the truth. `No. I'm afraid I wasn't.'

`I see... but you must have been happy at some point,' he persisted.

She looked uneasy with his questioning. `Why are you asking me this?'

`Just routine. It helps me build up a picture of what Mr Hamilton was like as a person.' Sarah nodded. `We were good friends until shortly after we were married. He sold his father's business and then began to drink heavily.'

`This was when he was a solicitor?' The inspector asked.

`Yes.'

`Was the business in trouble?'

`Yes I believe so. He expected me to keep him after that.' She said voicing her thoughts out loud, then quickly regretting it.

`And did you?' He raised his eyebrows.

`I had no choice. Bills had to be paid.' She sounded indignant.

`Did your husband have any hobbies...play sport - was he part of a club for example?' Sarah gave a short laugh. `The only hobby he had was drinking himself into a stupor and gambling.'

`They are expensive hobbies, where did the money come from?'

`From me, he made me give him the money.' She was starting to feel uneasy again.

`Made you?' The inspector raised his eye brows with surprise. Sarah looked away from him. She wasn't sure just where all this was leading to and how much she should be saying to him. It was all irrelevant now and it had nothing to do with the murder enquiry.

`Mrs Hamilton, was your husband a violent man? Did he ever hit you?' he continued. He was starting to build a very interesting picture in his mind and the pieces of the jigsaw puzzle were starting to fit and even if they didn't, he was going to make them. With a promotion hanging in the wings he was not going to let it pass.

176

`Yes.' She replied in barely a whisper.

`Is that how he got you to pay him money... by using violence on you?'

`Not all the time... I lost my' she stopped what she was saying and began to cry.

`I know this is painful for you, but I need to know these things. You lost your what? Mrs Hamilton.'

`I lost my baby because he hit me. He put me in hospital.' There was something strange in her voice and he detected resentment, even hatred maybe?

`That's terrible. Unforgivable! You must have hated him?'

`Yes, I did hate him.' She confirmed without thinking.

`Enough to want him dead?' Sarah suddenly looked shocked, appalled at his question.

`No of course not. I didn't kill him.'

`Well it would be understandable if you did. He was violent to you. You lost your baby, he took your money and you lived a miserable life with him. You certainly have a motive to kill him.

`I may have a motive, Inspector but I'm telling you I didn't kill him.' Just then a police officer interrupted them and handed him a letter. It was the letter Sarah had written to Emma on the night Edward had raped her, and on the same night he had been murdered. The inspector read it with interest. He nodded his head from side to side. `Mrs Hamilton this letter was dated on the very night Mr Hamilton was murdered.'

Sarah swallowed and took a deep breath. `We had an argument and I was upset when I wrote it.'

`Who is Emma?'

`Emma is my friend, she lives in Devon.'

`What had you and Mr Hamilton been arguing about on the night you wrote this?' He waved the letter in front of him.

`He had stolen my jewellery to pay off a gambling debt.' She pushed a lock of hair from her eyes and wiped away her tears.

`I see. It says in this letter, to your friend, Emma, that you hate him and that you wish he was dead.' Sarah's eyes grew wide with fear and she bit her bottom lip nervously. `I was angry and upset.'

`Because he had stolen your jewellery? It must have been very valuable.' Somehow he was making it all sound so trivial.

`Because he had raped me,' she felt ashamed and humiliated but she had to defend herself. `But I didn't kill him I swear to you... I didn't.'

`But you admitted to me that you hated him and here in this letter, written on the same night your husband is murdered, you wrote that you wish he was dead. This is your hand writing isn't it Mrs Hamilton?'

`Yes, but I was nowhere near the castle that night... I was here.'

`Do you have any witnesses, who can confirm you were here all evening?'

`No, but I couldn't have killed him... he is twice my size.' She was desperately clutching at straws trying to prove her innocence.

`It was one brutal blow to the back of the head that killed your husband, easily done, even by a woman your size, with enough anger and hatred of course,' he quickly added.

`I'm sorry Mrs Hamilton but I'm afraid this doesn't look good. I need you to come to the station for a formal interview.'

`But why? I didn't murder my husband. I didn't!'

A moment later they had bundled her into the back of the police car parked outside and drove her off to the station. It was after many hours of questioning and integration she was formally charged with the murder of Edward Hamilton. She was sent to a prison in Portsmouth to await trial.

Twenty-four

Frank had taken Tommy to see Pompey play Brentford. He had also taken him to the Guildhall square a month earlier to see Churchill as all the crowds cheered with delight to see the Prime Minister make a personal appearance in Portsmouth after his illness. He had made another one of his inspiring, famous broadcasts lifting people's spirits. `The hour of our greatest effort is fast approaching,' he had announced. 'Our greatest effort,' Frank mumbled. How could anyone make any greater effort than they already had, yet somehow he believed in this determined leader who had so much strength and courage.

A ten mile stretch of coastland from Lands End to the Wash was declared a protected area and closed to the public. It was strictly prohibited to enter the area and there would be checks on all public transport as well as hotels and public places.

Audrey felt apprehensive when she heard about the news from her sister in Portsmouth. `They are expecting an invasion, that's what it is, Frank. This is what it's been all about, all those troops and secrets. `She stared at him as he pottered around the garden. He was re-potting some tomato plants that had grown too big. He liked to keep a few in the back garden, even though he had plenty up at the allotment. It was just handy to have them there whenever he fancied them in a sandwich. He was busy patting down the soil around the roots. Tabby sat observing him – watching his big hand moving up and down and without notice, he pounced on him.

`Oh Frank, we're gunno be invaded and we'll be taken over by Jerries like all those other countries `ave.' Audrey stood up from the chair she had moved into the garden to catch a few rays of sunshine peeking through the scattered clouds. She looked a little flushed.

`No, we're not,' Frank had an amused tone to his voice and Audrey wasn't sure it was directed at her or Tabby the cat. He stood up straight and brushed off the soil from his hands. `There's not gunno be an invasion, Audrey, - at least not in England anyow.'

She wasn't convinced. So what d'you reckon it's all about then?' She narrowed her eyes and frowned at him.

`Something big, something very big is gunno `appen. He smiled. They're getting ready to invade Europe. They are sending our boys into France and this time, Audrey,' he paused for a second before continuing, `we're gunno win.' He swung his fist, punching the air with certainty and then grinned at her. He had a gut feeling that this was the beginning of the end.

As soon as it was common knowledge to everyone that the country was moving into a full scale invasion of Europe, all military leave had stopped. There was still no word about Joe and the Lambert's only hope was that the war would soon be over and Joe would be found safe and well in POW camp somewhere. They refused to believe he was dead.

Mail and telephone communication was only allowed under the strictest supervision. The British Isles were sealed off and the south coast of England was awash with uniforms until there wasn't space for even the smallest cadet.

`Let's hope they get it right this time,' Audrey said. `We don't want another disaster like Dunkirk or Dieppe.'

`No they won't get it wrong this time, lots of preparation has gone in to this. You mark my words, Audrey... it'll soon be over... you'll see.'

*****

`Your solicitor is here to see you.' The prison warden's sudden entrance startled Sarah. She got up and walked out of her dark, small cell, looking dishevelled and just thankful that a familiar face was waiting to see her.

`Mrs Hamilton, I'm as shocked as you are to find you in here.' Mr Shaw extended his hand for her to shake it. She accepted his hand shake and he then pointed to an old wooden chair in front of him for her to sit down. One table and two chairs were the only items of furniture. The white bright lights of the room made her look even paler than she already was. Her eyes were sunken with deep dark circles and her tiny frame looked pathetic. `They think I murdered, Edward.' Her voice was soft and pitiful.

`I know, Mrs Hamilton – Sorry may I call you Sarah?' She nodded in agreement.

`Sarah, they have no other leads to go on other than you. You see - you have the motive to kill him, even though you *say* you didn't do it.' She looked surprised at his choice of words. `I may have the motive, but I'm telling you Mr Shaw, I didn't kill him. They have no reason to believe that I did.' She sounded indignant.

`I'm afraid they do.' Mr Shaw rubbed his chin, he appeared a little edgy. `They came to see me. They found my contact details in your flat. I had to tell them about you wanting to make a will and about the fact that your husband was after your money. They also have the letter that you wrote to your friend which says you wished Edward was dead, which may I add, was written on the same night he was murdered.' He raised an eyebrow at her.

`I know but it still doesn't prove anything.' Sarah tilted her head back and rubbed her face with the palms of her hand. She was exhausted. She then looked back at him again. `But what about the two men who came looking for Edward on the night he died?' She was sure they had something to do with it.

`They both had alibis – witnesses that confirmed exactly where they were at the time of the murder.' Mr Shaw declared reluctantly. He sat forward on his chair. His voice was low and just a fraction louder than a whisper. `The prosecution will have a field day with this information I have here. He waved his notes, taken from his brief case. They will turn all this information around, twist it to make it look like you killed him out of rage and hate.' Sarah cupped her hands over her face again. A second later she looked up at him in desperation. `But isn't it your job to defend me and make them see I am innocent?'

`Yes it is.' He confirmed peering at her through his spectacles. `What are you going to do?'

He chewed his bottom lip pensively. `Can anyone at all vouch for where you were between 2am and 6am on that night? A neighbour perhaps?'

`No, I was alone at home. I've already told the police that too.' She sounded impatient.

`We need new evidence to come to light. It would be enormously helpful if the murder weapon would be found.' He was thinking out loud now.

`And if it doesn't?' Sarah enquired apprehensively.

Mr Shaw gave a sigh. `Best not to think about that just yet. Let me see what I can do first.'

`Mr Shaw I want to know what I'm up against here. If I'm found guilty what will happen to me?' Their eyes fixed. He cleared his throat with a small nervous cough. `The sentence would be death by hanging. If found guilty of murder of course.'

Her head began to spin and for a moment she felt as if she was about to faint. What little colour she did have had completely drained away. `When is the trial?'

`The 10th of June. We have a few weeks to prepare your case.'

The 10th of June – the anniversary of her father's death. He would have turned in his grave if he knew she had been locked up in prison, accused of murder and equally so if he knew how Edward had treated her. She shuddered at the thought and suddenly noticed she was crying as a tear dropped down her cheek.

Mr Shaw took a deep breath. `I'm straight on the case now and I want you to know I will do everything in my power to help you, Sarah.' He gave a reassuring smile.

She forced a small smile back and then her eyes grew wide. `Can you hire a private detective? I can pay... whatever it costs. Just get someone on the case who can find the real murderer... Please Mr Shaw, I'm begging you.'

Mr Shaw grabbed his brief case by the side of his foot. `If that is your wish, I can arrange it. I will be in touch soon, and Sarah – sit tight, I'm doing everything I can.' A moment later he was gone and the prison warden ushered her abruptly back to her cell.

Germany was now under attack as troops swept across the Siegfried Line. Towns, cities and even villages were destroyed as the armies advanced, driving the enemy out. The greatest battles were being fought by air, day and night. Bombers crossed the channel and hurled destruction on Germany.

There was no mercy and there was no mercy for Sarah too, as Mr Shaw frantically worked day and night on her case with no success. There was a private detective also working hard but to no avail. No new evidence as yet had come to light. Sarah's future was looking extremely bleak as the court case drew rapidly closer.

Twenty-five

VE Day. That was what they were calling it. It stood for Victory in Europe and it seemed that Portsmouth, Portchester, Fareham and the whole of the country and the rest of the world for that matter had gone mad with delight.

`Let's go to Portsmouth to the Guildhall square. Let's all go.' Audrey hugged Frank. Her emotions were all over the place. `Oh Frank – I know our Joe will be found now the war is over.' Frank gave her an unconvincing smile. He wished more than anything he could share her optimism. He had a feeling of dread in the pit of his stomach that kept nagging away at him day and night. As the years had gone on his hope of them finding Joe had slowly diminished, not that he had ever told Audrey that.

`Oh can we Mum? That'll be great. There are loads of people going down to the thanks giving service at the Guildhall.' Maureen piped up excitedly from the sofa. Tommy sat reading the newspaper. He was still quiet although he had spoken a lot more lately. He loved to reiterate stories in the newspaper, mumbling comments under his breath, but there was a definite progress in his recovery. It was Frank he spoke to the most they seemed to have an unspoken bond between them. `I see the murder trial is coming up for that chap they found dead in Portchester Castle.' He said glancing up to see if Frank was listening.

`Is it son? I've not read about it. Never seem to get the time to read the local paper.' He always read the national paper to keep up to date with what was going on in the world but the local paper was a luxury and something he rarely had time for with working and the allotment to keep him busy.

`Sarah Hamilton her name is' Tommy read out loud, turning over to the next page. Just before he had a chance to finish reading the rest of the story that explained she was formally known as Sarah Whittington before her marriage to Edward Hamilton, he was interrupted by his mother. `Go and get ready, Tommy. We'll catch the bus in half an hour. You don't have time to sit and read the newspaper.' With that Audrey dashed upstairs to get changed. Tommy sighed and folded up the paper before throwing it behind the sofa. It landed amongst a pile of other old newspapers that were waiting to be thrown in the rubbish.

The Lamberts caught the bus to Commercial Road and walked the rest of the way up to the Guildhall square. The place had been bombed to a pulp and the proud city was in a terrible state. So many streets were laden with waste and debris. There were empty burnt out shells that were once shops or houses and like a symbol that stood out, the Guildhall itself stood gutted, just a blackened empty shell. Yet surrounding it in the square were thousands of people who had come from all over Portsmouth to join in the thanks giving ceremony.

They crammed into the big square, trying to find the best place to stand to view the procession that would soon be arriving. The police were clearing a space and Frank led his family to the perfect spot to watch the parade.

`Look, Mum, there's Uncle Ed and Auntie Shirley.' Maureen pointed out, grabbing tightly onto little Nancy's hand for fear of losing her in the crowds.

`Oh yeah – Look Frank, shall we go and join them?' Audrey was busy waving to them.

`Don't be daft - you won't make it on time.' Frank shouted out above the noise of the thumping drums.

The Royal Marines were the first to start marching into the square.

`Don't they look smart, Mum.' Maureen stood watching in admiration at their gleaming trumpets and trombones as they played `Land of Hope and Glory' and `Rule Britannia!'

At the sound of the patriotic tunes the crowds stood proud, singing at the tops of their voices, defiant to the enemy who had made their lives hell for so many years.

The marines were followed by soldiers, sailors and airmen and not just British but with French, American and Canadian too. Audrey watched with tears rolling down her face. Her thoughts drifted to Joe and she just hoped and prayed that now the war was over, he would be found alive and well, and if not well, at least alive. She had never given up hope that one day he would be found. A mother knows if her son's alive it's something you wouldn't understand; she had told the rest of them whenever they tried to tell her otherwise.

Tommy watched with a glazed look in his eyes, remembering his days at sea and then his thoughts wondered to Joe too. Frank turned to check on him. `You alright son?'

`I'm fine, Dad.' He swallowed the lump at the back of his throat and sighed.

184

`Good, lad... it's all over now.' Frank smiled proudly at him.

`Is it? What about all those men that lost their lives and what about our Joe?' He sounded bitter and angry again. The terrible things he had witnessed at sea were engraved heavily into his memory and soul and probably would be for the rest of his life. He wasn't the same Tommy Lambert any more. It was as if a part of him had died on the ship when it had sunk.

`I don't know, son.' Frank sighed. Everyone you spoke to had paid the price of this ugly, terrible war and he could understand Tommy's bitterness, although there was nothing he could say to help him, but at least he was alive and he was home where he belonged. He didn't think he could have coped with losing both sons.

The service was short but very emotional, led by the Bishop of Portsmouth and the Provost of the Cathedral. After the last hymn the Bishop raised his hand in blessing and there was a moments silence as they all stood and bowed their heads, remembering those who had been killed. Nobody moved or spoke; you could have heard a pin drop. Each of them lost in thought about friends and relatives who had gone to war and never returned or who had been killed in the blitz. Audrey gave a small and quiet sob and the strain on her face said exactly what she was thinking, and sensing her thoughts, Frank gripped her hand tightly and put his other arm around Tommy, who was silently crying. Maureen wiped away a tear clinging onto little Nancy in her arms.

The white ensign – the flag of peace, flapped in the wind forcing everyone to raise their heads and as if it had been rehearsed, Portsmouth erupted into the most glorious cacophony of rejoicing and celebrating ever known in history. Every ship in the harbour, from war ships down to the little Gosport ferry-boat, sounded its siren. Bells rang from every church tower and people everywhere were cheering and dancing in the streets, pouring out their joy and relief that at last, the world was a safe place.

Sarah sat huddled up in the corner of her dark cell. There was a glimmer of light that shone into the middle of the room from a tiny window up high. There was an old mattress that she sat on, her knees drawn to her chest, her tatty auburn hair hung over her face. She had been lucky that she didn't have to share the cell with anyone else. There was a terrible stench in the air which resembled the smell of urine.

She looked up towards the little window. It was too high for her to even get close to it but she could hear the faint noise of bells in the distance. It was hard to make out what it was with all the shouting and crying of the inmates. There was always so much noise day and night; she had hardly slept in weeks. She buried her head again in between her knees and shuddered at the sound of jangling keys and the big heavy iron door screeching open then slamming closed in the cell next door to her. She hadn't seen Mr Shaw for over a week now and was starting to think if he had given up on her. It was her trial in a few days. She had resigned herself to being found guilty and wished now that it could be over and done with as soon as possible. If she was to die, she would rather it be sooner than later. The only bit of comfort she could find, was knowing that when she died, she would be reunited with all those who she loved most.

Twenty-six

The keys jangled noisily and the heavy iron black door squeaked and swung open, revealing Mr Shaw standing in the doorway. He dismissed the guard and walked towards Sarah who looked up at him, startled by his sudden appearance.

He was smiling broadly at her. `This certainly is *our* VE Day.'

Sarah's expression changed to a deep frown. She was so weak and tired and really didn't have the energy to think any more. `I don't understand.'

`The murder weapon that was used to kill Edward has been found. Tests confirm it is Edward's blood, but the finger prints on the weapon don't match yours.' Mr Shaw walked towards her, still beaming proudly.

`Whose does it match... do they know?' Sarah looked baffled.

`Oh yes they know who it is... in fact they have him in custody right now. Eric Simons is his name and he apparently was a gambling partner of Edward's.

`Eric Simons - but that was Edward's best friend, he was his best man at our wedding.' She was totally bewildered and confused. Sarah, who cares who he was? You, my dear, are a free woman.' He rubbed her arm affectionately and without warning she turned and hugged him, crying with relief. He felt a little embarrassed by her sudden affection and patted her back lightly before slowly prizing himself away from her. `There will be some paperwork involved which will take no more than a day or two and then you are free to go.'

She looked up at him, her eyes wide and dancing with happiness. `Thank you so much Mr Shaw... I just don't know what to say.'

`There is nothing to say... it's all over, Sarah. Now do you want me to collect you when you come out and take you home?' He peered at her through his specials, carefully observing her.

`No... it's alright ... you've done more than enough for me.' She smiled at him. It was a smile full of gratitude and he nodded.

`I'm going to have a word with the authorities here to give you some better food and I want you to use these last few hours here to eat and rest, you need to build up your strength for the outside world.'

`Thank you,' she smiled again through her tears.

`I look forward to seeing you outside of here.' He grinned and then turned on his heel, walking out of the cell feeling proud of himself and delighted for her.

It was forty-eight hours after Mr Shaw had delivered his good news and when Sarah was released from prison. The sunlight was bright in her eyes and the warm air felt wonderful on her skin. She stood for a few moments absorbing the sunshine and she didn't know if she wanted to laugh or cry. She had resigned herself to dying for so long whilst waiting for her trial and now she had her life back, a life she had no idea what she was going to do with.

She didn't laugh or cry but instead she walked along the narrow cobbled street away from the prison, trying to work out what she would do now. Edward was gone and she was no longer tied to him. There was no family left, perhaps Thomas, but goodness knows where he was or if he was even alive and she wondered if she would ever see him again. She contemplated going to see Emma for a while, just to get away, time to lick her wounds and build her strength again. She turned the corner of the street and stopped in her tracks. She was in the back streets of Portsmouth somewhere and wasn't sure where, but there was a long row of terraced houses in front of her, many of them displaying welcome home banners and union jack flags. She found herself standing staring at a house with a large banner hanging above the doorway that read `Welcome home our Joe.' A lady with grey curly hair wearing an old blue pinafore was busy cleaning the windows of the little terraced house and as if sensing there was someone standing behind her, she stopped and turned around to see Sarah watching her.

`You look a bit peaky my love, - you alright?' She was a plump woman with rosy cheeks, she reminded Sarah of Annie in many ways.

`I'm fine, thank you.' She stood staring at the banner. Just seeing Joe's name written like that made her ache for him.

`That's my son... he'll be back anytime now.' She announced following Sarah's stare.

`Is the war over then?' Sarah glanced up the street at all the other banners and flags flapping in the warm summer breeze.

The lady gave a chuckle `Of course the war is over. Where 'ave you been hiding, on the moon? The whole world has been celebrating this past week.'

`I... well I've not been well.' Sarah felt awkward, her cheeks coloured with embarrassment. That would explain the bells ringing, they must have been church bells ringing, she realised as she looked all around her. Why hadn't Mr Shaw mentioned it? How could she not know the war was over?

`Oh I see... well, it's most definitely over.' The old woman confirmed. 'Ave you got anyone coming home from the war?' As soon as she had asked the question she wished she hadn't, so many loved ones were not coming back from the war and the girl looked like she herself had been through the mill.

`No' Sarah replied softly.

`Do you live around here?' The woman was curious about this mysterious well-spoken girl.

Sarah shook her head. `No I live in Portchester.'

`Do you want to come in for a cuppa before you carry on with your journey?' The front door was open and she pointed inside. She was concerned for the girl. She didn't look like she even knew what day of the week it was. She must have been very ill if she didn't know the war had ended.

`No - but thank you... I really must be going.' Sarah turned and started to walk on past the old woman.

She caught the bus from Commercial road and sat staring out of the window, and without thinking, she got off at the bus stop on the outskirts of Portchester, only five minutes away from where she used to live. It was almost as if her mind had been set on auto pilot as she walked home to Whittington Manor, trying to forget that she had a home in Fareham that she had once shared with Edward. She had only ever had one home and that was Whittington Manor. It was engraved in her heart. It was where she had lived almost all her life and it was the happiest time of her life, when her mother, father, Charles, Thomas and Annie where all there, living together as a family, all those years ago. They were years she would treasure in her heart for the rest of her life and she only wished she had appreciated them more in those days. Now they were all gone and she was alone in the world. She couldn't bring them back but she could bring the house back and that was exactly what she intended to do, even if it meant living there alone. She owed it to her father to keep the house in the Whittington name.

When she arrived at the old oak tree at the bottom of the gravel path, she stopped and stared at it wistfully, remembering all the times she and Joe had kissed there, shaded under its great big leaves. She rubbed her hand along the roughness of its trunk and noticed something she had never seen before. There was an engraving. It read Joe loves Sarah and it was inscribed inside a heart. Tears stung her eyes and taking a deep breath she turned and started up the old gravel path. A moment later the path disappeared into the over growth of weeds and long grass that had taken over the grounds during the past few years.

She picked up a long stick and thankful that she was wearing trousers, she stumbled and battled her way through the overgrowth, hacking at the grass and weeds, creating a way through to the entrance of the house. The front door which was hanging off its hinges, behind a wooden plank, had come lose and was hanging precariously to one side. Most of the house was an empty burnt out shell but surprisingly there were a couple of rooms near the front of the house still standing. She pushed cautiously back the plank of wood acting as the front door, and it banged onto the original front door, creaking loudly. She stood for a moment peering inside from where she was standing. The only noise that could be heard were the birds singing in the near by trees. Very gently she placed her foot onto the floor board inside the house to feel if it was safe to walk in. It felt strong enough, and so she continued.

The once long sweeping staircase had been ripped completely in half, making it impossible to walk upstairs. She stood for a moment staring above her. The air was cold and damp and she felt a shiver go down her spine as she glanced to the side of her, down the long hallway that led to the kitchen. It was nothing but a black hole now, an empty space where her mother and Annie had been killed, right there in that very spot. She shivered again and quickly turned away to walk towards the second drawing-room. There was no door left to the room any more and as she entered in a pigeon flew towards her, causing her to shriek and leap backwards.

The room was dark, apart from a strip of day light that poured in through the crack of the heavy red velvet curtains, framing the broken window. She walked towards it and pulled back the curtains to let in the daylight. The chesterfield leather sofas were still standing covered in think dust and rubble. Many items of furniture were broken and strewn all over the room including the old grandfather clock that had smashed from the impact of falling to the ground, but to her amazement, in the far corner, stood the old grand piano.

She dusted it off with her arm and carefully pulling back the lid she could see it was in pristine condition. The little stool that had once sat beneath the piano had disappeared, and then she spotted it, it had rolled away and was lying on its side. She bent down and reached out for it and as she placed it up right she jumped, startled by a big black spider which fell out from under the seat and scurried across the room.

She stood rubbing her arms with her hands staring at it as it disappeared under a piece of debris. There was a noticeable chill in the air. There was nothing warm or happy about the house any more. It was cold, eerie and depressing.

She turned back to the piano remembering how much her parents had loved her to play and a sob caught the back of her throat. She missed them all...`Why?' Her cries of despair echoed the room.

She brushed off the stool and sat down on it, hitting a few random keys, as if testing it out first, and then without thinking, she began to play. It was only after playing the first few notes that she realised she was playing the old familiar tune `Nocturne' by Chopin. She played each note with passion, straight from her heart, displaying all the heartache and anguish built up inside of her during the past years. Music filled the air, and as if it was bringing life back into the house again, the whole room lit up with a sudden burst of sunshine that shone so brightly through the broken window.

There was warmth to the room as she played relentlessly, unaware that tears were cascading down her face. She played for all those she had once loved and who had once loved her. And like a vision she saw them all, standing there around the piano watching her. Her mother, father, Charles, Thomas, Annie, Joe... they were all there, smiling at her and encouraging her to continue playing. She was afraid to stop for they might disappear. She continued playing so beautifully until eventually one by one they faded just as the bright sunlight also faded away.

There was a deathly silence and the room became dark once more. Placing the lid over the keys, Sarah rested her head on her arms and sobbed loudly, her crying echoing once more the cold and lonely deserted house.

Finally, she stopped crying and sensing someone was watching her, she turned, but there was no one there. There was a noise, a floor board creaking, and she sat very still listening intently, watching for any movements. And there in the cold grey light, beyond the doorway, she could see a figure standing in the far distance.

`Whose there?' She called out but no one answered. She stood up and crept across the room.

`Who is it?' She repeated. This time there was a tremor of fear in her voice.

`Sarie!' The voice called out echoing around them.

Her heart skipped. It couldn't be...

`Joe! `Joe is that really you?' she ran frantically in the direction of the voice.

`Yes'

she paused and squinted. It was Joe. He looked older, thinner, but still incredibly handsome.

`Oh my God... Joe! She ran straight into his arms and they kissed in desperation and with passion.

They paused for breath as she looked anxiously at him. `They said you were dead.' Her hands were around his face as she sobbed, staring into his familiar green twinkling eyes. He was beaming at her, equally thrilled to be in her arms again. `Who said I was dead?'

`Two soldiers at the hospital. They said they saw you get shot in France and you fell in a ditch surrounded by Germans. They were sure you were dead.' She was speaking so quickly he could hardly understand her.

`I almost was... `I was shot in the shoulder but when their backs were turned I made a run for it into the woodland.'

`And what happened' Sarah's eyes were wide with amazement.

`Eventually an old retired French doctor found me... Just on time. I collapsed at his feet so he took me and treated me wound.'

`And then?' She wanted to hear it all, she could hardly believe he was standing there in front of her, - alive and well. It was like a dream, a very good dream and she never wanted to wake up from it. Her eyes were dancing with excitement.

`He took me to his cousin's farm and they hid me in his cellar.'

`Until the war ended?'

`Yes, until the war ended.' He grinned at her, so thankful to be with her again. There had been times when he had been locked away in the cellar that he had doubted if he would ever get out of France alive and even if he did, he wondered if she would still be waiting for him?

`Oh... Joe.' They kissed and held each other tightly.

`What 'append?' he asked, finally, pulling away from her and looking around at the derelict house surrounding them.

`It was bombed.' Her face clouded over in a mist of anguish.

`And your mother?' She shook her head from side to side, tears filling her eyes.

`Oh Sarie.... I'm so sorry.'

`Nanny too... They destroyed everything. There's no one left.' Her head hung low and he placed a finger under her chin softly forcing her to look into his eyes. `My darling...I'm here now.' He stroked the side of her face and pulled her back into his arms. `Come on let's go home, Mum and Dad are waiting for us and tomorrow, first thing, I promise, we will make a start on fixing this place up. We will get Dad and Tommy involved if we have to.' He gave a short laugh. Sarah smiled at him through her tears. She was safe now. He was the only man she had ever loved and he had come back for her. He was back home and this time to stay.

Yet despite her happiness, her smile faded and a look of sadness replaced it. `Joe there is so much I have to tell you.' She had to tell him about Edward.

`Shush, there's time...plenty of time for talking later.'

`But Joe, I need to tell you so much.'

He nodded knowingly. `It doesn't matter Sarah. It's all over... It's in the past and I love you, that's all that matters now.

Smiling through her tears she took his hand as they left the house. She looked up at him with a big bright smile. `And I love you too Joe Lambert.'

Authors website: www.clairevoet.co.uk

See Book trailer on youtube

http://www.youtube.com/watch?v=sY_SxnY0Tx8

Lightning Source UK Ltd.
Milton Keynes UK
UKOW050714280812

198148UK00001B/160/P